"I'm

"Why not?

"For one thing," Cassie reminded her, "I wasn't invited."

"Yes, but I was," Diane pointed out, then fluttered the envelope under Cassie's nose. "Diane Krensky *and guest*. You can come as my guest."

Cassie was surprised to find herself actually considering the possibility. Nearly a year had elapsed since Phillip Keene had vanished from her world, and she'd thought she'd gotten the hang of coping. But the appearance of this wedding invitation had disabled all her coping mechanisms.

She could feel the tears gathering in her throat. "I don't want to be there to see Phillip pledge his troth to another woman."

"You could go and cut off his troth with a kitchen knife."

"I can't believe how bloodthirsty you are!"

"Any guy who does to my best friend what this guy did to you whets my thirst for blood. I say, let's go and wreak havoc."

Dear Reader,

When my editor invited me to write a book that would be part of a Superromance "In the Year 2000" promotion, I was thrilled. I was doubly thrilled when she asked if I would write a book with a "revenge" theme. A book that was all about getting satisfaction.

Revenge. All that passion! All that dark, dangerous emotion! All that intrigue and malevolence! I couldn't wait to get started.

"Oh, one last thing," my editor said. "Could you make it a comedy?"

Many successful comedies arise from the darkest subjects. Maybe it's because when we're feeling bad, when we've been betrayed like Cassie Webber, the heroine of *The Wrong Bride*, when our hearts have been broken and our ability to trust is lying in tatters, one of the most effective weapons we have is humor.

So laugh along with Cassie as she plots her revenge against Phillip Keene, the man of her dreams and her nightmares. And remember that revenge is sweetest when it's exacted with a smile.

Sincerely,

Judith Arnold

THE WRONG BRIDE
BRIDE
Judith Arnold

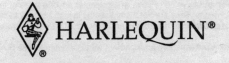

TORONTO • NEW YORK • LONDON
AMSTERDAM • PARIS • SYDNEY • HAMBURG
STOCKHOLM • ATHENS • TOKYO • MILAN • MADRID
PRAGUE • WARSAW • BUDAPEST • AUCKLAND

ISBN 0-373-70830-0

THE WRONG BRIDE

Printed in U.S.A.

THE WRONG BRIDE

PROLOGUE

"I LOVE YOU, Cassie."

They were naked, their limbs entwined, their bodies slick with perspiration and heavy with exhaustion. Cassie's brain was so misty with heat and passion she was certain she'd misheard him. What he'd probably said was, "I'm *above* you, Cassie." He *was* on top, and he'd never before even hinted that he loved her.

She, however, had loved him from the start. Well, all right, maybe it had begun with infatuation—infatuation as unexpected and staggering as a sharp blow to the solar plexus. In very little time it had evolved into the kind of friendship in which two people seemed magically connected, linked in innumerable and undefinable ways, viewing the world through the same prism and seeing the same rainbows. It hadn't taken her long to admit she was madly in love with Phillip Keene.

Unfortunately, he was planning to leave town tomorrow.

She gazed up to see him smiling. His smoke-gray eyes glimmered with emotion. Slowly, as if with great reluctance, he eased out of her embrace and propped himself up with his arms.

"I wanted to make love to you the first time I saw you," he confessed.

"That day you helped me carry the footlocker down the hall?"

"That instant."

She mirrored his smile. She'd wanted to make love with him from that first moment, too. "Why did you wait so long?"

With his fingertips he traced her cheekbone, her nose, her lips. "How could I get involved with you when I knew I'd be leaving in June?"

It was June now. June meant his graduation from business school and his return to Ohio to run his father's furniture factory. Cassie had been aware of his plans. He'd never misled her. She'd known all along that he wouldn't remain in Boston after he finished his schooling. But she'd let him into her heart anyway.

"Are you sorry?" she asked.

"About this?" He bowed and kissed her mouth again. "Are you kidding?"

"No, I'm not kidding."

"No, I'm not sorry." One final, lingering kiss, and then he rolled off her and pulled her into his arms. "It does complicate my life, though."

"Why?"

He sighed. "You know why. I'm going home."

She wished he wouldn't refer to Ohio as *home*. She wished he could think his home was in Boston, in her life. If there was anything she could say to keep him here, anything she could do...

There was. She could take a chance, expose her soul, declare the truth. She could be brave. She could fight for what she wanted.

"What did you say before?" she asked.

"About going home?"

"No, before that. Right after we…" She felt a blush heat her cheeks.

"Oh. Right after *that*." He grinned. A dimple creased his cheek, but his eyes were solemn. "I said I loved you, Cassie. And I meant it."

"I love you, too, Phillip." She leaned back in his arms so she could view his face. "Maybe…maybe you don't have to leave?" It was a question, a plea.

A series of emotions seemed to glide across his face: frustration, disappointment and then resolution. And love. She saw love in his eyes, as true and honest as her love for him.

"I do have to go," he said gently. "I've got to explain to my parents that I'm not going to settle in town and run Keene Furniture. I can't tell them something like that over the phone. I've got to see them, tell them in person."

Was he saying what she hoped? Once again, she was afraid to trust her ears. "You're not moving back to Ohio?"

"How can I? I love you, Cassie, and you're here."

She had never wept for joy before, but she wanted to weep now. She wanted to sob and sing and cheer. And then make love with Phillip all over again.

"My parents are going to be upset that I want to stay in Boston," he said. "It goes against everything they've ever wanted for me—"

"And for themselves," she suggested.

"For the family. They have dreams, too, you know."

"But you have to follow your own dreams," she said, feeling sorry for his parents but ecstatic for herself and Phillip.

He cupped her face in his hands and kissed her.

"I'll explain it to them. But I can't do it long-distance. I can't break their hearts that way. I've go to go home."

"If that's what you think is best."

"It's what I have to do," he said firmly. "I'll tell them, and then I'll come back to you."

"I love you, Phillip," she whispered. "I've loved you for a long time, and I love you even more now."

"I'll come back," he vowed. "I promise. I'll come back, and we'll be together forever."

CHAPTER ONE

Mr. and Mrs. Harold Riggs
request the honor of your presence
at the wedding of their daughter
Tricia Lynn
to
Phillip James Keene
Saturday, the seventeenth of June
the year two thousand
at two-thirty o'clock
Linden Hills Country Club
Lynwood, Ohio

CASSIE WEBBER STUDIED the embossed silver letters that curled and swirled down the center of a very stiff, very creamy, very formal card. She'd seen wedding invitations before, and this one had little to distinguish it, except for one detail: the groom's name.

"Phillip Keene?" she said, trying to suppress the panic in her voice. "Oh, my God. Diane, where did you get this?"

"I found it in my mailbox." Diane preferred sitting on tables to sitting on chairs, so she ignored the empty chairs scattered about the room and planted her butt on Cassie's worktable. A long, battered, remarkably ugly piece of furniture, it looked as if it had spent its better days in the visitors' lounge of a maximum security prison. Currently it served as the primary work surface in the production office of *Dream Wheels,* the children's television show Cassie produced for the public-broadcasting network. Most of the table was taken up with notes, photos, drawings and pages of script for an episode concerning the Alamo, scheduled for the upcoming season.

"I take it you didn't find one in your mailbox," Diane stated.

Cassie's view of a photograph of the Alamo was obscured partly by the wedding invitation Diane was waving under her nose and partly by the rush of tears into her eyes. "Phillip Keene is getting married," she repeated, stupefied. Her legs felt weak. Her heart felt weaker. She'd been standing and now she sank into her chair, batting her eyelids furiously, trying to keep the tears from spilling over.

"So it seems," Diane muttered.

"Oh, my God."

"Oh, my God is right."

Diane was Cassie's production assistant and best friend. She'd known that Cassie was in love with Phillip even before Cassie had been ready to admit it to herself. And once Phillip had left Boston and days had stretched into weeks, weeks into months without a word from him, Diane had figured out that he'd given Cassie the shaft long before Cassie had been willing to acknowledge the painful truth.

Diane had sat with Cassie through many bottles of cheap chianti, listening to her friend alternately lament her own foolishness and cast aspersions on Phillip's character. Diane had taken Cassie to their favorite tennis court at the high school in Lexington, around the corner from where Diane's parents lived, and told Cassie to pretend the ball was Phillip, and she'd let Cassie win set after set with her vicious serves and lobs. Diane had bought Cassie cannolis in the North End and furry-skinned kiwis at Stop-and-Shop and assured her that, yes, indeed, Phillip Keene really deserved to burn in hell for all eternity.

It wouldn't require a big leap for Diane to predict how Cassie would feel when she learned that Phillip intended to welcome the start of the twenty-first century by tying the knot with another woman.

"I can't believe it." Cassie's voice emerged faintly.

"Of course you can believe it," Diane said, gentle and caustic at the same time. "Phillip Keene is a piece of slime. Why wouldn't he do something like this?"

"I mean, it's bad enough he's getting married. No, worse than bad. It's horrible! Despicable! And then to invite my best friend to the wedding. Why would he do that, Diane? Is he a sadist?"

"We could add that to the list of things he is," Diane said sympathetically. "A piece of slime. A pathetic excuse for a human being. A thug. Satan's spawn. A lousy lover."

"No, not that," Cassie mumbled.

"A lying, two-timing bastard. And a sadist." Diane considered her list and nodded. "Of course, it's possible he invited me for some other purpose than just to rub your nose in it. He might have invited other people from the station, too."

"Why would he invite other people?" Cassie scanned the room. Like the worktable, her office was a place to which the word *classy* would not apply. The institutional-green walls were covered with bulletin boards, blackboards and whiteboards, holding schedules, cast lists, *Dream Wheels* posters, plot ideas, memos and persnickety budget reminders from the financial office. File cabinets crowded one corner. Hip-high bookshelves held rows of bound scripts along another wall. A lava lamp shared desk space with a Rubik's Cube, a box of dominoes, a statue of Kermit the Frog and Miss Piggy in a cozy embrace, and a computer.

The *Dream Wheels* production office was no more or less glamorous than the public-broadcasting station as a whole. The only reason Phillip had ventured into the humble world of public broadcasting a little more than a year ago was to volunteer a few hours of telephone duty, taking calls during one of the station's pledge breaks. He'd arrived with a group of classmates from the Harvard Business School, intent on performing a good deed on his way to the top rung of the economic ladder.

Phillip had hated working the phones with his buddies during that pledge break. But the experience had inspired him to come up with other ways the station might raise money. He'd convinced both the station's budget director and one of his own professors that he could prepare useful case studies on the fund-raising programs of public-broadcasting stations.

He'd made friends among the people he worked with at the station. But Cassie had been the only person there with whom he'd formed a real bond. Some bond, she thought bitterly. A bond constructed of sex and betrayal.

"Who else from the station would he have invited?" she challenged Diane.

Her friend shrugged. "I don't know. He spent a lot of time with some of those number-crunchers in finance."

"He spent a lot of time with me, too."

"Well, maybe he was in a magnanimous mood. Maybe he invited lots of people. Maybe he's thinking if everyone gives the happy couple an official mug with the station logo on it as a gift, they'll wind up with a complete set."

"Great." A watery laugh escaped Cassie. "He probably did invite everyone except me. Just to add a little salt to the wound."

"Come on, Cassie—that wound should have healed by now. Salt can't hurt scar tissue."

Cassie let out a shaky breath. Either salt could hurt scar tissue, or her wound was a long way from healing, because merely looking at the invitation hurt as badly as having someone tear her heart out of her chest without anesthesia.

"Actually," Diane noted, "it's also possible that his mother invited me."

"Phil's mother?" Cassie frowned.

"I met her that time he brought her to the station. Remember? You met her, too—but you were in the middle of a studio taping, and Phil was busy doing his usual stuff in the finance office. He asked me if I could keep his mother entertained for the afternoon. I wound up taking dear old Dorothy Keene all over town—the Old North Church, Faneuil Hall Marketplace, the Public Gardens. We took a Swan Boat ride, and then we had tea and pastries at the Ritz-Carlton. We really hit it off."

"I remember," Cassie said vaguely, her gaze riveted to the invitation.

"Of course, if I'd have known Phil was going to love you and leave you, I wouldn't have been so nice to his mother." Diane grimaced. "She seemed so sweet. It's hard to believe her son could have turned out to be such an ass.''

''Maybe he takes after his father.'' Cassie fought off a fresh surge of tears. ''What am I going to do?'' she asked plaintively.

''What *can* you do? Hey, how about you buy a voo-doo doll and stick pins in it? Two voodoo dolls, if you want to put a hex on—'' Diane craned her neck to read the invitation ''—Tricia Lynn Riggs, whoever the hell she is.''

''No,'' Cassie muttered. ''Just Phil. Just him. He's the one who deserves a black-magic curse.'' She fingered the invitation dolefully. Had she ever actually thought he would come back to her? Had she been stupid enough to assume he'd live up to his promises?

Of course she had. He had never lied to her in the months they'd known each other. At least, she didn't think he had.

On the other hand, maybe he'd been lying all along. Maybe he'd already been engaged to marry Tricia Lynn Riggs when he'd met her. Maybe he'd spouted a bunch of empty promises just to get her into bed.

He wouldn't have had to lie to get her into bed, though. She hadn't asked for any promises before they'd made love. The promises had come afterward.

They were a postscript. A sop he'd felt obligated to toss her. A beer chaser after a belt of two-hundred-proof passion.

Cassie stared at the invitation like a passerby at an accident scene, unable to avert her eyes from the hor-ror. The graceful lettering, the glossy silver ink, the textured paper—all drew her gaze like iron to a mag-net.

''Actually, he invited me and a guest,'' Diane said,

displaying the envelope, which was addressed, in beautiful calligraphy, to "Ms. Diane Krensky and Guest."

"You and a guest? What guest?"

"I don't know. Now that Bobby is history, I suppose I could bring Howser," Diane said, swinging one leg and grinning wryly. Howser was her surly, overweight cat.

"Are you seriously thinking of going to the wedding?"

Diane laughed. "Oh, sure. There's nothing I'd rather do than travel all the way to Lynwood, Ohio, to see that jerk get married. And I'm sure Howser would sacrifice his entire supply of Fancy Feast tuna for the chance to go with me." She thought for a minute, then added, "If Howser were a real tiger, instead of a tiger-striped tomcat from the pound, I'd consider bringing him. Then, just when Phil's about to say, 'I do,' I'd unleash Howser and he'd leap for Phil's throat. He'd tear Phil's face to ribbons with his claws and—"

Cassie shuddered and held up a hand. "Enough!" she groaned. Voodoo dolls she could handle, but violent imagery nauseated her.

Ignoring Cassie's protest, Diane sat straighter, energized by the gruesome idea. "You know, I think this has possibilities. I could rent a tiger."

"Rent one?"

"Or borrow one from the Franklin Park Zoo. It says 'and guest'," she emphasized, jabbing the words on the envelope. "Why not? I could take some huge, predatory beast with me to the wedding and set him loose on the guests. As I unhooked the leash, I'd smile and say, 'Cassie wasn't able to attend the wedding, but she asked me to bring you this.'"

Diane often helped Cassie out as a script doctor; plotting was her specialty. Once she got going on a plot, she revved up until her engines were firing in overdrive. She was well into overdrive now, Cassie thought, not exactly pleased.

"Better yet," Diane continued, eyes bright and both legs pumping, "in order to spare myself any possible injury and to stay out of trouble with the animal-rights crowd, I could skip the tiger and, instead, plant time bombs around the wedding venue. Then I could disappear, and at the moment Phil is about to say 'I do,' the bombs would all explode. Think of the carnage!"

Cassie swallowed and pressed her hand to her queasy stomach. "That's exactly what I'm thinking of."

Diane pretended to be disappointed by Cassie's squeamish reaction. "You don't like my idea?"

"It's too commercial." That was a joke they shared with other staffers at the station: whenever anyone came up with a concept that was violent or sensational or at all likely to generate rabid audience enthusiasm, the rest of the staff would shake their heads, click their tongues with feigned disgust and say, "Too commercial."

Diane smiled. "Okay. No time bombs. A few small grenades?"

"Not funny, Diane."

Subsiding, Diane cut back to swinging only one leg. "All right, I'll behave. Seriously, what should we do?"

"You should go to the wedding, so you can come back to Boston and cheer me up by telling me Phillip's

gained thirty pounds and lost half his hair, and Tricia
Lynn Riggs is terminally ugly with a voice like Daffy
Duck's and green warts all over her face.''

"I don't want to go," Diane said.

"But I think you should," Cassie argued out of or-
neriness. "You said his mother was sweet."

Diane curled her lip. "Ohio?" she muttered, making it sound like a toxic waste dump. "Why would I
want to go to Ohio? Okay, so his mom is sweet, but
Ohio? If he were getting married in New Orleans, I'd
give it serious thought. Or San Francisco. Or even San
Antonio."

She picked up a travel brochure about San Antonio's River Walk from the array of Alamo information
scattered across the worktable, and the topic of conversation abruptly veered in the direction of work.
"You really think kids are going to want to see a show
about a bunch of cafés along a canal?" she asked as
she skimmed the article. "The Alamo, sure, Davy
Crockett and all that. But the River Walk?"

"It's supposed to be beautiful."

"It is," Diane assured her. "I was there once.
Those little cafés along the canal, so romantic, with
candlelit tables and mariachi music and double-sized
margaritas...." She sighed dramatically, causing her
shaggy brown mane to quiver around her face. "Unfortunately I was there with Bobby, and this was right
about the time I was beginning to realize he was a
first-class turd. But it was awfully romantic. Not nec-
essarily suitable for a kids' TV show, though."

"I was figuring the episode would focus mostly on
the Alamo," Cassie assured her, plucking the brochure
out of Diane's hand and putting it back on the table.
She didn't want to discuss San Antonio right now. She

wanted to discuss Phillip Keene and his abhorrent wedding—and her own misery.

Diane seemed to read her mind. "Assuming I went to the wedding," she began, "what would *you* do?"

Cassie sighed, compulsively touching the invitation, tracing the letters, sliding her index finger along the creamy edge of the card. "I would buy a quart of black-cherry ice cream, rent *Brief Encounter* and go home and wallow in self-pity."

Diane shook her head. "Wallowing in self-pity is an indulgence you can't afford. You need to become proactive, Cassie."

Cassie wrinkled her nose. "About what?"

"About this wedding."

"How can I be proactive? The guy deceived me. I was an idiot. And now he's gone. It's over and done. Where's the proactive scenario in all this?"

Diane ruminated. "Maybe *you* could go to the wedding and plant the time bombs."

"Me? I wasn't invited."

"Oh, I see. You want me to go and cause mayhem, while you stay home and play the innocent."

"Mayhem?" A tiny smile threatened the corners of Cassie's mouth.

"Well, you said no bombs—but hey, how about planting stink bombs? That way, no one would get hurt. They'd just smell godawful."

A full-fledged grin hijacked Cassie's lips, even as fresh tears stung her eyes. "You have a sick mind," she scolded her friend. "And I'm not going to the wedding."

"Why not?"

"For one thing," she reminded Diane again, "I wasn't invited."

"Yes, but I was," Diane said, then fluttered the envelope under Cassie's nose. "Diane Krensky *and Guest.* You can come as my guest."

Cassie was surprised to find herself actually considering the idea. "You don't think Howser would mind my taking his place?"

"Of course Howser would mind. Howser minds everything. But if I let him decide what I was going to do, my life would be confined to tossing toy mice across the living-room floor and replenishing the supply of Fancy Feast. Forget about Howser. He simply has to learn how to cope."

Cassie tried to hold on to her smile, but all the humor drained from her. Maybe it was because she knew that, even more than Diane's cantankerous cat, she herself had to learn how to cope. Nearly a year had elapsed since Phillip Keene had vanished from her world without a trace, and she'd thought she had gotten the hang of coping. But the appearance of this wedding invitation—the invitation she couldn't stop fondling, as if she had some kind of fetish—had disabled her coping mechanisms.

"I don't want to go," she said mournfully, hating the fact that more tears were surging through her. She could feel them gathering in her throat, rising through her sinuses, flooding her eyes, then seeping through her lashes and making the return trip down her cheeks to her mouth. She tasted salt on her upper lip. "I don't want to be there to see Phillip pledge his troth to another woman."

"You could go and cut off his troth with a kitchen knife."

"I can't believe how bloodthirsty you are."

"Any guy who does to my best friend what this

guy—'' Diane stabbed at the invitation with her index finger ''—did to you whets my thirst for blood. I say let's go and wreak havoc.''

"I'm trying to put together the fall schedule for the show," Cassie argued, surveying the worktable as if she needed to see all the outlines and notes to convince herself. "I can't just drop everything and fly off to Ohio."

"You're right," Diane said too quickly. "You can't. Forget the whole thing."

Diane was deliberately pushing her buttons—Cassie knew all her friend's manipulative ploys. Knowing them didn't make them any less effective, though. As soon as Diane told her she couldn't do something, she wouldn't be able to stop thinking about doing it. "Unless…"

Diane's eyes sparkled. She knew she'd piqued Cassie's interest. "Unless what?"

Cassie didn't even *want* to be thinking what she was thinking. What she wanted to be thinking was that Diane was a troublemaker who ought to be ignored when she got this way. But that thought simply didn't seem as important as the ideas churning inside Cassie, bubbling up and bursting with gleeful little pops. "Unless there's something going on in Lynwood, Ohio, that we could turn into a show."

"A show," Diane said, her expression dubious but her gaze unflagging.

The premise of *Dream Wheels* was flexible: a group of children owned magic bicycles that could carry them off on adventures. Sometimes the adventures involved traveling through time, like the upcoming Alamo episode, where the *Dream Wheels* kids would join up with Davy Crockett and Jim Bowie in the battle against Santa Ana. Sometimes the adventures involved traveling through space; since the show first went on the air two years ago, the *Dream Wheels* kids had visited Bermuda, Hudson Bay and—thanks to some deft editing and the generous assistance of NASA—the surface of Mars.

Not that Phillip Keene's hometown promised to be a particularly exotic location. But if the *Dream Wheels* kids could meet Crockett and Bowie and learn all about the River Walk and double-sized margaritas, why couldn't they fly their *Dream Wheels* bikes to Lynwood, Ohio?

Diane shook her head. "What could you possibly tape out there? I mean, come on, Cassie. *Ohio.*"

"Do you know what's right in the middle of Lynwood, Ohio?" Cassie slid her chair back so she wouldn't have to twist her head to look at Diane. "Keene Furniture."

"A store? Wow."

"A furniture factory." She shouldn't waste her creative energy even framing such a show in her mind, but once she'd latched on to a notion, she couldn't abandon it. If she talked it out, it would probably start to sound inane to her, and she wanted it to sound inane so she could forget about it. "Phil's grandfather founded the firm during the depression," she told Diane. "They make high-quality wood furniture. Top-of-the-line stuff, Phil used to tell me. Lots of hands-on carpenter work, topnotch craftsmanship and all that. It could turn into a terrific 'how' show." "How" shows were episodes that demonstrated how something was made or done. Last season, she'd produced shows on how crayons were made, how cartographers drew maps and how turbine engines worked. "Think about it,'' she said, realizing with some dismay that the concept didn't sound the least bit inane. "We could start with a tree and show how it gets cut down, how it gets sawed into lumber, how it gets shaped and sanded and constructed into a chair. How does a tree become a chair? That would be our episode.'' She studied Diane's face, half hoping Diane would insist that it was a really bad idea for a show. "What do you think?''

Diane looked troubled. She bit her lip, toyed with a strand of her hair and scowled. "It sounds great,'' she admitted reluctantly.

"We could fly to Lynwood, and the show's budget will pay for it. We could film our chair-building sequences at Keene Furniture, cut off Phil's troth and come home.''

"And you say I'm bloodthirsty,'' Diane complained.

Cassie ignored her. "We'd have to bring a cameraman with us. You think Roger Beckelman would do it?'' A few months ago Cassie had stolen Roger from one of the local news broadcasts up in Maine. He had an easygoing nature, blessedly devoid of artistic temperament. He did his job and took satisfaction in it without throwing tantrums or making demands. Cassie wasn't sure she could count on him to plant bombs for her, but if the mission was to film sequences for the show, he was her man.

"Roger Beckelman,'' Diane said, "would stand out in Lynwood, Ohio, like Gulliver in Lilliput.''

"You don't know that.'' True, Roger was well over six feet tall and bone-thin, with blond hair that fell to his waist and a wardrobe that ranged from torn denim to nearly torn denim, with a few T-shirts and flannels thrown in for variety. Roger wore an earring and had a tattoo of a flower on his left forearm. Beyond his tattoo and his mellow attitude, Cassie didn't know much about the man, but she believed that an even temper and a respect for flowers were enough to distinguish him as a man of quality. "For all we know, Lynwood is a mecca of sophistication in the heart of Ohio."

"For all we know, Lynwood is a mecca of soybean fields and cow dung. With a furniture factory stuck in the middle of it."

"All right, look." Cassie had forgotten how depressed she was about Phillip's marriage. She was too excited by the idea of filming a "how" sequence for her show at a furniture factory. She would have to get permission to film there, and to do that she'd have to circumvent Phillip, who would never grant her permission to do anything that might put her in the path of his wedding. But if she had Diane contact Keene Furniture's public-relations department and kept her own name out of it, she might be able to pull it off.

And then she and Diane and Roger could fly to Ohio without having to pay their own transportation or housing costs. They could get some fabulous footage for *Dream Wheels* and...do something. She wasn't sure what, but the idea of planting stink bombs at Phillip's wedding appealed to her. "Can I count on you?"

Diane slid off the table and smoothed her T-shirt into the waistband of her jeans. "Can you count on me for what?"

"Filming how carpenters transform a tree into a chair and helping me take revenge on Phil."

Diane's face broke into a wicked smile. "Of course you can count on me! I'm proud of you. Isn't this more fun that pigging out on ice cream and watching an old tearjerker on the VCR?''

"I'm not sure it's more fun," Cassie said. "It's certainly more proactive. The wedding is in less than two months. We've got work to do. The first item on your agenda is to RSVP that you and a guest are going to be there. An anonymous guest. Don't you dare mention my name." Cassie handed the invitation back to Diane, who slid it into its envelope and started toward the door.

In the open doorway she turned back and gave Cassie a measuring look. "What's the first item on *your* agenda?"

Cassie drew in a deep breath. "To convince myself that this isn't the dumbest thing I've ever done."

"It isn't," Diane assured her. "The dumbest thing you ever did was to fall in love with Phil."

Cassie couldn't deny that. She waved her friend off, then dropped back into her chair and stared blankly at the San Antonio materials strewn across her table.

Giving her heart to Phillip Keene had definitely been dumb. Traveling to Ohio with the intent of sabotaging his wedding to someone else probably ran a close second.

But if she survived stink bombs, troth amputation and the likely demolition of her own fragile ego, she might at least get a fabulous episode of *Dream Wheels* out of it.

CHAPTER TWO

FROM THE WINDOWS of his office, Phillip could see the river. It flowed slowly now, the locks and sluices eroded, crumbling in disuse.

In the nineteenth century the building had been a textile mill, dependent on the river's current to power its looms. But the mill had closed down, following cheaper labor south, and when Phillip's grandfather had bought the old brick building, gutted it and converted it into a carpentry shop during the Great Depression, the river had meandered back to its original course.

Keene Furniture Company had grown bigger over the years, while the river had grown older and calmer. Now it was nothing more than a bit of picturesque scenery outside Phillip's window. Actually, it was a hell of a lot more picturesque than the figures Phillip had been crunching on his computer in an effort to tame the company's torrential river of debt.

A knock at the door drew his attention from the view beyond the glass. His office was long and high-ceilinged, the walls unadorned brick, the windows tall and multipaned. At one time, teenage girls from the outlying farms had spun cotton into thread in this room. Now the pine plank floor was covered with a rug, the inner wall was lined with built-in bookshelves and the room was filled with Phillip's massive desk, a computer workstation, a sofa, several chairs and a coffee table. His father was still the firm's CEO in name, but Phillip's office shouted *I'm in charge.*

As he glanced toward the door, it opened and his secretary, Edie, peered in. "Tricia's here," she announced.

Before he could speak, Tricia nudged Edie aside and swept into the office, a vision of pastel silk and bouncy red hair. "Hello, there!" she chirped, waltzing across the room and flinging her arms around him. She planted a noisy kiss on his cheek, then leaned back and appraised him. "What? No smile for me?"

Phillip dutifully smiled.

"Edie said you were working, but I see she was wrong." Tricia tossed a teasing smile over her shoulder to Phillip's dour secretary, then turned back to him. "You were staring out the window and moping, weren't you? You were thinking about how desperate you were to take a break and get some fresh air. And have lunch with me, of course."

His smile this time came naturally. Tricia liked to manipulate and manage him, but her efforts were so transparent he wasn't offended by them.

If he really hadn't wanted to take a break, he would have declined her invitation without hesitation. But the cash-flow problems with Keene's retail store in Chicago were so ghastly contemplating them had given him a headache. If he continued to study the numbers throughout lunchtime, his skull might split open from the pressure. "I can spare a half hour," he said.

Tricia pouted prettily. "Forty-five minutes?" she wheedled.

"Forty, and count your blessings." He crossed to

his desk, scooped his jacket from the back of his chair and put it on.

"It'll take me that long just to go over the flowers with you," she said, hooking her hand through the bend in his elbow and urging him toward the door.

Phillip didn't give a rat's ass about the flowers. Tricia was the one staging the most elegant wedding Lynwood, Ohio, had ever seen—Tricia and her mother. It was their show, and as far as he was concerned, their flowers. "You can tell me about them at lunch," he said.

"But we'll be eating then."

"So you'll talk with food in your mouth."

She gave him a stricken look; evidently she didn't realize he was joking. He tried to convince himself that her obtuseness amused him.

There were worse things in life, he reminded himself, than marrying a woman who failed to get your jokes eighty percent of the time. It would be far worse to marry someone you couldn't tolerate. Or to watch the Keene Furniture Company sink like a stone to the bottom of the river after sixty successful years because Phillip's father had expanded too rapidly into the retail side of the business, running up debts the company couldn't pay on any sort of reasonable schedule.

Phillip admired Tricia. He didn't have to think too hard with her, or try too hard. She had a pleasant disposition and great legs. He honestly believed he could build a life with her while devoting the bulk of his energy to restoring Keene Furniture's profitability.

"Lunch," she reminded him, giving his arm a tug.

She must have sensed that his thoughts had veered far from the subject of flowers. The process of planning a wedding struck Phillip as much too complicated, especially since the entire affair was going to occupy all of one June afternoon. So much hoopla for a few hours of partying. So many decisions, so many demands. So much money.

It was mostly Tricia's father's money, though. And Phillip's mother was making most of the decisions for his side, thank God. He had enough on his mind without having to make wedding decisions, too.

He descended the stairs to the first floor with Tricia. The high heels of her shoes clicked loudly in the stairwell, and his headache threatened to return. He'd never had a headache in Boston, he recalled. Educating himself at a high-pressure business school and living amid the incessant cacophony of the city that labeled itself the Hub of the Universe had never triggered cranial pain in him. But ever since he'd returned to Lynwood, his placid, picturesque hometown, with its pristine air and its leisurely pace, he'd been plagued by headaches, low-level pulses of tension above the bridge of his nose, behind his eyebrows, at his temples.

The spring sunshine as he and Tricia emerged from the building was as bright as a shiny new tack—and it stabbed his eyes like a tack, too. He pulled his sunglasses from an inner pocket of his jacket and slid them on.

Seemingly impervious to the glare, Tricia tucked her hand more snugly around his arm and led him across the parking lot toward the gate in the chain-link fence that surrounded the factory property. Her walk had a regal air of entitlement. She didn't gloat about being the daughter of the richest, best-connected man in Lynwood, but, as his mother would say, she didn't hide her light under a bushel, either. At times Phillip felt Tricia viewed him as no more or less than her due. Who else but Tricia Lynn Riggs, fair and pretty, a homecoming queen and the one-time captain of the cheerleading squad, should be engaged to marry the heir to the Keene Furniture dynasty?

They went through the open gate and up the shaded drive to Main Street. The "malling" of America seemed to have bypassed Lynwood. There was a mall fifteen miles away, and Columbus lay just beyond that, if a person had a serious hankering for the big city. But Lynwood hadn't changed much in the century since the textile mill was built. Main Street cut a graceful curve through the heart of town, a broad boulevard lined with stately shade trees, clean sidewalks and shops built to human scale. Sleek luxury cars shared the road with bicycles and rickety pickup trucks. Litter wound up not in the gutter but in the trash cans that stood on every corner.

It was, frankly, a bit dull. But Phillip had enough excitement in his life just going through Keene Furniture's accounts. Every time he located another loan his father had signed for, his heart skipped a beat and his blood pressure jumped a notch. What he needed was a tranquillizer. Lacking that, he'd dose himself with a steady regimen of Lynwood.

Tricia ushered him past the hardware store, past Leona's Hair Salon and Bingo's Pet Supplies—Yes, We Have Live Crickets! a sign in the window boasted—to the corner where Main and Elm intersected. Across the way, the sign above the bank indicated that it was sixty-eight degrees. The post office, a squat brick mausoleum-like building, stood directly opposite, and catercorner to it was Tricia's favorite downtown lunch spot, a dangerously cute café that specialized in pseudo-organic sandwiches on bread that always seemed to have seeds in it. If he hadn't warned Tricia that he was pressed for time, she might have wanted to drive out to Linden Hills, the dining room of which served the closest thing to gourmet cuisine available in Lynwood. But for a quick bite and a conference on flowers, Harvest Bounty would do.

Phillip hoped it wouldn't be mobbed. The bank crowd always overran the place at twelve-thirty, but it was just barely noon. He noticed only three people perusing the menu posted in the window. The man was lanky, dressed in fraying blue jeans and an untucked flannel shirt, his blond hair pulled into a ponytail that dropped halfway down his back. He was flanked by two women, one built like an athlete, with wide shoulders and stylishly shaggy light-brown hair. She wore sweatpants and sneakers and looked fully prepared to embark on a marathon run.

The other woman was slim and petite, her hair the color of dark chocolate, straight and blunt-cut at her shoulders. Peering into the window, she presented only her back to Phillip, but he found it an unnervingly familiar back. Did he actually recognize the shapeless brown blazer? Had he ever seen a woman fill khaki slacks exactly the way that woman did?

The light turned green and Tricia stepped off the curb, her hand still hooked around Phillip's elbow. Inexplicably shaken by the sight of the woman's back, he accompanied Tricia onto the crosswalk. His pulse accelerated the way it did whenever he found anything ominous in the company records. And an orchestra comprised of nothing but snare drums played inside his head.

He knew those shoulders, damn it. He knew that

stance. He recognized the slight tilt of the woman's head as she scrutinized the restaurant's menu.

Tricia seemed oblivious to the sudden shift in his mood. She strolled blithely across the street, beaming a smile intended, apparently, for anyone privileged enough to glance her way. When they reached the opposite corner, Phillip swallowed and took a deep breath, bracing himself as the threesome turned from the window.

Cassie. What the hell was she doing in Lynwood?

He was vaguely aware that he knew the other woman, but who she was didn't interest him. His gaze zeroed in on Cassie, her heart-shaped face, the dark arches of her eyebrows, her tentative smile. Her eyes, searching his face. Her teeth, working her lower lip as she stared up at him.

Oh, God. Cassie.

She looked good—the way a favorite hammock looked good, the way a glass of lemonade looked good on a scorching August day, the way the ocean looked good when the surf rolled in a curl of silver onto a hot white beach. He wanted to dive into her and feel her all around him.

"Hey, Phil!" the other woman exclaimed. "Hey! Great to see you!"

It took all his concentration and energy to complete the simple act of turning from Cassie to acknowledge the other woman. "Diane?" he mumbled, utterly perplexed. What was Diane Krensky from the public-TV station in Boston doing in Lynwood? Why was Diane grinning at him, rising on tiptoe and kissing his cheek?

Who cared? The only important question was, what was Cassie Webber doing in Lynwood?

"Who are these people?" Tricia asked him, her fingers squeezing his elbow and her teeth clenched behind her smile, so the words came out cramped.

He ignored her. Not deliberately, not to be rude, but because, with Cassie standing right in front of him, less than ten inches away, he couldn't deal with his fiancée, or Diane Krensky, or the tall guy with the skinny ponytail…or anyone at all. Anyone but Cassie.

His heart felt thick in his chest, dense, straining to complete each pulse. His headache vanished, but so did the tranquillizing effects of a gorgeous spring day in his picturesque midwestern hometown. He wanted…

Heaven help him, but he wanted to be back in hot, humid, noisy Boston, in Cassie's tiny, stuffy apartment with the rattling air conditioner and the scent of vanilla and orange spice in the air, Cassie's scents. He wanted to be naked with her, loving her, feeling her hot and wet around him. Feeling her come around him.

What he most definitely didn't want was to be staring at her on a street corner in Lynwood less than a week before he was scheduled to marry another woman.

"I'm Diane Krensky," Diane introduced herself to Tricia when it became obvious he wasn't going to do the honors. "I'm a friend of Phil's from Boston. And this is Cassie Webber, another friend of his from Boston," she said, nudging Cassie slightly.

Was it only Phillip's imagination, or had Diane emphasized the word *friend* when she used it in reference to Cassie? Had she known he and Cassie had been lovers? Had Cassie confided in her?

"And this is Roger Beckelman," Diane said, completing the introductions.

Phillip found the strength to shake the tall guy's

hand. If Roger had been a friend from Boston, too, Phillip didn't remember him.

Nor could he begin to grasp why any of them were in Lynwood, this week of all weeks. Couldn't they have come next week, when he and Tricia would have been out of town on their honeymoon? Or couldn't they have not come at all?

It didn't matter. For whatever reason, they were here. *Cassie* was here. *Cassie Webber,* the smartest, sexiest, most tantalizing woman he'd ever known.

He noticed the way dimples formed at the corners of her lips, the way her left eyebrow arched slightly higher than her right, the way her jacket sloped off her shoulders as, doing his best to be courteous, he reached for her hand and gave it a bland shake. Despite the fact that Tricia was still clinging to his arm, Cassie shook his hand, her fingers small but strong around his. He remembered the way her hands had felt on his body, and he shifted his stance, grateful to be wearing pleated trousers.

Her smile remained shy, uncertain, lacking in warmth or trust. Well, hell, how could she trust him after what he'd done to her? He hadn't meant to hurt her, hadn't wanted to—but sometimes life got in the way of the best-laid plans. Life had hurt him, too, but he'd worked hard to put her out of his mind. What troubled him was that, a full year later, she apparently hadn't succeeded in putting him out of hers.

Who was he kidding? He hadn't succeeded, either. Not really. He'd only tossed a blanket over her so she wasn't visible to him. But she'd always been there, a hot spot in his memory, just waiting for something to happen that would knock the blanket off and reveal her.

Like this. Like her turning up in Lynwood with her good friend Diane and some scarecrow-looking fellow with a diamond stud in his left earlobe.

He had to say something. Tricia was staring at him quizzically. "Um…this is a real surprise," he said stupidly. "What brings you to Lynwood?"

"Surely you didn't think we'd miss it!" Diane answered, even though Phillip hadn't addressed the question to her.

His gaze remained on Cassie: the soft, pale skin of her throat, her gently rounded hips, her short, unpolished fingernails, the chunky gold signet ring on her right ring finger and the watch on a thick leather strap around her left wrist.

"Miss what?" he asked.

"Your wedding! We're here for your wedding. Well, Cassie and I are. We just dragged Roger along for work."

"Work?"

Ignoring him, Diane turned to Tricia. "You must be the lucky bride-to-be. Tricia, right?"

"Yes." Tricia flashed another curious look at Phillip, who was scrambling to keep up with Diane. Why was she here for the wedding? Why was Cassie here? How had they even heard about it?

"It was such a surprise to get the invitation," Diane continued, answering his unvoiced question. "I mean, we never would have guessed you'd gone home to Ohio and found yourself a fiancée. It was the last thing any of us would have expected. Right, Cassie?"

Pink shot through Cassie's cheeks. Her eyes glistened slightly; Phillip assumed the noon sun was irritating them. He wanted to lend her his sunglasses, but how could he with Tricia still hanging off his arm?

He tried to stop letting Cassie's lovely brown eyes mesmerize him. He had to contend not only with Tricia but with Diane and her startling revelation. She'd gotten an invitation? He was even more surprised than she was!

Who'd invited her? And for crying out loud, who'd invited Cassie?

Someone must have, because here they were.

Lowering his gaze, he glimpsed her hands again. Such delicate-looking hands. He remembered the first time he'd seen her, those small, blunt-nailed hands clutching the corners of a splintery wooden footlocker so tall it blocked her face from his view. All he'd seen when he'd stepped out of the business office at the public-TV station was the towering footlocker, its green paint peeling, a pair of slim legs in blue jeans extending below it and at its outer edges her little-girl hands, clinging.

"Let me help you with that," he'd said.

Her voice, dark and husky, had reached him from behind the footlocker: "That's all right, I've got it."

Even more than he'd wanted to assist her, he'd wanted to see the face that went with that sexy voice. He'd lifted the trunk out of her hands, discovered that it was actually rather light, although definitely unwieldy, and he'd found that the face was remarkable. Not stereotypically pretty but fascinating, a contrast of creamy skin and dark hair, a pug nose and soft coral lips, and eyelashes so long and thick he wouldn't have been surprised to learn that she had to comb them every morning to keep them from tangling.

He'd known right away that he wanted to be friends with this woman. More than friends.

But they weren't friends anymore. If they had been friends, he would have invited her to his wedding.

Maybe he *had* invited her and he just didn't remember. The past few months had been so hectic, what with the threat of financial disaster at Keene Furniture and Tricia's frenetic preparations for the wedding, that for all he knew, he might have jotted Cassie's and Diane's names onto a preliminary list of invitees. He couldn't believe he could do something so utterly brainless, but standing just inches from Cassie, under the current circumstances, made him believe he was fully capable of doing all sorts of brainless things.

Everyone seemed to be waiting for him to speak. "The wedding isn't until Saturday," he said. "Why are you here now?" Even allowing for the bizarre possibility that he had somehow authorized someone to send Cassie and her buddy Diane an invitation, he couldn't understand why they'd come to Lynwood almost a week early.

And who the hell was this Roger Beckelman? Even if Phillip had been insane enough to invite Cassie and Diane to his wedding, who was their male escort? Diane's friend or Cassie's? Why did the possibility that he was Cassie's friend cause Phillip to suffer a twinge of jealousy?

None of it made sense. But for some reason, the drum ensemble in Phillip's skull had stopped playing and decamped. Simply standing close to Cassie seemed to cure him.

Stupid thought. His headache had vanished because he'd left the office and the ghastly debit-red blot his father had made of the company's bottom line. If anything, Cassie's presence should make him feel worse, not better.

"You know," Tricia was saying, "Phillip doesn't talk much about the time he spent in Boston. I'm so glad he invited some of his Boston friends to our wedding so I could meet you. Say, here's an idea!" She steered her radiant smile from Beckelman, who stood a good six inches taller than she did, past Diane, who was about her height, down to Cassie, who stood a good three inches shorter. "Why don't you folks join us for lunch, and you can tell me all about Boston."

"We'd love to," Diane said.

Her swift acceptance roused Phillip's suspicions, though he wasn't sure why. "I thought we were going to talk about the flowers," he reminded Tricia.

"Like you really care," she shot back. "White, pink and red roses in the bouquets, red rose boutonnieres for the men. It's going to cost a fortune. Come on, let's see if we can snag a table before the bankers get here." She reached for the restaurant door and Beckelman swung it open for her.

Phillip shot Cassie a perplexed look before gesturing her ahead of him into the restaurant. She smiled back, a smile that reminded him of exactly what had drawn him to her in the first place, what had made him treasure her friendship, what had made him regret that friendship as much as he craved it.

It was a smile that did nothing to ease his apprehension.

SO THIS WAS the lucky bride-to-be, Cassie thought as she shook her napkin open across her lap. This was Tricia Lynn Riggs, the woman to whom Phillip had committed himself, the woman for whom he had abandoned Cassie.

Tricia looked uncannily like Fergie, the redhead ex-wife of whichever English prince it was. Cassie couldn't keep the royal family straight, but she had the feeling Tricia Lynn Riggs was the sort of woman who could.

She was definitely beautiful. She had lovely proportions, unlike Cassie, who'd always felt her limbs were too long and thin, her knees and elbows too big for her slight frame. Cassie would never look good in pastels, and while she could probably afford a silk dress if she found one on the rack at Filene's Basement, the bulk of her wardrobe ran to slacks and blazers.

It wasn't that Tricia was glamorous, but she was…*feminine.* Cassie was a woman, no question about it. But feminine? Not in a groomed, gorgeous, pastel-silk way.

Just the thought that she could never look good in pastels was enough to make Cassie want to weep.

No, it wasn't. She'd never cared one way or another about pastels, and she wasn't going to start caring now. She wanted to weep because, as much as she hated Phillip, as much as she wanted to wreak revenge on him, as much as she wanted to ensure that the year 2000 would go down in his memory as the absolute worst year of his life, seeing him reminded her of how much she had once loved him.

Thank goodness she had Diane and Roger to buffer her. Roger wasn't much of a talker, but he was tall and he was male. Diane could do the talking for all three of them.

Looking at Phillip churned up too many memories, too much emotion. Cassie turned her attention to the menu, buying time to collect herself. The lunch offer-

ings were tame, the most exotic sandwich a concoction
of grilled eggplant and melted mozzarella on a seven-
grain roll. That must be Lynwood's idea of Italian
food, she thought wryly. Only a few hundred miles
from Boston, she felt as if she had landed in a foreign
country.

A waitress approached their table, pencil poised
above her pad. "Hey, there, Tricia," she greeted Phillip's fiancée. "How's it going?"

"Busy," Tricia confided, her smile as sweet and
light as powdered sugar. "Crazy. Too much to do, too
little time."

"Well, it's gonna be a fantabulous wedding, I just
know it. Me and Doug can't wait. I mean, try to get
him to put on a suit and tie and take me anywhere?
He says to me, 'Hey, Janelle, this wedding is just a
week before our wedding anniversary. So we don't
have to go out for our anniversary. We'll just do this
big wedding at the country club and call it a date.' I
mean, is he cheap or what?" She directed her grin to
Phillip. "So, whaddaya say, Phil? Any premarital jit-
ters?"

"No," he answered laconically. "I'm pressed for
time, Janelle, so…"

"Sure." She adjusted the angle of her pencil and
gazed expectantly around the table. Both Tricia and
Roger ordered tuna melts. Diane requested the turkey
club. Cassie and Phillip ordered grilled-cheese-and-
tomato sandwiches. Iced tea all around. Janelle
bounced away to pass along their orders to the chef.

"Janelle was a cheerleader with me in high
school," said Tricia. "Lynwood is a small world. Everybody knows everybody. That's why we've invited

everybody to the wedding. But it's so neat that we're going to have some of Phillip's Boston friends here, too. How many people from Boston did you invite, honey?'' she asked him.

He shrugged helplessly and shook his head. "I don't remember," he murmured, glancing pointedly at Cassie. His frown informed her that he did remember she wasn't among them.

"So, how do you three know one another?" Tricia asked, eyeing Roger.

"We all work together," Diane explained. Cassie felt a poke in her shin—Diane's sneaker, a signal that she ought to say something. Diane was right. If she remained silent, Phillip was going to figure out that she was under emotional siege.

"I produce a TV show for public broadcasting," she told Tricia, relieved when her voice came out sounding normal. "It's called *Dream Wheels*. Diane is my right-hand person, and Roger is our chief cameraman. He joined the staff at *Dream Wheels* after Phillip left Boston," she added, glancing briefly at Phillip to demonstrate how unaffected she was by his nearness.

"Cassie stole him from a news show up in Bangor, Maine. The best theft she ever committed," Diane added. Roger chuckled modestly. As far as he was concerned, their primary reason for being in Lynwood was to tape some segments for the show.

Phillip seemed to be sizing him up. Cassie could guess what he was thinking: this fellow needs to meet a barber. But then, Phillip wasn't the most obsessively well-groomed fellow she'd ever known. True, at the moment he looked like nothing so much as a young executive on the rise, but back in Boston she'd often seen him in jeans, old polo shirts and deck shoes without socks, a day's growth of beard darkening his jaw.

"Dream Wheels?" Tricia asked.

"It's a children's show," Cassie told her. "Once you and Phil have kids, you'll be watching it all the time." Good. She could mention Phillip in the context of marriage and parenthood and sound totally unperturbed.

Even better, Phillip *didn't* look totally unperturbed by her comment. "You still haven't explained why you're here almost a week ahead of the wedding," he said.

Janelle the waitress arrived at their table. Cassie waited until the drinks were distributed, then took a sip of her iced tea. Sitting so close to Phillip jangled her nervous system. Trying to pretend she was calm jangled it even more. But she was going to put on an Emmy-caliber performance. She was going to stay cool and calm and charmingly vindictive. She was going to ruin his life before he ever even figured out what she was up to.

If she herself could figure out what she was up to, and *if* she could pull it off.

And those were a couple of huge *if*s, she admitted grimly. "We're going to film some segments in the area for next season's *Dream Wheels*. There's a working dairy farm about an hour north of here we may be visiting if we have time, and the Audubon Society runs a bird-banding project at a state park not too far away."

"But primarily we're here to do the Keene Furniture feature," Diane said.

Phillip flinched. "What Keene Furniture feature?"

"Cool!" Tricia spoke simultaneously. "A feature about Keene Furniture? For a TV show? Wow! That's so cool. What's it going to be about?"

Cassie immediately turned to her. She knew Phillip was upset—just as she'd hoped he would be. She wanted him rocked and rattled. "The premise of *Dream Wheels*," she explained, "is, a group of city kids have these magic bicycles. When conditions are just right, the bicycles turn into flying machines and carry them off on escapades. The conditions aren't always just right, though, and they can't always control where the 'dream wheels' take them. But they have all kinds of adventures. We intersperse animated excerpts with film footage. We try to make the films educational, about exotic places or different periods in history—or about how chairs are made."

"What gave you the idea of filming at Keene?" Phillip asked tightly.

"You gave me the idea." She smiled, feeling her cheeks cramp from the effort.

Phillip's answering smile was deadly. "How did I do that?"

"You used to describe the place to me. The design shop, the carpentry shop, the lathes, the sawdust. Soaking and bowing the wood. Staining it. It's perfect for a 'how' show."

"What's a 'how' show?" Tricia asked.

"Where the film excerpt shows how something is done. I thought that how chairs are constructed would make for a terrific show."

Diane took over again. "Keene Furniture's PR guy—Lowell something?" She glanced at Cassie, seeking help.

"Lowell Henley," Cassie said.

"Right. He gave us the green light. So we're going to be spending a few days taping there."

Phillip was clearly displeased. "Just what we need. A film crew traipsing around the building."

"Not a crew," Diane assured him. "Just the three of us. We'll be discreet. You won't even know we're there." Her smile could have taken paint off a car, Cassie thought. Of course Phillip would know they were there. She and Diane would make sure he knew, if only to make his final days of bachelorhood more difficult.

Diane took a sip of her iced tea and nodded. "Lowell Henley gave us all the clearances we needed to tape the segment. It'll be great publicity for Keene Furniture."

"Keene Furniture doesn't need publicity right now," Phillip muttered, glowering at Cassie.

"Why not?" Tricia broke in. "I think it's a cool idea." She sent Phillip an adorable pout. "You never told me you hobnobbed with TV people in Boston. You never told me *anything* about Boston."

"I...I didn't think you'd be interested. And anyway—" he studied his drink, studied the checkered tablecloth, studied the cuticle of his left thumb, anything to avoid looking at Cassie "—there wasn't much to tell."

Like hell there wasn't, Cassie thought bitterly. There was plenty to tell, and if Tricia wanted to hear about it, she'd be glad to oblige. If nothing else came out of this trip to Lynwood, if the film segments turned out lousy, if the wedding proceeded without a hitch, if Phillip and Tricia wound up happily ever after with each other... Cassie reassured herself that if she got to tell the joyous bride everything there was to tell about Phillip's promise and his betrayal, his lovemaking and his lying, his two-faced, two-timing faithlessness, maybe the trip wouldn't be a total loss.

CHAPTER THREE

"THIS PLACE IS STRANGE," Roger announced.

Cassie looked up from her laptop. She was ensconced in one of the deeply sloping Adirondack chairs on the front porch of Bailey's Bed-and-Breakfast, a rambling farmhouse-style building on a residential road a few blocks north of Main Street. She, Diane and Roger had considered setting up their base of operations at the motel on the highway just outside the town limits, but the motel had seemed sterile, and Bailey's had been within walking distance of civilization.

Besides, Bailey's screamed charm, with its rambling porch, flower boxes, white clapboard siding and barnred shutters. Unfortunately Bailey's advertised more charm than it delivered. Cassie had generously allowed Roger and Diane to take the two empty rooms on the second floor and had settled into the third-floor attic room beneath the eaves because she was the shortest. Roger in particular could not have survived in the attic room, with its dormer windows and sloping ceiling. He would have run the risk of slamming his head against the ceiling and knocking himself out cold if he'd stood too quickly.

Cassie hadn't seen Diane's and Roger's rooms, but the attic was dark and dreary, the rug threadbare and one of the windows painted permanently shut. She had

noticed that Diane and Roger had access to a shower
on the second floor, whereas the third-floor bathroom
featured only an antiquated claw-footed tub. So, after
dinner, when she'd hoped to have a shower, she had
to resign herself to a bath beneath the eaves.

Sometimes things worked out for the best. Lying in
the deep porcelain basin, gazing up at the slanted ceiling, she'd felt herself decompress in the water's
steamy embrace. She hadn't realized how tightly
wound she was until she began to unwind.

Now, clean and refreshed, she sat on the porch, trying not to wind tight again. The evening was mild, a
slight nip spicing the air. Tissue-thin layers of pink
and golden light rode the horizon, and the muted drone
of insects was punctuated by the occasional gruesome
sizzle of a bug hitting the zap-light that stood on an
aluminum post in the grassy front yard. Curling strips
of flypaper dangled from the porch roof, and several
bright-yellow bags hung on stakes in the shrubbery,
waiting to trap Japanese beetles. The owner of Bailey's, a surly woman of late middle age named Mrs.
Gill, seemed to have invested more in anti-insect war-
fare than in basic plumbing and decor.

Cassie glanced at Roger, sprawled in another Adirondack chair next to her, holding an unopened can of
beer and gazing out at the front yard and the road
beside it, a slab of asphalt edged in grass. She couldn't
argue with him; the place was indeed strange. This
entire trip was strange. If anyone could cope with
strangeness, though, it was Roger Beckelman. Defiantly unkempt, oblivious to style, he was a walking
billboard for strangeness. Yet he was shrewd and talented with a camera, and Cassie had never seen him
lose his temper.

"You think this place is strange, huh?" she said.

"Yeah."

"Care to be specific?"

"There's no minibar in my room," he said.

Cassie considered absence of minibars much less strange than the grisly hisses emanating from the zaplight every time a bug flew too close. "Do you think we should have stayed at the highway motel?"

"Nah. They wouldn't have minibars in that dive, either." He popped the tab on the can. A wisp of white vapor rose from the opening as he lifted it to his lips. He, Diane and Cassie had stopped at a convenience store to stock up on necessities on their way back to the B-and-B after dinner. He'd purchased beer and potato chips. Diane had bought a gallon jug of wine and two half-gallon bottles of Gatorade. Cassie had bought a six-pack of diet soda and a package of chocolate-chip cookies, figuring she would need them either for strength or for solace, depending on how the next few days progressed. She'd bought a few Granny Smith apples to compensate nutritionally for the cookies, and a box of Cheerios in case she didn't like the breakfast served at Bailey's.

"Is there a problem with your room?" she asked Roger.

"Besides the obvious?" He grinned. "There's something scratching in the wall. I think it's a mouse."

Cassie shuddered. "At least you won't get claustrophobia like me."

He took another sip of beer. "It's not this place. It's the whole town. It's like a freaking Norman Rockwell painting."

She grinned and nodded. "I'll bet Phil and Tricia

will get some pretty photographs for their wedding album, surrounded by all this scenery.'' She gestured toward the lilac hedges, dense with pale-lavender blossoms, and the soldierly rows of daffodils framing the front walk. She couldn't care less what kind of wedding photos the lovebirds got, but she was fishing for Roger's opinion of them, and this seemed as good a way as any to introduce them into the conversation. ''What do you think of the happy couple?''

''Well, I'd describe her as ripe and eager,'' he replied, gazing past Cassie as he recollected Tricia. ''I think your old buddy lucked out.''

''You do?''

''A lady like that?'' Roger gave a loose-limbed shrug. ''I wouldn't kick her out of bed.''

Great, Cassie thought sourly. Phillip Keene, an intelligent, compassionate exemplar of high values and depth of character, was going to hang his future on a ripe, eager duchess clone, a woman even Roger wouldn't mind fooling around with.

''So, are we going to film at the dairy tomorrow?'' Roger asked, pointing at her laptop, where she'd been outlining a script for the farm visit.

She shook her head. ''I'm not scheduling the dairy until I see how things go at Keene Furniture.'' After their awkward lunch, she was pretty sure things wouldn't go smoothly.

Running into Phillip so soon after arriving in Lynwood had jarred her. No matter how many pep talks Diane had given her back in Boston and on the flight to Columbus, and no matter how much Cassie wanted to take her revenge on him for shattering her heart, no matter how much she wanted to see him stagger into the new millennium broken and humbled, coming face-to-face with him hadn't gotten her vindictive juices flowing.

Quite the contrary. She'd turned to look at him on that sun-washed street corner and had to summon every ounce of willpower to keep from hurling herself into her arms.

She still loved him. Oh, sure, she hated him with a vengeance...but he was Phillip, *her* Phillip. He was the friend who'd sat with her for hours, listening as she'd described her vision for *Dream Wheels,* her hopes for the show's future, her fears and ambitions. He hadn't scoffed and told her she was as caught up in her own fantasy as her cycling characters were. Instead, he'd given her pointers on how to license *Dream Wheels* toys and assured her that whatever she could dream, she could do.

Phillip had respected her, believed in her, insisted she was a genius. He'd sworn that he considered intelligence and creativity the sexiest attributes a woman could possess.

And then he'd proved it by making love to her, whispering his love to her, swearing his love, promising his love to her forever.

The bastard.

She ought to have reacted to the sight of him with venomous rage. But for some reason, gazing up into his beautiful gray eyes, all she could remember was the love.

Hours later, soaking in the tub in the oddly shaped attic bathroom, letting the warm water embrace her body like a lover—only without the emotional fallout that followed her last experience with a lover's embrace—she managed to wash away most of that romantic claptrap. She wasn't exactly sure she was ready to don her armor and set out to wreak havoc with his life, though.

As if aware of Cassie's faltering resolve, Diane swept through the screen door, letting it swing shut with a hiss. She'd been in the kitchen, explaining to Mrs. Gill that since a full sixty percent of her paying guests were high-power TV professionals from Boston, they deserved access to at least one shelf in the kitchen's refrigerator to store the soda and beer they'd purchased.

"What are you doing?" she asked, circling Cassie's chair and hoisting herself onto the porch railing. "Cooking up devious revenge plots?"

"I don't know how to plot revenge," Cassie confessed with a sigh. "I was actually trying to write a shooting schedule for the chair-making episode." Revenge wasn't her forte, either as a scriptwriter or as a woman scorned. Cassie excelled at conciliation, not getting even. She had achieved what she had by being creative, not destructive. "I don't know what to do about revenge," she said wearily. "Maybe we should just pack up and go back to Boston."

"No," Diane said firmly.

"We can't leave," Roger added. "I brought too much videotape. I want to film a chair."

The crunch of tires on gravel broke into their conversation. Cassie turned in time to see a late-model Mercedes coast to a halt where the grass met the road, right beneath the hinged wooden sign identifying the old farmhouse as Bailey's Bed-and-Breakfast.

In Boston, Phillip had owned a ten-year-old Toyota, which he'd bought secondhand. "If you live in a city," he used to say, "there's no point in owning an expensive car." Cassie hadn't criticized his vehicle.

Since she didn't own a car at all, she'd considered it the height of luxury to travel around town in Phillip's rattletrap.

Here in freaking Norman Rockwell land, of course, he could cruise the streets in a luxury car without worrying about vandalism or theft or the inevitable dings and dents that came from driving on narrow, twisting roads that had been designed four hundred years ago for horses and wagons. In Lynwood, drivers probably stopped at red lights. They probably yielded at yield signs. A pricey car could survive this town unscathed.

She watched as Phillip emerged from the cream-colored sedan. He'd changed out of his business clothes and into the neatest pair of blue jeans she'd ever seen—compared with them, Roger's frayed dungarees looked like a rag doll's rejects—and a crisp white oxford shirt, open at the collar. His car door made an expensive-sounding click when he closed it.

He sauntered up the front walk to the porch and said, "Hi."

In the twilight, Cassie couldn't get a clear reading of his expression. He seemed to be smiling, but it was a taut, uncomfortable smile. His eyes were solemn, dark and probing. Despite his apparent tension, he was still obscenely handsome.

Which wasn't why she'd fallen for him, she hastened to remind herself. Just because looking at him sparked a low heat in her abdomen, and her pulse always got a little jagged when he was in her vicinity, her breath a little shallow.... That they could be talking and arguing, analyzing the meaning of life and bickering over whether *Titanic* was a better flick than *A Night to Remember*, with sex the furthest thing from her mind—and yet her body was always, always tuned to his frequency, picking up signals he probably wasn't even aware of sending....

That wasn't why she'd loved him.

She still seemed to have her dial set to WPHIL, she thought with a blend of disgust and dismay. As he stood at the bottom porch step, gazing up at her, she couldn't help but pick up his signal. Reminding herself that in a matter of days he was going to be entering into a legal, spiritual, lifelong commitment to another woman didn't help. Nor did reminding herself that she'd come to Lynwood to make his life as unpleasant as possible.

"Are you busy?" he asked.

She gave him a chilly smile. "As a matter of fact, we were discussing our plans for filming at Keene Furniture tomorrow."

A muscle flexed in Phillip's jaw. "I was hoping we could talk."

"Sure," she said, pretending the idea delighted her. "Pull up a chair and join us."

He eyed Roger and Diane, then turned back to Cassie. "I meant you and me. We'll go somewhere in my car." With another quick look at the others, he added, "I hope you don't mind."

"No problem," Roger said affably. Cassie would have liked to kick him in the shins. She glanced toward Diane, who sent her a shrug and an encouraging smile. No help there. Neither of her friends was going to rescue her.

Lacking an escape, she clicked off her laptop, snapped it shut and handed it to Diane. Then she sighed, emptying her lungs so she could fill them again with Norman Rockwell air. Maybe talking to Phillip would provide inspiration with regard to her revenge plans. Maybe spending a few minutes in his company would remind her that she hated him more than she desired him.

"Okay," she said brightly, hoisting herself out of the chair. "I'll see you guys later. If I'm not back by ten o'clock, call the police." That last comment was for Phillip's benefit, so he would know she didn't intend to spend more than a couple of hours with him.

Phillip nodded a farewell to Roger and Diane, then stood aside so Cassie could precede him down the walk to the car. With impeccable manners, he opened the passenger door for her and offered her his hand, which she had to take because not taking it would broadcast her hostility toward him. With a polite smile, she let him assist her into the leather bucket seat. It was much too comfortable, especially after the stiff porch chair. As soon as she settled into the contoured cushions, she slipped her hand from his and tugged her door shut, forcing him to back off or risk having his fingers crushed.

She watched him through the windshield as he strolled around the front of the car to the driver's side. He wasn't as tall or skinny as Roger, but there was a lanky grace in his movements, an ease in the way he fit into his body. Unlike his fiancée, he didn't look ripe. Rather, he looked a little raw, despite his refined grooming. He had a hunger in his eyes, an angularity about him, something that made him seem on the verge of breaking into a sprint.

He settled in the seat beside her, and she commanded herself not to think about his appearance—or about the deep warmth his nearness stirred in her. He was her foe, the man who had broken her heart. And her immediate concern was to make sure he didn't know how much damage he'd done.

"Lynwood is such a cute little town," she said in her most saccharine voice.

He shot her a swift, skeptical look. He must have heard the phony lilt in her words. Gritting her teeth and resolving to sound less sarcastic, she stared straight ahead as he ignited the engine and pulled away from the Bailey's sign.

Unlike his old Toyota, this car hummed. "Nice wheels," she observed, this time without a trace of irony.

He shot her another look but said nothing.

So he didn't want to make small talk. All right, then. She wasn't going to knock herself out trying to do so.

He drove down Main Street, past the tidy shops and leafy trees, past the town hall and the library, past the high school, and west toward the salmon-pink horizon. The houses flanking the road beyond the town center were enormous and stately. No doubt the Riggs family lived in one of those elegant homes. No doubt the Keene family did, too, and when the Keene and Riggs families merged through the process of holy matrimony, no doubt Phillip and Tricia would claim a stately, elegant Lynwood mansion of their own.

He kept driving, enveloped in silence. His face shimmered in the dusk light. His hands draped loosely around the leather-wrapped steering wheel. His seat was pushed way back, maximizing his legroom.

Her impatience began to build. What did he want? He'd said he wanted to talk, so why wasn't he talking? Was he abducting her for some nefarious purpose? Would he drive her into the woods somewhere, murder her and hide her body beneath a blanket of leaves and twigs so she wouldn't be found until his marriage was a fait accompli?

The countryside became hilly and the road narrowed. After cruising past a small orchard, Phillip veered onto an even narrower road, this one unpaved. The murder-in-the-woods scenario began to seem more likely.

At last he coasted onto a flat clearing on a bluff. He pulled to the edge of the bluff, from where Cassie could see a patchwork panorama of the rolling fields below, and shut off the engine.

"Where are we?" she asked.

"High Point."

She unfastened her seat belt and leaned forward, resting her forearms on the dashboard. Under other circumstances, she would have admired the view, but she had little interest in the scenery tonight. It did, however, give her something to look at so she wouldn't have to look at the man beside her. "Do you bring women here for sex?"

She sensed more than saw him flinch.

"Cassie," he murmured, a hint of pleading in his tone, and a large helping of hesitation.

Unable to keep her eyes on the view now, she turned to study him. Why had he brought her here? Surely he had no intention of having sex with her, not less than a week before his wedding. If, God forbid, that *was* his intention, she'd shut him down fast. With a fist to the nose, if necessary.

Now, there was an idea. Why not break his nose before the wedding? Then, instead of pretty wedding photos, Phillip and Tricia would remember the happiest day of their lives with an album full of pictures in which Phillip sported two black eyes and a swollen schnozzola.

Interesting idea. Violent, but interesting.

"Cassie," he said again.

She turned back to the windshield and wondered how violent she was willing to be. "Yes?"

"What are you doing here?"

"You're the one who drove us to this place. You tell me," she said, pretending to misunderstand him.

He didn't answer right away. In her peripheral vision, she saw him sink back in his seat, his gaze aimed at the tinted strip along the top edge of the windshield.

"I brought you *here* because I figured it would be quiet and out of the way, and we could talk."

If he wanted to talk, let him. She said nothing.

"Why," he asked slowly, as if addressing an imbecile, "are you in Lynwood?"

"I came for your wedding." Just saying *your wedding* was like feeling a knife cut open her chest, but she managed not to wince.

He sighed. She smelled his crisp, windswept fragrance. She forced herself not to watch as he raked his hand through his hair. It was such a familiar gesture that she didn't have to look at him to see the motion, the way the silky black locks parted around his fingers and then fell back into place.

"I honestly don't remember including your name on the invitation list."

"Well," she huffed with exaggerated indignation, "aren't *you* the gracious host! Are you going to *un*-invite me?"

"I'm sorry. You must think I'm pretty rude."

Rude was the least of it, she thought bitterly.

"But, Cassie—" he sighed again, a long, slow

breath that seemed to originate in his toes ''—come on. You don't really think I would have invited you to my wedding on purpose, do you?''

"You mean, after you shafted me? Well, gee, I don't know." Too caustic, but she couldn't seem to help herself. Where she'd felt that stab in her chest, now she felt pain oozing out. Hemorrhaging, in fact. She might just die from the pain, right there in his fancy Mercedes.

Her tone obviously annoyed him. "Look. We're both adults here. Let's be reasonable."

"Sure, let's be reasonable. You shafted me, and here I am for your wedding. Who would have thought I'd be here after you treated me like dirt?"

"Cassie."

If he groaned her name one more time, she was definitely going to break his nose. Maybe his jaw, too. Violence actually seemed like a pretty nifty idea, the more she considered it.

"When I came home to Ohio last year," he explained vaguely, "nothing was as simple as I'd thought it would be."

"I see. And I was…what? A complication?"

"As a matter of fact, yes." He gazed at her. "I'm sorry, but you were."

"And I'm sorry I made your life difficult," she muttered, not the least bit sorry.

"Then maybe you'd be willing to simplify my life by leaving."

"Oh, right!" She tossed back her head and laughed. "You think that after everything you did, I should do you a favor. What could possibly make more sense?"

"Cassie." His voice had lost its irate edge. He sounded muted, almost diffident. "I didn't want things to come out the way they did. I mean that. I'm sorry about what happened.''

Wonderful. He was sorry he'd tumbled into bed with her, sorry he'd stripped off her clothes and his own and touched her, kissed her, tasted her everywhere. Sorry he'd taken her body with his and loved her until they were both gasping and moaning and clinging to each other in helpless surrender.

Sorry he'd told her he loved her. Sorry he'd promised to return.

''So, what do you want from me? Forgiveness?'' she asked, surprised that her voice had lost its edge, too. She sounded almost…forgiving. She didn't mean to, but that was how it came out.

He ruminated, tracing the curve of the steering wheel with his thumb. She ordered herself not to stare at his hands, but she couldn't seem to look away. He had long, nimble fingers, chiseled knuckles, square nails. Sexy, masculine hands.

''Is it really not possible for you to forgive me?'' he asked, his gaze curiously hopeful.

''You broke your word, Phil.'' *You broke my heart! You hurt me!*

''And saying I'm sorry isn't enough?''

''You're getting married on Saturday,'' she retorted. ''What do you care whether I forgive you or not? What difference does it make? I'm just a wedding guest. Someone you once knew. What do you care what I think?'' She was blowing this encounter, she knew. Her anger was too obvious. She wished she could stay poised and patient, but she couldn't.

''All right,'' he finally said. ''Let's start at the beginning.''

What did he mean by ''beginning''? Did he mean

the day he'd lifted that cumbersome footlocker from her hands and their eyes had met, and after he'd lugged the thing to the studio and he'd loitered there, asking her whether she could use some help building pieces for her sets, and whether she thought pledge breaks were the most efficient way to raise money for the TV station? Was that it?

"I'm not going to let you film a *Dream Wheels* sequence at Keene Furniture," he said.

She flinched. Of all the things he might have said, all the things that existed between them, all the hurt, all the anger, why was he talking about *Dream Wheels?*

She wanted to film the creation of a chair. Given the many negative urges she was experiencing, she needed to film a sequence for the show so she'd know she was still capable of something positive. Yes, she lusted for vengeance; yes, she was vindictive and enraged; yes, she wanted Phillip to suffer. But if she got some good footage for her show, she might be able to believe she still possessed a shred of humanity.

Besides, the only way she'd been able to afford this trip had been to bill *Dream Wheels* for the bulk of the expenses. If not for Phillip's wedding, she would have been planning an itinerary to film the Alamo.

Besides, Roger had brought lots of videotape.

She tried to present her argument calmly. "You didn't bring me to this bluff so we could talk about *Dream Wheels.*"

"As a matter of fact, I did."

"Get real, Phil. You brought me up here to tell me to go home."

"And to tell you this, too. I don't want you filming at the factory."

"Why not?" she asked in a surprisingly rational voice. Somehow she could separate herself from her show, her grief from her ambitions for the episode. "I made all the arrangements with Lowell Henley. He was enthusiastic. He recognizes the importance of children's television—especially when it's both educational and entertaining. He understands that—"

"No," Phillip cut her off. "I can't have you roaming through my buildings with cameras and cables. I would have said no if Lowell had bothered to discuss it with me first. He didn't clear it with me."

"Why should he clear it with you? He's in charge of publicity for the company. You're in charge of…what? Making sure the payroll checks don't bounce?"

Phillip's gaze grew icy. "I'm in charge of everything," he said.

"Well, well," she muttered. "A degree from Harvard Business School is enough to qualify you for the job of God? I'm in awe."

His mouth twisted in irritation. "I'm not God, Cassie. I'm the chief operating officer of Keene Furniture, and I'm telling you, you aren't filming there."

"I've got written approval for the project from Lowell."

"I could fire Lowell," Phillip snapped, then directed his gaze to the windshield's tinted strip and sighed yet again. "Not that I would," he added.

"That's a relief." Acid dripped from her every word. "I was beginning to think you might not be God after all. You might be the devil, firing any employee who dared to take the initiative without kissing your butt first."

Phillip sent another look her way but didn't respond

to her insinuation. "Lowell's a good man," he conceded. "But he should have cleared this with me first. It's just a real bad time for people to be wandering through the plant with cameras, interfering with everyone's workday."

"I'm not *people*," Cassie said. "I'm Cassie Webber."

"Exactly."

She made the mistake of glancing his way. His eyes were turbulent in the fading light, burning into her. His mouth was grim—and devastatingly attractive. She had a sudden, visceral memory of the way his mouth had felt on hers, and more pain poured through the wound in her chest.

"You're Cassie," he confirmed quietly. "And you shouldn't have come here."

She heard regret in the words, and the hint of a warning. "Well, it's too late," she said defiantly. "I'm already here."

"Yes. You're here."

He reached out and brushed a strand of hair off her face, then traced the hollow of her cheek with his fingertips. Her face tingled. Her entire body tingled. Her muscles clenched, aching to feel his fingers here and there and all over.

"You're right. Maybe it *is* too late," he said softly, stroking his fingers over her cheek again, to the edge of her jaw, down to her chin, to her throat.

Too late for what? she wondered frantically, knowing Phillip wasn't talking about her having traveled to Lynwood for his wedding. Did he think it was too late to suppress her desire for revenge? Too late for apologies and forgiveness? Too late to remember what should have been, what never was?

Too late to keep him from kissing her? To keep from kissing him back?

It took enormous strength for her not to lean toward him as his fingertips grazed her skin. It took her entire supply of self-control to pull back, to grope behind her for the door lever and yank it. The door swung open and she nearly tumbled backward. The night spilled into the car, the cool air agitated by the raucous chorus of crickets.

"Stop it," she whispered—to herself as much as him. She wanted him to stop touching her, but even more, she wanted herself to stop wanting his touch. Bolting out of the car, she stood on shaky legs, hugged her arms around herself and prayed for the fresh evening air to clear her mind.

How dare he? How dare he pierce her defenses, arouse her, gaze at her with such yearning? How dare he run his fingertips over her skin and fill her with desire for him? The nerve of him! Telling her it was too late, when she was the one for whom it was too late, the one who'd lost everything but her dignity—and nearly lost that, too, alone in a car with Phillip, on a bluff a few miles west of Lynwood.

She was the one who had lost everything worth having, the one who was dangerously close to losing herself. The only thing it was too late for was leaving him without first inflicting some damage. It was definitely too late for that.

CHAPTER FOUR

EDIE LOOMED OVER Phillip's desk. "You haven't heard a word I've said," she chided.

"Yes, I have." He smiled faintly. "I've heard at least three words you've said."

She clicked her tongue in annoyance and flipped through her notepad once more. "Lowell Henley says he's got everything under control and you should just leave the TV people to him," she recited, ticking items off her list of notes. "The florist wants you to call and confirm the total cost of the flowers Tricia ordered for the wedding." Tick. "The retail outlet in Chicago wants you to go there and fix their inventory problems." Tick.

"Forget it. We've got phones, faxes, e-mail, voice-mail and snail-mail. We can fix Chicago's problems from here—assuming their problems are fixable." He sighed. He knew he had to solve the mess in Chicago, but he'd been trying to straighten things out with that store for months now and had made no progress. "Whether or not I meet with them in person, their management sucks."

"They want you to help."

"I'm getting married this weekend," he retorted, trying to ignore the chill that slithered down his spine as he spoke the words.

He closed his eyes briefly and swiveled his chair

toward the window. He was in bad shape—belligerent, frazzled, unwilling to contemplate how much money the flowers Tricia had ordered were going to cost him, let alone how to fix the problems in Chicago. Cassie Webber was in town. How the hell was he supposed to *think?*

Last night…cripes, last night he'd come very close to betraying his fiancée just days before his wedding. He'd sat in his car, his fingers brushing over Cassie's smooth, soft skin, and he'd wanted her. Just as intensely, just as insanely, as he'd wanted her the very first time he'd seen her, staggering down the hall at the public-broadcasting station with her arms wrapped around that damned footlocker.

Some men possessed more self-restraint than others. Given the way he had felt with Cassie last night, he must have more self-restraint than all the men in the world put together. How else to explain why he hadn't hauled her into his lap, torn off her clothes and his own and made hot, sweaty love to her?

Granted, he hadn't done what his heart and his hormones and his brain had been screaming at him to do, because Cassie had fled from the car. Wisely. She must have known what he'd been thinking. If she'd made the mistake of glancing in the general direction of his crotch, she couldn't have helped knowing.

"Phillip?"

Edie broke into his reverie.

"I'm not done here."

He turned to face her and forced himself to pay attention. Edie glared at him, her notepad raised like a shield, although he knew it was, in fact, an offensive weapon. Ever since he'd settled in to run Keene Furniture, he'd been asking her to connect his calls to his voice-mail so she wouldn't have to waste her time writing down his messages on her pad and reciting them to him. She claimed she preferred to do things the old-fashioned way, but Phillip suspected the real reason was that she preferred to stand before him, ticking off items on her list.

"I know you've got your wedding to think of," she lectured, "but there's too much to do. The Chicago store—"

"—can wait," he told her, completing the sentence. "Whatever is going on there, it can wait."

Edie pursed her lips. She looked as if she'd been drinking battery acid; her entire face seemed puckered. "The musicians called to confirm. Not the band for the reception, the trio for the ceremony. Harpist, violinist and flautist. She was very particular about that. She said she was a 'flautist,' not a 'flutist.'"

"Fine." He wanted to close his eyes again and go back to last night, back to the instant before Cassie had bolted from his car. The instant when she'd been just inches from him, and he'd inhaled her clean, vanilla fragrance and gazed into her eyes and remembered how wonderful it had been with her in Boston a year ago, when they could sit beside each other and talk, and breathe in each other's scents, and wonder whether they were ever going to get beyond talking and breathing.

"I mistakenly called her a 'flutist,'" Edie went on, "and she threw a fit. I thought you'd appreciate the warning."

"I do. You can't begin to know much I appreciate it," he muttered.

"And last but not least, Harry Riggs wants to see you."

That got Phillip's attention. He sat up straighter. "Why does he want to see me?"

"He didn't say," she answered. "I assume it's because you're going to marry his daughter on Saturday. He probably wants to offer some final words of advice, or one of those sentimental lectures about taking good care of Tricia."

"Of course." A high-decibel, distinctly unmusical headache began to pound in his head. All percussion—not a flautist in the mix. He recognized the piece: "The I-Don't-Want-to-See-Harry-Riggs Sonata." "I'll phone him."

"He said he wanted you to visit him. As a matter of fact, his exact words were—" she read from the pad "'Tell that boy to come to my office.' He was quite specific. He seems to think you're a boy."

"That's just the way he talks." Actually, Phillip suspected that his future father-in-law truly did see him as just a boy. If Keene Furniture weren't so vulnerable to Harry's manipulations, Phillip would have explained to him that he was a full-grown man, nearing the end of his third decade on the planet, and Harry had better start referring to him that way.

But he had to behave deferentially toward Harry, at least as long as Harry had the upper hand.

"He sounded kind of angry," Edie said. "You haven't done anything wrong, have you?"

The only thing Phillip had done wrong was to indulge in a moment's lustful yearning for another woman. Or, more accurately, a long, sleepless night of lustful yearning.

But he doubted that was what Tricia's father wanted to see him about. Harold Riggs, president of the Lynwood Bank and Trust until a major regional bank had absorbed it and paid him a staggering sum, and currently an independent financial consultant and venture capitalist, was wealthy enough to call anyone anything he wanted and suffer no ill effects. He was powerful enough that when he wanted to see Phillip, all he had to do was issue a summons and Phillip would feel obliged to answer it.

The drumming in Phillip's head increased in volume. "Tell the folks in Chicago I'll get back to them by the end of the week. Tell them to fax me their records and I'll have a look at them in my spare time—of which I have none." His skull filled with the crash of cymbals, followed by a kettledrum roll. "Tell Henley I don't want some noncommercial kids' show filming in our factory. Tell the musicians everything's copacetic."

"And Harry?"

"Tell him I'll stop by before lunch."

Tick, tick, tick—Edie applied her pencil to her pad. "Anything else?"

"If Tricia comes by, tell her I can't see her."

Edie frowned but didn't argue. With a parting look of extreme disgruntlement, she spun around and stalked out of the office, closing the door behind her.

Phillip ought to call up his most recent figures from Chicago. Or he ought to have a look at the financial data Harry no doubt wanted to discuss with him. Or he ought to give Lowell Henley a buzz and make sure he understood that Cassie Webber and her colleagues were not welcome in the building.

Cassie. Just conjuring up her name was enough to make him ignore everything he ought to be doing. How could he think about Harry and Chicago and the flautist when his mind was crammed with memories of Cassie, memories of their friendship in Boston, memories of their lovemaking, memories of sitting with her in his car less than twenty-four hours ago?

He recalled the angle of her jaw, her big brown eyes, her prickly personality. He remembered the way her breath had caught when he'd touched her cheek. He had been all alone with her at High Point last night, just the two of them, the car and the sunset, and he pondered all the things he'd wanted to do to her and with her, all the things he would never do.

He swore to himself that he wasn't in love with her. Not anymore. He couldn't be. He couldn't *let* himself be. Too much else had happened.

Water under the bridge, he thought morosely, rising from his desk and crossing to the window to stare at the river. Water over the dam. A river that had proceeded along its course, eroding a bit of his soul as it flowed. It didn't matter what he'd once felt for Cassie—or what he felt for her now.

He was marrying Tricia Riggs. This Saturday, he would exchange vows with her, and a little more of his soul would wash away. But the river would keep on flowing.

"LISTEN TO ME, Tricia, dear—you don't want flowers in your hair," Constance Riggs declared.

They were seated in matching floral-upholstered chairs in Leona's, the finest hair salon in town, and mapping out Tricia's coiffure for Saturday. Tricia's mother sat primly in her seat, the satin veil folded neatly in her lap, with the pearl-studded tiara atop it. At one time, Tricia had thought it was the most resplendent headpiece in the world. But now...she wasn't sure why, she thought maybe just weaving some silk ribbons and flowers into her hair would look kind of cool. A touch of whimsy amid all the formality. Why not?

Because her mother would have a cow, that was why not.

Leona sat facing the Riggs women on a little round stool. She couldn't weigh more than ninety pounds, and she had one spandex-wrapped leg twisted around the other so many times she looked like a piece of twine from the waist down. Her hair was short and spiky, brown with ash-blond highlights, and her eyes were caked with black liner and mascara. But for all that, she was pure Lynwood, homey and small-town. She just liked to *think* she was cutting-edge.

"Well," she said, leaning forward and pawing through Tricia's wavy hair, "we could do something interesting with flowers. Something very sweet."

"I don't want her to look sweet," Constance said. "This isn't a sweet wedding. We spent several hundred dollars on this veil. You don't spend that much money on a veil and expect to come out looking sweet."

"Well," Leona argued gently, "we could use the veil along with some flowers. You'd just want to go light on the styling, that's all."

Constance turned to Tricia, her expression exasperated. "*Everything* has already been decided," she said sternly. "Now is not the time to start changing your mind."

Tricia sighed. She'd always thought she had the right to change her mind until the moment she said, "I do."

Of course, she had no intention of changing her mind about that. Phillip was going to be the perfect husband. Everybody said they made an ideal couple, and Tricia thought so, too.

She and Phillip looked good together. She loved picturing the babies they would have—cute, round, redheaded babies with dimples and pretty blue eyes, just like hers. As a matter of fact, the babies would look exactly like her. But they'd have Phillip's reliability. And his intelligence, because he was smarter than she was, at least in an academic sort of way. And maybe they'd have his athletic ability, too, if they were boys. He'd been a hotshot athlete in high school. His team photos were still on display in the trophy cabinet in the school lobby. Long before it had even occurred to Tricia that she might marry him, she used to pick him out from the rows of suited-up players in the old varsity photos. He'd always been easy to pick out. He was the best-looking guy on every team.

If she and Phillip had boys, they would be the best-looking boys on their varsity teams, too. If they were girls, they'd be cheerleaders like her. Not that Tricia was sexist or anything, but Lynwood cheerleaders had it so much better than the jocks. They got the coolest outfits and were the envy of all the other girls. If Tricia had daughters, they'd be cheerleaders-in-training. She might even buy little letter sweaters for them to wear, in toddler sizes.

But rethinking her hairdo for the wedding was allowed, wasn't it? Especially since the headpiece was kind of stiff. When it was on, it pinched the sides of her skull. Plus, it made her ears stick out. She was going to be wearing the pearl-and-diamond earrings her father had given her for Christmas, so she didn't mind the bottoms of her earlobes sticking out. But not the tops, like Dumbo the elephant.

She gazed past her mother to Leona. "Can't we just try it?" she asked. "I mean, experiment with my hair a little, just to see. I was thinking, with all the roses and everything—"

"Which, you understand, Phillip has to pay for," her mother pointedly reminded her. "You ordered enough flowers to bankrupt the poor boy. And now you want more flowers? Have you thought about the people with allergies? Do you want people sneezing at your wedding?"

"I'll pay for these flowers," Tricia said. "If they're part of my outfit, we'll pay for them, just like we paid for the dress. I just thought…I mean, it would be kind of, I don't know, like I'm a flower child."

"*Exactly.*" Constance Riggs shuddered. At fifty-two, she was young enough to have been a flower child herself, if she'd chosen that route in her youth. But she would never have chosen it. Like Tricia, she was a daughter of Lynwood. A cheerleader emeritus.

Tricia didn't mind her heritage. Although she kept thinking that maybe she ought to try something a little different, just a tiny taste before she was no longer allowed to change her mind. Something like…oh, say, getting to know that fellow with the long hair and the earring, that friend of Phillip's friend.

She envied Phillip the time he'd spent in Boston. Granted, Massachusetts wasn't exactly the Riviera, but it seemed almost that exotic to Tricia. She'd visited the city once, a long time ago, and toured a few historic sites, just as she'd visited San Francisco and Disney World and Cancún. It wasn't as if she'd never been out of Lynwood.

But to live in Boston, to experience such a different culture—that was what she envied. She'd never lived in a big city, surrounded by all kinds of people, including men with earrings and hair all the way down their backs. At college she'd known about the weird kids, the ones who had metal hoops piercing their nostrils and eyebrows and wore heavy black boots even when it was eighty degrees out, and who invariably made the dean's list. But she hadn't had anything to do with them. She'd stayed safely in her sorority and majored in early childhood education because it would come in handy when she had children of her own. She certainly hadn't troubled herself to make the dean's list.

She'd never gotten to know people like the multi-pierced, smart kids on her campus or like, for example, Roger Beckelman. She wouldn't mind becoming acquainted with him for no other reason than that he was different. When she recollected his hair and his bedraggled clothes and the tattoo of a flower she'd glimpsed under his sleeve, she realized that he'd lived his life in a way she couldn't begin to imagine. She wouldn't mind living *her* life in a way she couldn't begin to imagine, too, even if she could do it only in the most trivial manner, like wearing flowers in her hair as she walked down the aisle.

"An upsweep," her mother was explaining to Leona. "Loose curls, nothing too poodle-y. We don't want Little Orphan Annie up there. Just a luxurious, relaxed perm, and then we'd sweep the front locks up and back and affix the tiara so a drizzle of curls would frame her face. That's how I picture it."

"Is that okay with you?" Leona asked Tricia.

Tricia sighed. In the grand scheme of things, she supposed, the particulars of her wedding-day hairdo weren't that important. What mattered was that she was marrying Phillip, a good man, an intelligent man, a man who ran Keene Furniture, one of Lynwood's most important businesses. No matter how Leona styled her hair, on her wedding night Tricia was going to yank off the tiara, pull out the pins and let her hair tumble down. Although frankly, Tricia didn't think Phillip would even notice her hairdo. She was always dressed to the nines for him, always groomed herself impeccably, and he never mentioned it, except in the broadest terms: "You look good, Tricia," or if he was in a really expansive mood, "You look great."

Now, a fellow like Roger Beckelman...would he be the sort of guy who'd notice her magnificent designer gown, her elaborate tiara and her beautiful earrings? Or would he be more likely to notice a bride who'd woven flowers and ribbons into her hair?

Tricia shouldn't care. But until Saturday, until she said, "I do," she could let herself care, a little.

HARRY RIGGS'S OFFICE consumed the second floor of a modern building on the eastern side of the town square. He owned the building and rented the downstairs office suites to an accountant, a chiropractor and a dentist. The upper floor, with its broad gleaming windows overlooking the square and town hall, was all his.

He obviously didn't need that much room to work in, since much of the suite was empty; the parts that weren't were taken up by sitting areas and huge potted plants. The cavernous entry at the top of the granite stairway could have doubled as an art gallery between shows; two inscrutable paintings hung on the walls, and an area rug featuring an abstract pattern covered nearly the entire floor. The first time Phillip had visited the place, he'd been stymied trying to find his way to the receptionist's desk.

He understood that the sparse furnishings and vast empty spaces were simply Harry's way of intimidating his visitors, announcing to anyone who ventured inside that he was an important person, that compared with him, everyone else was an insignificant twit.

Phillip refused to be intimidated by Harry Riggs. He often suspected Harry of trying to overwhelm him, but he was stubborn enough to deny Harry that satisfaction. Even with the power he currently wielded over Keene Furniture, even with the stakes riding on his ability to work with Harry, Phillip refused to get all shaky-kneed around the man.

He was marrying Harry's daughter, wasn't he? What more did Harry want?

Phillip's father had never been shaky-kneed around Harry, either, which was perhaps unfortunate. If James Keene had been a bit more prudent in his dealings with his dear friend Harry, he might not have taken out so many loans from Harry when Keene Furniture Company started its too-rapid expansion, nor would he have borrowed against the company. Of course, Phillip's father had borrowed all this money from Harry because Harry's terms had been better than the bank's—and because Harry kept urging him to take out the loans long past the time the bank would have turned him down.

Now Keene Furniture was tottering on the edge of financial collapse. All that kept it from tumbling was Harry Riggs's willingness not to call in those loans.

Phillip hadn't learned about the company's dire financial straits until he'd returned to Lynwood after earning his business degree. He'd devoted much of his life to the family business. He'd worked there summers as a teenager, learning basic carpentry and quality control, sweeping floors and running errands, getting to know the folks on the floor and the folks behind the desks, familiarizing himself with what they needed and wanted in their jobs. He'd gone home knowing his parents expected him to apply his fancy Harvard B-School training to the company.

But within days of his return, he'd realized that by expanding the company to operate its own Keene Furniture retail outlets, his father had taken on a debt burden that would stagger a Fortune-500 enterprise. And at the other end of that debt loomed Harry Riggs.

Phillip's future father-in-law.

This was not the way he'd planned his life. But when he'd discovered what his father had done, how close to the precipice he'd driven the company, Phillip hadn't been able to turn his back on his family. Keene Furniture was his father's identity and his own heritage. He hadn't been able to walk away.

So he'd started working with Harry on restructuring the loans. And there Harry's pretty young daughter had been, and Harry so eager, so pleased that Phillip smiled every time Tricia offered him a drink when the families had gotten together... It didn't take a business degree from Harvard to figure out what Harry wanted, and to figure further that if Phillip made Harry happy, Harry wouldn't bankrupt his dear old friend James Keene.

Even before Cassie Webber had turned up in town, Phillip had found himself wondering whether he would have asked Harry's daughter to marry him if Harry hadn't been holding the Keene family's economic future in his meaty hand. Fortunately Phillip was fond of Tricia, because if he'd chosen not to become Harry's son-in-law, Harry might have taken title to the furniture company.

Unfortunately, however, marrying Tricia wasn't enough to satisfy Harry. Phillip also had to race across town to pay homage whenever Harry demanded it, which was what today's visit was all about. Thus, instead of remaining at his office to review the documents the Chicago store had faxed, Phillip was climbing the imposing granite stairs to Harry's upper-floor domain so he could kiss His Lordship's ring.

"I'll tell him you're here," Harry's secretary said after Phillip had hiked through the airy emptiness to her anteroom. She appeared no older than twenty or so, and she could have moonlighted as a model for *Playboy*. Phillip didn't think Harry was personally involved with her, though. He would employ a secretary with pneumatic breasts and fat-free thighs for no better reason than to prove to the world that he could hire anyone he wanted.

Phillip watched with detachment as the secretary strutted across the anteroom to Harry's office and vanished inside. He knew he was going to have to wait. That, too, was part of Harry's game.

After the expected five-minute delay, the secretary gave Phillip permission to enter Harry's inner sanctum. Harry lounged in his high-back leather chair, chewing on an unlit but elegantly long cigar. His hair had faded from strawberry blond to something approaching a yellowish-gray, and his complexion was perpetually ruddy. He was shorter than Phillip by a few inches, which was probably why he preferred to remain seated whenever Phillip called on him.

"Well, son," he greeted Phillip in a booming voice. "How are you holding up?"

So the old man was going to play it friendly. "Pretty well," Phillip said, shoving his hands into his trouser pockets and striking a relaxed pose.

"You've got just a few days of freedom left. Getting cold feet?" Harry asked, waggling his bushy eyebrows.

Phillip hoped his face gave nothing away. Surely Harry couldn't know about Cassie's being in town—or about Cassie's having once been in Phillip's life. Besides, the fact that she was in town and that merely thinking about her caused a certain part of his anatomy to grow warm didn't mean his feet were getting cold.

"I'm looking forward to the big day," he said calmly. He eyed one of the several visitors' chairs positioned around Harry's oversized office but decided to remain standing. He hadn't come here to schmooze. If he made himself comfortable, Harry might think he actually enjoyed stopping by.

"Tricia tells me you've got some friends in town for the week. Old friends from Boston."

Damn—did he know? Could he guess what kind of an old friend Cassie had been, and where Phillip had taken her last night, and what he'd wanted to do with her? "They're here for the wedding," he said vaguely.

"Well, I'm sure you've got a lot on your mind, you and Tricia both, so I won't keep you," Harry said, feigning benevolence. "I just wanted to let you know I've been reviewing some figures with my accountant, and we're a little concerned about how overdue some of the loans have become. I hate to pressure you at a time like this…"

You love to pressure me, Phillip thought.

"...but I need to show some activity on those loans."

"You've seen activity on them," Phillip argued. "We've restructured the debt and begun payments."

"Way below the terms your father agreed to."

"Better than what you'd get if we had to file for bankruptcy protection."

"You're going to have to do better." Harry's voice grew quieter, steelier. "There should have been real movement on these loans six months ago. Right from the start, when your father signed those notes, I worried that we'd reach this point."

"If you were that worried," Phillip said, infusing his voice with even more quiet steel than Harry's, "you shouldn't have provided the loans. No smart businessman makes loans to enterprises he thinks are losers."

Harry opened his mouth and then shut it.

Phillip knew he'd won the point. "The name Keene on a piece of furniture has always meant top quality. The company's going to get back into the black eventually. My father overextended himself—we both know that. He's got me now, and I'm going to make this come out right—but I need time, Harry. I need time. We've had this discussion before."

If Phillip were paranoid, he'd think Harry had decided to have this discussion again today because he'd heard that Phillip had taken Cassie up to High Point last night. Harry was amazingly aware of what went on in his town.

But Phillip had been with her for less than an hour yesterday. And she had come to Lynwood to film a sequence for her TV show and to attend Phillip's wedding—although God only knew how she'd been sent an invitation. And during the time Phillip and Cassie had been at High Point, nothing had happened. Nothing physical, anyway. Nothing outside of his tortured imagination.

"Was there anything else you wanted to talk about?" Phillip asked. The mouth end of Harry's cigar looked soggy. Although Phillip didn't particularly like Tricia's mother, he felt sorry for her for having to kiss a man who sucked on cigars. Assuming Constance Riggs even bothered with kissing.

Harry backed down reluctantly. "Not at the moment. But this situation with the loans is getting tight, Phil. I don't intend to carry your company much longer."

"Don't worry about it," Phillip said. "I've got to go. It's a busy week." *And if I stay here any longer, I'll want to kick something. Or maybe shove your cigar down your throat.*

"You're right. It is a busy week for you. I want that wedding to go off without a hitch for my baby," Harry warned. "And then you'll be carrying Tricia forever. When it comes to loans, that's a bad thing. But in a marriage, forever is the way it should be."

Words of wisdom, Phillip thought sourly as he said goodbye and strolled out of Harry's office, keeping a smile on his face and a bounce in his gait so Harry wouldn't think he'd gotten to him. A marriage was forever, and it shouldn't have anything to do with loans. Or indebtedness. Or power plays.

Just because it shouldn't didn't mean it wouldn't. For his parents, for his grandfather's memory, for the many fine people who worked at Keene Furniture, Phillip would marry Harry's daughter. He didn't like it. He didn't want it. A year ago he couldn't even have imagined it.

But this was how it would have to be—if not forever, at least for now. At least until Keene Furniture was back on solid ground, no longer in danger of floating down a river of debt and into Harry's hands.

CHAPTER FIVE

CASSIE WOULD HAVE enjoyed her bath much more if Diane hadn't been seated just outside in the hall, shouting through the locked door.

"The way I see it," Diane bellowed, "you can destroy Phillip's wedding or you can destroy Phillip. Of course, there could be some overlap. You might be able to accomplish both simultaneously. Anyway, you've got several options."

Thank goodness Cassie was the only person boarding on the third floor of Bailey's. She wouldn't want anyone—especially the sour Mrs. Gill—to hear Diane. If the B-and-B owner knew her Boston guests were conspiring against Lynwood's favorite son, she might poison their breakfast muffins, or at the very least make them remove their beer and soda from her refrigerator.

"I've worked up a list," Diane went on. Working up lists was one of her most important functions as *Dream Wheels*' assistant producer. Apparently it was a talent she could apply to all sorts of ventures. "You're sure you don't want to aim for violence and mass destruction? Because we could—"

"No." Cassie pushed away from the cradling curve of the tub, splashing water onto the floor. "I don't want anyone hurt."

"You're hurt," Diane reminded her.

Cassie sighed. Her hurts were all internal and they probably weren't fatal. Whatever scars Phillip's betrayal had left her with were invisible.

Last night she'd studied her face in the mirror above the dresser. Throughout her silent drive back to the B-and-B with Phillip, her face had seemed to tingle where his fingers had brushed, and she'd almost expected to see pink streaks there, or a rash. She'd noticed nothing, of course, but her eyes had seemed to have a feverish glow, and her body had felt heavy with arousal hours after they'd parted company.

She'd managed to avoid him all day today, even though she and Roger had begun videotaping outdoor scenes at Keene Furniture. The day had been balmy and sunny, perfect for shooting the factory's exterior, the gates and outbuildings and parking lots, as well as the lumberyard on the outskirts of town, where wood was delivered and stored. After spending the day making sure she didn't run into Phillip, she was now soaking in a tub filled with tepid water. But it was hard to stay cool when, almost twenty-four hours after he'd touched her, she still couldn't forget the shimmering sensation of Phillip's fingers gliding over her face.

"I know you'd prefer the kinder, gentler approach," Diane called through the door, "but the point is revenge, isn't it?"

"I want to destroy him," Cassie conceded, "but I don't want any violence."

"Okay," Diane said. "How about ruining his business?"

"If we ruin his business, that'll ruin the *Dream Wheels* stuff we're filming this week."

"Film first, then ruin it."

"And what about his parents? It's a family business,

you know. If we ruin Keene Furniture, we ruin his parents. You said his mother was nice.''

"His parents created him. They have to take responsibility for raising a creep, don't they?''

Cassie smiled. Lifting the corners of her mouth seemed to lift her mood, too. "What else do you have on your list?''

"Doing something to his fiancée.''

"No,'' Cassie said swiftly. "Keep her out of it.''

"Come on,'' Diane scolded. "The woman is suffering from terminal perkiness. For that alone she deserves to die.''

"It's not her fault Phillip did what he did,'' Cassie pointed out. "Besides, if we want her to pay, we should just let her go ahead with the wedding. Being married to a guy like him might be punishment enough.'' Cassie actually felt a bit sorry for Tricia. And she kind of liked the woman, even if she was young, pretty and rich—or, as Roger had put it, "ripe and eager.''

Well, all right, maybe Tricia didn't deserve Cassie's pity. Maybe Tricia had so much going for her she deserved whatever peripheral pain resulted from Cassie's attack on Phillip.

But Phillip was the two-timing bastard. He was the one who'd sworn his love and broken his pledge. He was truly the deserving one.

"You know,'' Diane chided, "you're really no help at all. I'm coming up with all these great strategies and you keep vetoing them. If you don't want to demolish Phil, what the heck are we doing in Lynwood?''

"We're filming material for *Dream Wheels*,'' Cassie answered, then sighed and pulled out the rubber stopper. The water gasped into the drain, gurgling and swirling and sending bubbles to the surface. "And yeah, I do want to demolish Phil," she added, easing herself to her feet and reaching for the towel.

"You just want to hurt him without bloodshed or collateral damage. I still like the idea of stink bombs. They wouldn't injure anyone. They'd just make everyone reek."

"No."

"Wimp," Diane muttered, just barely loud enough for Cassie to hear her through the door. She dried herself off, then dressed in the clothing she'd brought into the bathroom with her—lightweight linen slacks, a tank top and a lacy cardigan—and opened the door. Diane was seated on the floor, leaning against the opposite wall, a clipboard perched on her knees.

"Roger's managed to borrow some studio time at the public-access cable station in town to review today's tapes," Cassie told her. "He made nice with the locals. They think he's a famous cinematographer or something. Do you want to go check out the footage with him?"

Pushing to her feet, Diane wrinkled her nose in distaste. "Are you kidding? Spend an evening with a bunch of vidiots? Especially local cable vidiots." She shook her head vehemently.

Cassie slung her damp towel over a hook fastened to the door and grinned. "I don't want to spend the evening cooped up in a studio, either. I was thinking we could drop Roger off at the studio and then take a drive."

Diane looked intrigued. "Drive where?"

"Linden Hills."

"The country club where the wedding is going to be?"

"If we saw the place, we might get some ideas—"

"Of whether stink bombs might be viable." Diane nodded. "Let's do it."

Cassie supposed she was lucky that Diane was so over-the-top. In a good working relationship, the assistant producer was supposed to provide whatever the producer couldn't—whether it was outlandish concepts, technical expertise or organizational skill. The producer's task was to impose taste, focus and judgment on the enterprise. In this case, Diane was suggesting tactics and weapons systems. Cassie could provide the taste and focus, but as for judgment, well, if she had any judgment she probably wouldn't have come to Lynwood in the first place. In fact, she probably wouldn't have fallen in love with Phillip.

Diane trailed her back to her cramped attic room. "God, it's awful up here," she griped on Cassie's behalf. "How can you stand it?"

"I can't. Count your blessings I'm not bunking with you."

"You could bunk with Roger," Diane suggested. "I'm sure he'd be more fun in bed than me. Bobby used to complain that I snored."

"Yeah? What does Howser say?"

"Howser can't complain. He snores, too."

Cassie grabbed her purse and pocketed the rental-car key. "If I was going to seduce anyone," she said, combing her hair in front of the mirror, "it wouldn't be Roger. He's a great guy and I like working with him. I'd never do anything that might jeopardize our working relationship. Anyway," she added, setting down her comb, "he's not my type."

"Of course not. Your type is hunky midwesterners who trample on women's hearts."

"As far as I know," Cassie argued, "the only heart Phil ever trampled on was mine. And if I was going to seduce anyone—"

"You're not going to seduce him, are you?" Diane asked, wide-eyed.

"Of course not!"

Diane studied her curiously.

"I don't want that man near me," Cassie said.

"How are you going to wreak revenge if he doesn't get near you?"

"I'll destroy his business," Cassie resolved. "Or we'll use your silly stink bombs if we have to. Come on, let's go." She didn't want to give herself a chance to contemplate seducing Phillip. Seducing him—or being seduced by him—was the source of all her misery. Making love with him, falling in love with him—the two came together in her mind. She'd never been the kind of woman who could make love without being in love. If Phillip had seduced her last year, he'd succeeded only because she'd been madly in love with him.

She wasn't going to seduce him now. Sex with him would destroy her much faster than it would destroy him.

They found Roger on the porch, a can of beer in one hand and his camera tote bag slung over his shoulder. "All set?" Cassie asked briskly. "Diane and I aren't going to be able to view the tapes with you. I hope that's all right."

"No problem."

"So where's the studio?"

"It's 220 Maple Street, on the corner of Main," Roger replied.

"Can you believe this town?" Diane said with a chuckle as the three of them strolled around the rambling bed-and-breakfast to the unpaved parking lot in back. "Main Street, Maple Street—all we're missing is Mom and apple pie."

Roger shrugged. "Boston has Winter Street and Summer Street."

"And they're the same street, too," Diane said. It was true. The street turned from Winter to Summer as abruptly as Boston's weather changed from one day to the next.

Once her passengers were settled in the car, Cassie drove to Main Street and turned left, passing the Harvest Bounty and the bank, passing a pristine white church and the chamber of commerce building, in front of which a starchy American flag snapped in the evening breeze. A block ahead, she spotted Maple Street, aptly named for the trees shading the sidewalk.

"So what are you two doing that's more interesting than checking the tapes?" Roger asked as Cassie pulled up to the curb to let him out.

She sensed Diane shifting in the back seat, revving up to tell Roger what they were doing. Cassie had talked Roger into making the trip to Lynwood, but she didn't want him included in her own nefarious reasons for traveling there. She and Diane had been friends with Phillip a year ago; more than that Roger didn't need to know—at least not until the bombs started exploding. "We're going cruising," she told Roger. "It seems like just the thing to do on a June evening in a town like this."

"You going to pick up guys?" he teased.

"Only if we find some really cute ones. What time do you want us to pick *you* up?"

"Does that mean I'm really cute?" Roger grinned. "I'll get a ride back with Eddie. He said he'd give me a lift. Bailey's is on his way home."

"Great. Have fun. We'll see you later."

Roger swung his long legs out of the car, then hauled the rest of himself and his tote out. As Diane moved up to the front seat, he waved and loped toward the drab concrete block of a building bearing the number 220 above its glass door.

"Okay," Diane said cheerfully. "Next stop, Linden Hills."

"Where *is* Linden Hills?"

"Somewhere around here." Diane stretched, her legs almost as long as Roger's. "I guess we'd better ask someone."

"We're running low on gas. Let's tank up and get directions."

"Lucky we're women," Diane remarked as Cassie U-turned back to Main Street. "If we were guys, we wouldn't know how to do that."

Grinning, Cassie rolled down her window. For all its cloying charm, Lynwood had its assets, one of them being fresh-scented air. She could smell green in the breeze, the tang of newly mowed grass and budding trees, of spring leaves and June warmth. Boston had its share of trees, but the big healthy, majestic trees were all clustered in parks, and the trees in the neighborhoods were scrawny and scraggly. The sky appeared wider in Lynwood, too, not glimpsed in slivers between tall buildings. Even in the less ritzy neighborhoods of Lynwood, like the one where Bailey's was, the houses sat on emerald lawns and were framed by lush, blossoming shrubbery.

At the far end of Main Street, near the supermarket, she spotted a gas station. She pulled in, turned off the engine and got the hose inserted into the gas tank before the attendant, a gawky, pimply kid in a starched brown uniform, could reach the pump.

"This is a full-service gas station," he said, sounding annoyed and nudging her away from the nozzle.

"I'm sorry." Why was she apologizing for filling her own tank?

"You can get back into the car," he added, and she obeyed, not willing to get into a fight with him over who was pumping the gas. He busied himself cleaning her windows and checking her oil.

"That boy needs a life," Diane commented.

"I think it's kind of nice, getting serviced like this."

"Yeah, compared with the servicing you got from Phil, this isn't bad. Don't forget to ask him for directions."

The kid seemed genuinely pleased to be able to outline the route to the country club. Cassie paid him, satisfied that he was no longer annoyed with her, and steered out of the gas station.

"What exactly are we going to do when we get there?" she asked Diane as they traveled along the sinuous country road the kid had identified as the quickest route to Linden Hills.

"Reconnaissance."

Cassie visualized Diane and herself in combat fatigues, crawling through the underbrush with knives clenched in their teeth and flak exploding all around them. "Remember," she said, "the only person I want to hurt is Phil, and I want to hurt him emotionally, not physically. Physical wounds heal. I don't want him to heal.''

''Some physical wounds don't heal,'' Diane argued cheerfully. ''Physical wounds in his nether regions, for instance. Physical wounds along the lines of amputation.''

''Diane!'' Cassie said, shocked.

''You really are a wimp, Cassie. What would you do without me?''

Cassie sighed. ''I'd probably slap Phil in the face and call him an unspeakable cad. Then I'd go home.''

''Boring. It's a good thing I'm here.'' She thought for a minute, then turned to Cassie. ''Okay. Imagine the wedding. Imagine what you'd like to have happen during the ceremony.''

Without letting her concentration stray too far from the road, Cassie visualized an aisle with a long white runner for the bridal party. She pictured Tricia Riggs blissfully moving down it to the altar, where Phillip and the minister were waiting. Perhaps the organist playing ''The Wedding March'' could flub half the notes. Or Tricia could trip on a wrinkle in the runner and go sprawling, her dress hiked up around her hips.

Or, ''How about if we find a little girl to pose as Phil's out-of-wedlock child?'' she suggested.

Diane raised one eyebrow. ''Huh?''

''She could run down the aisle toward Phil shouting, 'Daddy! Daddy!' In a town like Lynwood, that would be a first-class scandal.''

Diane snorted. ''Not bad. But you've worked with child actors, Cassie. You know how tricky they can be.''

True enough. She'd worked with some talented juveniles, but even the most disciplined young troupers could be unpredictable. Mothers or agents had to be involved. The union demanded all sorts of rules and restrictions. And after all that, the child often screwed up. In a videotaped TV show, that wasn't a big deal, but at a wedding, with only a few days of rehearsal... No, Cassie couldn't chance it.

It was a wicked idea, though. Maybe instead of a self-propelled child, they could scrounge up an infant somewhere, a three-month-old baby, and Cassie could carry it in her arms. "I wanted our daughter to witness the marriage of her father," she could say to Phillip as she extended the swaddled infant to him.

Her amusement faded, the notion losing its appeal. It cut too close, brushed too hard against reality. Merely thinking about it caused Cassie's eyes to burn. Not that she wanted a baby—especially a baby whose father was Phillip Keene, the ass. But still...

The car rolled past meadows carpeted in manicured grass so green it looked as if the color had been painted on. They must be approaching the outer reaches of the country club's golf course. In the late-dusk light, the amoeba-shaped sand traps cut into the grass were so white they practically glowed, and trees and paths and ornamental bridges adorned the landscape with synthetic precision. Cassie slowed the car, watching for what the kid at the gas station had described as a stone wall flanking the entry.

A quarter mile of links landscape later, she saw the masonry walls and the elaborate wrought-iron gateway arching over them, from which hung a sign labeled in luxurious script: Linden Hills.

"Oh, brother," Diane muttered. "I smell pretension."

"What did you expect? It's a country club."

"I'm not sure I'm dressed for the occasion, dahhh-ling."

Cassie shot Diane a glance. Diane had on pleated shorts, a clean sweatshirt and sneakers. "At least you don't look like a mad bomber. They probably won't frisk you."

"I'll tell them I'm the new tennis pro," Diane joked as Cassie steered through the gate onto the paved driveway, which sliced across several verdant acres of lawn and ended in a circle at the awninged front door to the club's main facility. Like the stone walls and the surrounding acreage, the building was breathlessly grand, an expanse of white broken by Palladian windows, the front stairs beneath the awning covered in red carpet as if awaiting the arrival of royalty.

A road led from the circular driveway to a parking lot bordered by a tall white picket fence. Cassie parked in the lot and shut off the engine. "Do you think we'll get towed if I park here? I haven't got a membership sticker or anything."

"We've got a sticker with the name of the rental company," Diane said. "If anyone asks, we can say the Cadillac is in the shop."

Cassie waited until Diane was out of the car, then locked both doors. "I never realized you were so good at this kind of stuff."

"What stuff? Plotting? I think you should name me *Dream Wheel*'s executive story editor."

"You'd have to take a pay cut for that title," Cassie joked, eyeing the cars parked near theirs. She didn't notice any membership stickers, but more than a few cars displayed decals from prestigious universities.

Laughter drifted from behind the picket fence. She headed to the fence, Diane falling into step beside her.

Peeking through the narrow gap between two pickets, Cassie could make out a huge in-ground swimming pool. A few women lounged on upholstered chaises beside the pool, chatting; a few hearty children shrieked and splashed in the water, heedless of the setting sun.

"Maybe we could drown Phil," Diane whispered. Cassie laughed. Having Diane suggesting such gruesome ends for him made her feel comparatively civilized for thinking that simply pushing him into the pool in his formal wedding tux would be fun.

They strolled past the pool to the tennis courts, enclosed not by a picket fence but by a flexible mesh. Two middle-aged men, ferociously fit, their faces gleaming with perspiration, dueled on the clay center court.

"A little nicer than the courts we play on at Lexington High School," Diane conceded.

"Maybe we could brain Phil with a tennis ball." Cassie supposed she could be as cruel as Diane—although tennis balls weren't hard enough to cause much of an injury.

"That sounds pretty violent to me," Diane teased. "Are you having a change of heart?"

"Forget I said anything."

"Hey, I like the idea. A stray tennis ball could come sailing in from wherever and bean him just before he says, 'I do.'"

Cassie chuckled.

The evening was mild, and watching the tennis players sweat made her feel warm. Motioning with her head toward the main building, she pushed up the sleeves of her cardigan, crossed the parking lot and, Diane in tow, approached the red-carpeted entrance.

She imagined passing through the heavy glass double doors Saturday afternoon at two-thirty. The vaulted entry would be filled with well-dressed women wafting perfume and equally well-dressed men in tailored suits, all of them buzzing about the social event of the Lynwood season: furniture mogul Phillip Keene tying the knot with duchess of York clone Tricia Riggs. There would probably be music—not the treacly arrangement of an old Beatles tune currently being pumped into the vestibule, but something classy and tasteful. Harp music, maybe, or classical guitar. Ushers in tuxedos would be escorting the guests through the entry to…where? Cassie and Diane needed to find out. The site might suggest ideas for revenge.

"What was I just saying about pretension?" Diane murmured, checking out the open door labeled Pro Shop in curlicued gold script.

"What did you expect? It's a country club. People who belong to country clubs have money and play golf." Although Cassie's background was working class, it wasn't as if she never had anything to do with rich people. Public-TV employees frequently had to make presentations before executive boards and foundations, accompany celebrity visitors during pledge-break appearances or escort heavy-duty donors around the station. Working at a noncommercial station entailed rubbing elbows with rich people on a regular basis.

Phillip was rich, too. She'd known that back in Boston. He hadn't discussed his family's finances. He'd driven that old Toyota, and he'd dressed in typical student attire, nothing flashy or expensive-looking. But he'd had an attitude of confidence about him, an aura of privilege, the rock-solid breeding of someone who had grown up in a big house with both parents on the premises, someone for whom attending Harvard Business School would not cause culture shock. His wealth hadn't meant much one way or the other to Cassie, but she'd been aware of it the way she'd been aware of his dark hair and his sexy smile.

They passed a hallway labeled To Lockers And Pool and drew to a halt by the rear wall, an expanse of glass-and-brass-trimmed French doors that opened onto a spacious patio with steps leading down to a garden.

"This is where they're going to have the wedding," she stated.

"You think so?" Diane said.

"It's perfect for a wedding. Where else would they have it?"

Diane surveyed the patio, open to the pink dusk sky. "Let's start praying for rain."

"I'm sure they'll put up a tent," Cassie said. A few people, groomed with understated taste and armed with cocktails and goblets of wine, were enjoying the sunset on the patio right now. She supposed that on Saturday afternoon, the area could be cleared of outsiders, a canopy erected over the garden and chairs set up in rows on the grass. A white-satin runner would be unrolled from the French doors down the steps to the far end of the garden, where a portable altar, bedecked with flowers, would stand. The chairs would be white and festooned with ribbons. Or maybe more flowers.

It unnerved Cassie that she could see it all so vividly. She almost hoped Phillip and his bride had a few surprises in store for the guests. Maybe they would arrive in a hot-air balloon, or parachute to earth in jumpsuits, his black and hers white. Maybe the ceremony would be held on the tennis court.

No. She just *knew* it was going to be on the patio and in the garden. Her certainty ignited a tiny flame in her chest where yesterday she'd felt as if she'd been stabbed. By the afternoon of the wedding, she'd probably feel dismembered.

"Assuming they have a tent," Diane said, "we could sabotage the support poles. Just before the creep says, 'I do,' the tent could collapse on top of everyone. Can't you just see it? All those wedding guests, dressed to the nines, trying to fight their way out from under an acre of heavy canvas. Think of the deflated hairdos. Think of the crushed corsages."

Deciding she'd rather not, Cassie turned from the patio. A double door stood open on the far side of the lounge; through it emerged the hum of voices and the clink of silverware against china. Evidently, the Linden Hills dining room.

Just as she knew the wedding would take place on the patio, she was equally certain the reception would take place in the dining room.

Diane must have realized where Cassie's attention was. "A food fight," she whispered. "Forget the collapsing tent. We'll get a food fight started during the reception. By the time Phil and Tricia stand up to dance their first dance as husband and wife, the floor will be knee-deep in mashed potatoes and fruit cocktail."

Cassie didn't know whether to groan or laugh. "Maybe I *should* make you story editor," she muttered. "You've got such original, creative ideas." She moved toward the dining room and smiled at the hostess, who stood behind a podium just inside the doorway. The room was all white: textured white walls, white drapes on the windows, white linens on the well-spaced circular tables. Who would be able to find a bride in there? she wondered. In her white wedding gown she'd disappear right into the decor.

"Rats," Diane murmured into her ear. "Remember that pet store in town? Maybe we could buy a few rats—or some of those crickets—and unleash them just as everyone is sitting down to dinner."

"I don't want to be in the same room as rats," Cassie said with a shudder. "Or crickets, either, for that matter."

"A tarantula, then. Or how about a snake? Do you suppose the pet store might have snakes? A cobra or a rattler—"

"Phil's here," Cassie hissed, as if she herself were a snake. She lifted her chin in his direction. Diane's eyebrows practically merged with her hairline.

He was seated with an older couple at one of the smaller tables. The couple had their backs to the doorway, but Cassie could see that the man had a thick head of silver hair and the woman's hair was shoulder length, salt-and-pepper. Phillip was talking to them, his mouth moving, his fork poised in midair—and then he froze and stared directly into Cassie's eyes.

This was not good. She wasn't exactly sure it was bad, but it definitely wasn't good. She was going to have to come up with a quick explanation for what she and Diane were doing at Linden Hills. Something other than the fact that they were casing the joint, trying to come up with a way to bring about his downfall on Saturday.

He said something to his dinner companions, then set down his fork, placed his napkin on the table and stood. The couple twisted in their chairs to see whom Phillip was staring at. The woman looked familiar to Cassie.

Diane whispered, "That's his mom. I guess the man must be his dad. I never met Mr. Keene, but his mom—I'd never forget her."

Cassie nodded. She'd been introduced to Mrs. Keene the day she'd accompanied Phillip to the station during the woman's visit to Boston.

Phillip moved in long strides through the dining room, weaving among the tables, his gaze fixed on Cassie. Clad in tailored slacks and a forest-green shirt, he looked rugged but safe. He wasn't safe, though. Phillip Keene was never safe, at least not as far as she was concerned.

She took a deep breath and then another, refusing to succumb to panic or to the deep-set darkness of his eyes. "What are we going to do?" she asked Diane through clenched teeth.

"Be friendly and charming. Don't mention the food fight or the bombs."

"Thanks a heap—" He'd reached them, and she shut up.

"What the hell are you doing here?" he asked, his tone hushed but intense.

Cassie hoped her smile looked more natural than it felt. "Don't you ever say hello, Phil? You used to have better manners."

He glanced at the ceiling and swore softly, then said, "Hello. What the hell are you doing here?"

Diane jumped in. "Well, if you really want to know, we had some free time this evening, so we thought we'd see if we could find Linden Hills. We don't want to get lost on Saturday and arrive late for the festivities.''

Not bad, Cassie thought. Maybe she ought to make Diane story editor after all. Assistant producer *and* story editor. She could probably squeeze a tiny raise for Diane out of the budget. Diane deserved one just for being so perversely imaginative.

"We didn't mean to interrupt your dinner," Diane went on sweetly. "Why don't you go finish your meal."

Again he glanced at the ceiling, as if the solution to all his problems lay in the soundproofing tiles. "My parents want you to join us," he muttered.

Cassie nodded, her brain picking up speed as she assimilated this information. Should she and Diane join his parents? Was there a tactful way to refuse the offer?

She decided there wasn't.

"We've already eaten," Diane was saying, "but we could have a drink or some dessert. Right, Cassie?"

Diane seemed to know what she was doing—even when what she was doing was planning a disaster that was likely against the law in all fifty states. Cassie wasn't foolish enough to contradict her. "Sure," she said. "We could have a drink with your parents."

Phillip looked vexed, but his parents had left him with no alternative—and neither did Diane. He opened his mouth to say something, then reconsidered and pressed his lips into a thin line. With all the enthusiasm of a convict awaiting sentencing, he motioned Diane ahead of him, then touched his hand to the small of Cassie's back and ushered her through the dining room to the table where his parents sat.

His father immediately rose, beaming a high-wattage smile at Cassie. "Mom, Dad, this is Cassie Webber, a friend of mine from Boston," Phillip recited mechanically. "And this is—"

"Diane!" his mother exclaimed, extending both hands to Diane, who clasped them warmly. "What a pleasure. I'm so glad you were able to come!"

"I wouldn't have missed Phil's wedding for the world. I don't know if you remember Cassie—" Diane gestured toward her "—but the invitation said Diane Krensky and guest, and I just knew Cassie would want to be here, too."

Phillip stared at Diane, then at Cassie with dawning comprehension. Mr. Keene gave Cassie an enthusiastic handshake. "It's a pleasure," he said, pumping Cassie's hand. "We love meeting Phillip's friends. Please, sit down."

Phillip's mother smiled at Cassie and gave her hand a gentle squeeze. "Phil, why don't you bring over a couple of extra chairs," she suggested. "You two sit." She directed Cassie and Diane into Phillip's and his father's chairs while the men went off in search of unused ones.

Cassie was uncomfortably aware that the woman was studying her two guests. Did she know about Phillip and her? Did she know they had a history? Had Phillip told her, or could a perceptive mother figure it out on her own? Or did Mrs. Keene know nothing at all?

Phillip and his father returned lugging chairs, which they wedged in around the circular table. "You sit here, James," Mrs. Keene directed her husband, "and Phillip, you sit over there." Next to Cassie. So close to Cassie that if she laughed or sighed or her toes twitched, her leg would press against his.

"So, you gals are from Boston," Mrs. Keene said as Mr. Keene twisted in his seat, searching the room for a waiter. "You both worked at that TV station, right?"

"We're both connected to *Dream Wheels*," Diane confirmed. "It's Cassie's baby. I'm just the brains behind the operation." And then she was off, relating the concept of the show to Phillip's parents, telling them of the taping they'd planned for Keene Furniture during the days before the wedding.

"What a fine idea!" Phillip's father beamed at Phillip. "Isn't that a fine idea? Showing how a chair is made."

"It's a fine idea," Phillip growled. Maybe his toes had twitched, because suddenly his knee was digging into Cassie's leg. The effect of that contact wasn't quite as intense as his touch last night, but it stirred unwelcome sensations inside her, unwelcome memories. She recalled his legs entwined with hers, his knee nudging her thighs apart, his body penetrating hers, and felt her cheeks flame with heat.

"Excuse me—where's the ladies' room?" she asked. She couldn't sit at the table with Phillip's knee pressing her thigh and her face burning. She couldn't make pleasant conversation with his parents while reminiscing about her steamy, too-brief affair with their son.

"I'll show you," Phillip said quickly. And then he was on his feet and pulling out her chair for her.

Damn. She'd hoped to get away from him until she could compose herself. She might even have been subconsciously thinking about sneaking out of the building altogether and hiding in the car until Diane was done charming the socks off Phillip's parents.

She wasn't cut out for this revenge stuff. She wanted Phillip to suffer at least as much as she was suffering, but as long as his bumping a fully clothed body part into her was enough to set her heart pounding, she didn't see how she was going to exact any sort of revenge.

She'd said she wanted the ladies' room, and his parents were smiling expectantly at her, waiting for her to go. Phillip was waiting, too. Diane winked at her—hardly a reassuring sign. Cassie saw no other choice but to go find the ladies' room. With Phillip, damn it.

CHAPTER SIX

"SO, DIANE BROUGHT you to Lynwood?" Phillip asked the instant they'd crossed the threshold.

"I have to go to the bathroom," Cassie said coldly.

He clamped his hand around her arm. "What the hell is going on, Cassie? My mother invited Diane, and of all the guests she could have brought with her, she chose you? I'm not an idiot. Something's up."

She glanced at him and found herself transfixed by his handsome profile. Why was it that she could be so downright infuriated by him and yet so appreciative of his good looks?

It wasn't his appearance, she realized. From the first time she'd met him, she had been aware of him in a visceral way. Handsome men held an esthetic appeal, certainly; but with Phillip the appeal was different, more complex, more profound. With him there was a bone-deep connection, a blood-hot yearning. It had always been that way, and even now, just days before his marriage to another woman, it was still that way.

She hated herself for desiring him, and her hatred manifested itself in anger. "Why shouldn't I come to your wedding? Just because you once said you loved me, and you'd come back to me, and we'd be together forever? Well, not to worry, Phil. I'm over it—and obviously you are, too." She had never been a good liar. But in the soft, subtle lighting of the lounge area, with a string-orchestra arrangement of "As Tears Go By" floating through the air, he might not notice that she was a far worse actress than most of the cranky preschoolers she'd ever hired to perform in her show. He just might believe she'd recovered from their affair.

He didn't look persuaded, but that could be because she'd shaken loose some memories inside him, rather than because of her lousy acting. Maybe she wasn't the only one who hadn't forgotten what they'd shared. As his hand relented in its grip on her arm, his gaze also relented, his eyes growing darker, gentler.

"I'm sorry about what happened, Cassie," he murmured. "I really am."

"I'm not," she said, steeling herself against him. She didn't want his apology. As Diane had said, she'd been hurt, and she wanted him to be hurt, too. Apologizing was just his attempt to avoid punishment. She wasn't going to let him off the hook. "Could you please show me where the ladies' room is?"

He scrutinized her for a moment more, then released her arm and pointed her toward the hall leading to the pool. "Right there," he said, indicating a door with a filigreed gold-tone sign reading Women on it. Cassie gave him a frosty smile, then turned and strode into the rest room, her shoulders square and her head held high, even while she silently berated herself for being the worst liar in the world.

CASSIE WEBBER, he decided, was the worst liar in the world.

He'd wounded her. He knew it, and he hated that it had happened, but sometimes people had no alternatives. Sometimes they were forced to follow destinies not of their own making. They considered their options and found themselves obliged to choose not the best one—sometimes there was no best one—but rather the one that would cause the least damage.

Phillip could have devastated his family heritage and left his father to self-destruct. Or he could have jilted Cassie Webber, a bright, beautiful, sexy woman who would get over him, heal completely and give her love to someone much more deserving than him. Surely that was the less-damaging choice.

Once he'd decided not to return to Boston last year, he should have called her. He hadn't because he'd known that talking to her would have made his decision that much more painful. He would have heard her voice and his resolve would have disintegrated. He'd rationalized his refusal to contact her by assuring himself that the more abrupt the break, the easier it would be for her to realize she was better off without him.

He'd wanted her to loathe him. But he'd wanted her to keep herself and her loathing back in Boston, a safe distance from him.

Instead, she was in Lynwood, Diane's date for the wedding. And her nearness was making him crazy.

He wanted her. He wanted her to be the woman in white, marching down the aisle to join him before the minister on Saturday. He wanted Cassie—brilliant, luminous Cassie, who couldn't lie her way out of a paper bag—to be his bride.

And that would never happen. Not as long as Harry Riggs had it in his power to obliterate everything the Keene family valued, everything they'd ever been and ever would be.

He wished he could explain the stakes to Cassie. But then what? Would he ask her to wait for him until he could straighten out the company's finances and get Harry off his back? That could take years, and it wouldn't be fair to her, or to Tricia. Besides, Cassie would probably condemn him for choosing the family firm over her.

His only solution was to let her despise him so much she'd eventually consider herself lucky to have escaped a lifetime with him.

She emerged from the ladies' room. Droplets of water clung to her cheeks and lashes, and he wondered for a panicky moment if she'd been crying. But the arrogant thrust of her chin and the snide curve of her smile assured him that whatever she was feeling, it wasn't fragile and weepy.

"That bathroom leads down to the pool locker room," she said. "Too bad I didn't bring a swimsuit— I could have taken a dip."

Phillip refused to think about what she'd look like in a bikini.

"So, is that where your wedding is going to be? Poolside?"

"No. There's a patio and garden out back."

She smiled. "And then I guess you'll be having the reception dinner in the dining room?"

"That's what Tricia wants."

"What do *you* want, Phil?" she asked, a quiet earnestness in her voice.

You, he almost said. *I want to kiss you this minute, in this spot, just steps from where I'm going to be exchanging vows with Tricia in a few days. I want to take you in my arms and slide my hands up and down your back. I want you in my bed, under me, naked and moaning in ecstasy.*

His brain overruled his hormones. What he wanted,

he told himself, was to make Cassie resent him and reject him. He wanted her to leave Lynwood feeling good about herself, ready to forge ahead in her life, ready to forget about him, even though he would never forget about her. But he couldn't bring himself to say that.

"I want to go back and finish my dinner," he said.

"Of course." Her smile returned, patently phony. They had lost their chance for honesty. They were back to faking it, pretending things weren't what they were, pretending they wanted what they didn't want and didn't want what they did.

"OKAY, WHAT DO WE have?" Diane asked as Cassie steered out of the parking lot. "His parents are adorable. The country club is ritzy. Phillip is a turd."

Cassie sighed. She must be a really hopeless case, wishing she could defend him against Diane's nastiness even when her own heartbreak was the reason for the nastiness. Diane was her friend, her ally, her loyal accomplice. And Phillip was...well, a turd.

"He actually apologized," she told Diane.

"Big whoop. He's about a year late with his apology, isn't he?"

Cassie nodded glumly. "Anyway, we guessed right on the ceremony. They're getting married in that garden by the patio, and the reception is going to be in the dining room."

"Great."

Cassie didn't consider anything about this great. "He's suspicious about our motives for being here. He doesn't think we came just to celebrate his marriage."

"Well, duh." Diane was silent for a moment, then

she asked, "So, what's his weak spot? Where is he most vulnerable?"

"Me," Cassie blurted, startling herself so much she almost veered off the road.

"You?" Diane said disbelievingly.

Cassie recalled the way he'd held her arm, the way he'd stared into her eyes, the roughness in his voice when he'd said he was sorry. "I think he still…" She heard a rough edge in her own voice and cleared her throat. "I think he still has feelings for me. Sexual feelings."

"In other words, he isn't blind and his gonads are functioning. I'm not averse to performing some surgery between his legs. Just a little snip with pruning shears would put his sexual feelings to an end."

Cassie considered the possibility that even after such surgery, he would still want her. Last year in Boston, she'd believed that their desire was at least as emotional as it was physical. When they'd made love, it had been with their souls, as well as their bodies. She couldn't have responded so strongly, so completely, if it had been only sex.

For him, though, it might have been nothing more than that.

"You know," Diane continued, her tone devoid of humor, "you could be on to something. Maybe he does want you."

"I'm not repulsive," Cassie said, downplaying her previous comment. "I don't think it's such a big deal if he wants me. Eighty percent of the street people in my neighborhood want me, too. The other twenty percent are gay."

"No, no." Diane wagged a finger at Cassie's face to silence her. "I think you're right. You're his point of vulnerability. You're the weapon. We don't need bombs and pruning shears to ruin him. We've got you.''

Cassie began to regret she'd ever spoken. ''I could live with stink bombs.''

Diane ignored her. ''We could dangle you in front of him, the ultimate temptation. You know how to be tempting, don't you?''

''As a matter of fact, no.'' As a teenager, Cassie had always been an oddball. She'd had her share of guy friends—other oddballs. They used to hang around the English-department office and the tech-squad room, writing scripts and tinkering with the video equipment, staging scenes in the auditorium and recording them on tape. They'd taken the honors Shakespeare course and the creative-writing class, and they'd hung out at the local sandwich shop, eating Americanized fajitas at midnight and talking about how they would change the world once they ran all the major TV networks. But none of those guys had ever seemed tempted by her.

''What's the sexiest outfit you brought with you?''

''Diane.'' Now Cassie *really* regretted she'd spoken. ''I'm not a siren. I don't own sexy outfits.''

''Let's go shopping.''

''In Lynwood?''

''There must be a mall somewhere.''

''It's nearly eight o'clock. Even if there is a mall, it probably closes by nine.''

''Then you'd better drive faster. Why don't we go back to that gas station. That kid gave good directions. I'll bet he would know where the nearest mall was.''

Cassie let out a long breath. ''Even if we find a mall and go shopping, what exactly is the plan? Once you buy me sexy outfits, what am I supposed to do with them?''

"Wear them. Beyond that, I don't know. Yet." Diane grinned. She looked invigorated and dangerous. "We'll figure something out. Something less bloody than bombs and surgery, but just as gloriously destructive. To the mall, Cassandra! To the mall!''

Uneasiness gripped Cassie. But she couldn't think of a good argument against Diane's shopping expedition. Dressing herself in tantalizing apparel wasn't going to turn her into a femme fatale. But attempting to transform her might get Diane off her stink-bombs-and-surgery kick.

With another weary sigh, she drove toward the gas station to get directions to the mall.

ENTERING THE Keene Furniture factory building the following morning, Phillip nearly tripped on a cable. It sat coiled like a snake-charmer's cobra on the floor of the entry lobby, and like a cobra it seemed to snap at his ankle as he stumbled over it.

He cursed.

He used to pride himself on his eloquence. His high-school football coach always joked that Phillip had the largest vocabulary on the team, and when he won the Rotary Club prize for public speaking, no one had been surprised. In college and graduate school, he had always expressed himself with clarity and grace.

Yet in the past couple of days, for some reason, he seemed overly dependent on a limited lexicon of four-letter words.

No, not for some reason. For one very particular reason: Cassie.

He'd barely survived dinner last night. Naturally,

his parents had been captivated by her. His father had regaled Cassie and Diane with embarrassing stories about Phillip's childhood—the time he'd brought home a bucket full of toads he'd caught by the river and the bucket had overturned in the middle of a cocktail party his parents were hosting. Or the time he'd won the fourth-grade spelling bee and then misspelled his teacher's name in front of the entire student body. Or the first time he'd ever seen Tricia, when she was six and he was ten and a communicant in the faith of all ten-year-old boys: the I-Hate-Girls religion. "She's the most disgustingest girl in the universe," he'd declared. And now look—they were going to be married.

His mother had chatted a bit about the lovely day she'd spent in Boston with Diane last year—what a wonderful city Boston was, how much fun she'd had walking the streets and browsing in the shops. But mostly she'd observed Cassie. Her gaze had roamed between Cassie and Phillip, weighing and measuring, assessing. Dorothy Keene was nobody's fool. She'd always had a pretty clear idea of what was going on with Phillip.

He'd left Linden Hills right after Cassie and Diane had. He hadn't wanted to linger over a brandy with his parents and have his mother grill him on what exactly his friendship with Cassie back in Boston had entailed. As it was, Dorothy had expressed her doubts about Phillip's marriage to Tricia as recently as a month ago. "I know things are complicated between your father and Harry Riggs," she'd allowed, "but I don't want you to ruin your life."

"Marrying Tricia wouldn't be ruining my life," he'd insisted. "Tricia's a lovely woman." That was true. What was also true was that his mother had no idea how "complicated" things were between his father and Harry, and how dire the consequences would be if Harry decided to call in the loans. Phillip loved his parents. He couldn't bear to see them lose their business. If they did, they'd lose their heritage, their connection to the past and to the future, their security, their good name.

Compared with what could happen if Harry Riggs threw a tantrum, marrying Tricia seemed like a bargain.

He was spending too little time bracing himself for his new role as Harry Riggs's son-in-law. Too little time worrying about the management missteps at the retail outlet in Chicago and the company's crushing financial burdens. And he was spending far too much time thinking about Cassie.

Because of her, he hadn't been able to sleep for two nights in a row. Because of her, he kept experiencing erotic hungers at inappropriate times. Because of her, he had very nearly broken his neck because she, her big-mouth buddy Diane and her hippie cameraman had left a coil of cable in the entryway of Phillip's place of business.

She hadn't come to Lynwood to wish him well on the occasion of his nuptials. And he was far from convinced that she'd come because she wanted to film the crafting of a chair for her show. If he was a betting man, he'd wager that her real reason for being in Lynwood was to exact some sort of revenge for his betrayal. His insomnia was as much a result of fear as of lust. And in moments of brutal honesty, he had to admit he deserved whatever catastrophe she brought down upon his head, whether the catastrophe was that he would trip over her cable and break his neck or something else. Something worse.

Instead of heading directly up the stairs to his office, he shoved open the glass door that led to the hall linking design studios and carpentry shops. The first design studio was lit but empty, which was odd. It was nine-thirty; the design staff was usually hard at work by now. Peering through the open door, Phillip stared at the vacant drafting tables, the photos and sketches pinned to the pegboard walls, the scuffed hardwood floors. Then his attention was caught by the babble of voices from the far end of the hall.

His forehead knotted in a frown as he turned and stalked down the hall. The noise spilled from the biggest shop room, a spacious, vault-ceilinged carpentry work space filled with sheets and boards of wood, equipment and massive work counters. Ordinarily the room hummed with the sounds of power saws and lathes and sanders; ordinarily it held the scent of wood—pine, walnut, cherry, the musty fragrance of mahogany. Today, however, the only sound emerging was of human conversation and laughter, and perfume and aftershave overwhelmed the smell of sawdust.

Phillip stepped into the room. It was jammed with people—carpenters, clerks, the lumber-inventory manager and the fellow who kept the vending machines in the lounge stocked with soda and candy bars. Every fluorescent ceiling fixture was turned on, bathing the room in blinding light. People chattered and laughed. The atmosphere was festive.

Scowling, Phillip searched the room for Cassie. He had no trouble finding her tall blond cameraman, who held one video-cam and stood beside a second, stationary camera affixed to a tripod near one of the workbenches, atop which lay a smoothly cut sheet of oak. Once Phillip had located Beckelman, he spotted Diane standing not far from him, armed with a clipboard. But Cassie was short, easily lost in the crowd.

Then he saw her, crawling out from under the workbench, unfurling a cable behind her. She straightened up and he swallowed hard.

She was wearing a denim miniskirt and sheer panty hose that reminded him of a night he'd spent the past year trying to forget, a night in which her beautiful legs had played a significant role—along with the rest of her compact, curvy body. Dragging his vision upward, he swallowed harder. She had on a cropped jacket that barely covered what she was wearing underneath. He wasn't sure what it was—a slip or a camisole, or maybe a real blouse designed to look like underwear. All he knew was that it appeared to be more lace than fabric, and it was cut low enough to display a faint shadow of cleavage between her breasts.

His forehead grew damp with sweat. He wanted to believe he was uncomfortably hot because of all the people crowding the room and all the ceiling lights burning so brightly. Not because of Cassie's outfit and her glossy hair and the shine of her lipstick, a rich caramel shade that made him imagine the sweetness of her lips, the lush texture, the pleasure he'd have kissing them, devouring them...

"Isn't this cool?" Tricia chirped into his ear.

He spun around and his scowl deepened. A kettledrum thumped in his head, pounding the tempo of his pulse. Why was Tricia here? Why, when he was burning up from the inside out, did she think this spectacle was "cool"?

And why the hell was she wearing overalls? Granted, they were stylish overalls, crisp and starchy, nipped in at the waist and flared at the hips. The shoulder straps were edged in pale-blue stitching. Phillip had never seen them on her before.

"Isn't what cool?" he muttered.

"It's show biz!" Tricia gushed. "They're filming! Keene Furniture is actually going to be on TV. I swear, this is the most exciting thing that's ever happened in Lynwood."

"It's just a children's show," he reminded her, his gaze straying back to the dynamo overseeing the most exciting thing that had ever happened in Lynwood. Why did she have to be wearing such a short skirt? Her legs were perfectly proportioned, and the panty hose caused them to shimmer silkily. Her eyes—was she wearing mascara, or were her lashes that thick and dark naturally?

Her choice of cosmetics didn't matter. What mattered was that her extravaganza had lured practically his entire staff into the carpentry area to watch the goings-on, and thus no one was getting any work done. She was disrupting the rhythm of Keene Furniture with her cables and cameras, her bright lighting and her brighter smile. Even Edie was among the onlookers, her eyes round and her usually prim expression tainted by a smile.

And the guy from the vending-machine company was ogling Cassie. Didn't he have anything better to do? Didn't he have candy bars to stock or soda cans to recycle? Couldn't he ogle Diane, instead?

"Okay, everybody!" Cassie bellowed, and like magic everyone in the room fell silent. "I don't mind if you all want to watch, but you've got to be quiet. Richard, are you ready?''

Richard Bausch, Keene Furniture's expert on wood, stepped forward. His bushy, gray-tinged brown hair was a mess of untamable waves. He wore his usual outfit: a denim shirt and faded jeans that rode low on his waist, allowing his paunch to swell above his belt buckle. He should have been checking that morning's lumber delivery right now, determining which boards would be used for tables and cabinet fronts and which would be cut to construct smaller pieces, singling out those with the most appealing grain for Keene's top-of-the-line furniture.

That was exactly what he was explaining as he stood in front of the stationary camera and a room full of his spellbound co-workers. Phillip hadn't known Richard could speak so cogently about the different kinds of wood, the different degrees of hardness, the risks of using knotted wood and the decisions that would be made about stains and finishes based on the innate quality of a single board. ''You've got to listen to the wood, I always say,'' Richard explained with a combination of folksy affability and mysticism. ''It'll tell you what it's meant to be. It'll tell you if it's an end table or a chair or a hat rack, and it'll tell you if it needs a dark stain to look its best or if a light stain is the way to go.''

''He's good,'' Tricia whispered into Phillip's ear. Phillip had been thinking the same thing. If the company went bankrupt, Richard could get a job as a narrator of documentaries, or maybe as a lecturer on communing with lumber.

Glancing over his shoulder at Tricia, Phillip discovered she wasn't even looking at Richard. Her gaze was on Cassie's ponytailed cameraman. Beckelman stood at the foot of the workbench, aiming the lens of his handheld video-cam at one end of the broad board on the table and panning slowly, lovingly, down the length of the board to the other end while Richard lectured on the qualities inherent in the wood. Cassie stood to one side, her head and Diane's bowed together as they studied the clipboard and conferred quietly.

"Okay, cut!" she announced when Richard seemed to be losing steam. "That was great! Roger, do we need more?"

"I'm fine," he said, checking a setting on his camera.

Cassie glanced up from her clipboard, and her eyes met Phillip's. Her smile made the drumming in his head stop—and it almost made his heart stop, as well. It was a seductive smile, a knowing smile, a smile that said, *Don't I look fabulous?*

Without meaning to, he nodded.

Her smile faltered slightly, and she broke eye contact and addressed the rest of the crowd. "What do you think, folks? Should Richard win an Emmy?"

The room erupted in applause.

The sound jolted Phillip. The hell with Cassie and her show-business pizzazz. His employees had work to do, and damn it, they were going to do that work, even if Cassie had to be forcibly removed from the premises to get them back to their desks and workbenches.

He moved farther into the room, weaving his way through his throng. Before he got far, Lowell Henley snagged his arm and grinned. "Great PR, isn't it?"

Too agitated to risk speaking, Phillip pulled his arm

free and continued to wind his way to the bench where Cassie was filming Richard. He tried to figure out why he was so tense: because work wasn't getting done? Because Lowell Henley—a man of sound judgment most of the time—thought this was great PR? Because Tricia was dressed in farmer duds and behaving like a starstruck goofball?

Or because Cassie looked like a vixen in that revealing skirt and peekaboo top?

"All right," she bellowed above the din. "Richard, you're a natural. You're going to walk us through the cutting stage, right? How the board gets sawed into smaller pieces..."

She had her back to Phillip as he neared her. He threaded his arm between the shoulders of the human-resources director and the head of custom sales and clamped his hand on her arm. She jumped and spun around, then grinned at him.

Maybe it wasn't lipstick, he thought dazedly. Maybe her lips were always that caramel-sweet shade.

"We need to talk," he said, refusing to let go of her for fear the crowd would swallow her up. Or maybe he held on to her because the sleeve of her jacket was a soft brushed fabric and beneath it he felt Cassie, and because touching her had such a potent effect on him.

Although she was petite, her arms had genuine muscle on them. They were strong enough to lug a bulky footlocker down a corridor, strong enough to wrap around a man and...

Never mind. He did a little strong-arming of his own to guide her through the crowd and out of the carpentry shop.

They stood in the hall, which seemed markedly

chillier without all that body heat and glaring light. But Phillip still felt sweat on his upper lip and at his nape. He still felt a fever burning inside him, a conflagration of longing and confusion and disgust with himself that he couldn't just ignore her.

She gazed up at him. Her eyes turned him on as much as her mouth did. So did her outfit, and the curve of her arm against his fingers, and her very nearness.

"What?" she asked, slightly breathless.

"I told you I didn't want you filming your show here," he began. "I thought I made myself clear—"

The sound of heavy footfalls caused him to glance over his shoulder. Joe Renkawicz, the sixty-year-old maintenance supervisor, was clomping down the hall in his burly, overweight, work-booted version of a gallop.

"Hey, Boss!" he shouted to Phillip. "I heard they're producing a movie in there. This I gotta see!" Before Phillip could stop him, Joe barreled past them and into the carpentry shop.

Phillip sighed. He couldn't talk to Cassie in the hall, so close to witnesses—especially when he had no idea what he was going to say. He might remonstrate with her for defying his request that she not film at his plant. He might yell at her for dressing so appealingly. Or he might just lose control and—

No. That was not an option.

He was going to tell her to pack up and clear out, regardless of what his father had said last night and what Lowell Henley had said whenever he'd said it. Regardless of what all his ga-ga employees might think about the glamour and excitement of having a kiddy show filmed in their workshop. But he couldn't chew her out in public, where those same ga-ga employees might hear him and think he was an ogre.

Still holding her arm, he ushered her through the nearest doorway and let it swing shut behind them. It was only after he'd twisted the lock in the door so they wouldn't be interrupted that he realized they were in the men's room. A pair of urinals protruded from one green-tiled wall; the opposite wall held a pair of ceramic sinks topped with a wide mirror. The rear of the room contained several gray-partitioned toilet stalls. The air was tangy with the scent of antiseptic.

Phillip let the hand holding Cassie's arm fall. She surveyed the lavatory and quirked her mouth into an ironic smile. "Is this your conference room?"

He couldn't let himself respond to her taunting. In fact, he couldn't let himself respond to anything about her. He glanced away to avoid looking at her, but that move backfired when he found himself, instead, viewing her reflection in the mirror above the sinks. He admired the tilt of her chin, the pert angle of her nose, the tiny dimple in the corner of her mouth. He saw his own reflection, too—a man in a pearl-gray summer-weight suit in the grip of turbulent emotions.

His jaw clenched with tension, he turned back to her. "You can't film here."

"All right." She wrestled with a smile, then held her hand up as if swearing an oath. "We won't film any washroom scenes. I promise."

"Cassie." Exasperation boiled up inside him, making him even hotter. He loosened the knot of his tie and undid his shirt's collar button. He needed to breathe, to think. He needed to be in her presence without going insane. "I told you I didn't want you filming at Keene Furniture. Obviously I've been out-

voted by Lowell Henley and my father, but even so...
You saw the disruption you're causing. The company
can't handle that kind of turmoil right now. If you
have to film at Keene, do it some other time.''

"Lowell Henley told me I could do it this week,"
she reminded him.

"Lowell Henley didn't realize what kind of stress
I'm under at the moment.''

Cassie eyed him thoughtfully. "I didn't know getting married would be so stressful for you.''

"Well, now you do.''

"Why don't you just keep your distance from us,
then. Close yourself up in your office and enjoy your
stress. Lowell and I will handle the filming.''

"Cassie...'' He couldn't have her floating around
the building. Next week, when he was off on his honeymoon with Tricia, and Harry was satisfied that his
precious daughter had gotten exactly what she wanted
by becoming Mrs. Phillip Keene, Cassie could film all
she wanted. By next week, Keene Furniture would be
safe. Harry would never undermine his son-in-law's
company; he'd never jeopardize his daughter's future.
And if Phillip was out of town, he wouldn't run the
risk of bumping into Cassie in her skimpy little skirt
while she filmed.

She was waiting for him to finish. ''Did you happen
to notice how many people were crowded into the
shop?'' he said. ''Those are my employees. They have
work to do. As long as you're filming here, they won't
be doing their work. Do you see the problem?''

She peered up at him. Her eyes were so dark, her
skin so luminous. His gaze moved downward, along
her sleek, graceful neck to the faint shadow between
her breasts, barely visible above the lacy edge of her

top, and the idleness of his employees suddenly
seemed like the least of his problems.

He brought his gaze back to her face. She was still
watching him, her expression surprisingly solemn. Her
lips formed a tempting oval, sweet and inviting.

"I see a problem," she murmured. "I'm not sure
it's the same problem you see, though."

"I think it is," he said, his voice as subdued as hers,
his mood as solemn as her gaze. He no longer smelled
the industrial cleanser. He was aware only of Cassie's
familiar fragrance—spice and vanilla and womanly
warmth. His problem was that he was feeling exactly
the way he'd felt last year when he'd made love to
her and believed nothing else would ever matter to
him as much as she did. And her problem was the
same: that he was feeling the way he'd felt last year
about her—mere days before he was supposed to
marry someone else.

He reached out then and grasped her arms. He
pulled her toward him, gathering her to him, because
he knew that if he didn't taste her lips that very instant,
he would have to rip one of the urinals out of the wall
and hurl it through the window just to release some
of the tension burning to the point of explosion inside
him.

She didn't resist. Quite the opposite, in fact. The
instant his mouth touched hers, she opened to him.
The instant his arms closed around her, she brought
her arms around him. His tongue met hers and he was
lost. Falling. Plunging into sensation, a bottomless
chasm, the heart of a volcano, something deep and
endless and fiery, something he hadn't felt in the year
since he'd last kissed her.

He'd tried awfully hard during that year to avoid all

thoughts of Cassie. He'd actually succeeded a fair amount of the time. But now he was failing—disastrously.

He wanted *more*. More of what he couldn't have. More of the woman he shouldn't want. His body wanted her. His brain. His hands, meeting at her nape and digging into her hair, wanted to sift through its slippery texture, to feel it slide between his fingers. His skin wanted her skin against it; his bones wanted to bear her weight. His penis wanted her tight around him, throbbing as she came.

It was like the first time he'd kissed Cassie, when kissing her had felt so natural, so inevitable. Her mouth was like his own mouth's long-lost mate, molding to his, merging, moving with his in a dance of fierce intimacy. She took and gave as he gave and took. Her tongue danced with his, elegantly, competitively, carnally. Her body nestled into his embrace. Everything about this kiss was right.

Except that they were shut inside the building's first-floor men's lavatory and he was marrying someone else in less than a week.

"Cassie." It sounded like his voice, but distorted. Her name emerged from him twisted into a gasp, a groan, a plea.

Her arms tightened around him and her head arched back. When he pulled his lips from hers, he saw the pale line of her throat and had to put his mouth to it. As she drew in a sharp breath, her breasts pressed even more against him, and he knew he had to feel her with his hands, just once. Just once before the wedding.

Her jacket seemed to part for him, exposing the lacy white top, exposing the roundness of her breasts, the taut points of her nipples visible against the fabric. He wanted to sink to his knees and take her breasts in his mouth, one and then the other, but he knew if he did that he would have to make love to her completely. He wouldn't be able to stop.

So, with excruciating restraint, he limited himself to using his hands on her, cupping her, stroking, kneading until she whimpered. The low, tortured sound of her voice was enough to persuade him that he might not be able to stop after all.

She trembled in his arms and rocked her hips to him. Lifting his head, he saw that her eyes were closed, her lower lip caught in her teeth. She'd moved her hands to his arms, and he felt the bite of her fingertips through his sleeves.

How hard was the floor? he wondered. Maybe he could sit on one of the commodes and lower her onto him—or they could do it standing, leaning against the wall between the two urinals, with the mirror on the opposite wall reflecting them as they made love.

"Phil?"

Her eyes fluttered open and she stared up at him with such naked longing he had to stifle a groan. She slid her hands down his arms to cover his. For a split second, she held them tight against her breasts, and then she eased them away from her and sighed. The tip of her tongue flicked over her lips and he stifled another groan. "I don't think—" her voice was tissue thin "—this is a good idea."

If he hadn't been so miserable, he would have laughed at her understatement. It was the worst idea in the world. But for a few glorious moments he hadn't cared.

"I've got to get back to the taping." She sounded hoarse and tremulous. Her hands shook as she smoothed her blouse into the waistband of her skirt and adjusted her jacket over it. She shot a glance in the direction of the mirror, winced and ran her fingers through her hair.

Her hasty preening couldn't conceal the flush in her cheeks, the glow in her eyes, the swollen look of her lips. She could have been a poster child for female arousal. Not that Phillip was in a position to criticize; his arousal was, if anything, more obvious than hers.

He crossed to a sink, twisted the cold faucet and splashed water onto his face. It wasn't as effective as an icy shower, but it helped to clear his mind. He wished he had the nerve to drink some water, to wash the taste of Cassie out of his mouth, but he thought she might be insulted. Besides, he didn't really want to wash her away.

He pulled some paper towels from the chrome dispenser beside the sink, dried his face and hands and pivoted back to Cassie. She stood where he'd left her, squarely in the middle of the room, watching him. She wasn't the most beautiful woman in the world...but there was something about her, something that sucked him in, something that made him want to wad up the paper towel, toss it into the trash receptacle, cross the room to her and pick up where they'd left off.

"Maybe we ought to steer clear of each other," he said, wondering if not seeing her would be enough to keep him from wanting her.

"That's going to be impossible."

"It won't be impossible if you stop filming at Keene Furniture."

She smiled tentatively. "But I'll be at your wedding."

He stifled a curse. It would be difficult enough to

get married, feeling the way he did, without having the woman who sparked those feelings as a witness.

"You could sit in the back row where I can't see you."

Her smile lingered, but she didn't appear amused. "Or I could put a paper bag over my head." She checked herself one last time in the mirror, then moved toward the door. "I'm going to go film some people constructing a chair," she said briskly. "I really don't think you should make us stop. All your employees would be very disappointed if you closed us down. For the sake of staff morale, you'd better put up with me." Her smile was pensive as she strolled to the door, twisted the bolt to unlock it and stepped outside.

He watched the door swing shut behind her, hitting the jamb with a muted thump. There was a depressing finality to the sound. Alone in the harsh, antiseptic-smelling room, he stared at the mirror. His body might have cooled off, but he still looked vaguely delirious, his hair mussed and his eyes wild.

He forced himself to think about the company's debts. He forced himself to think about the man who controlled those debts, and about the man—his beloved, hapless father—responsible for that, and the damage that would be done to the second man if he didn't appease the first.

He thought about Tricia, a pleasant, attractive, good-natured young woman. He honestly liked her. But she couldn't drive him crazy the way Cassie could. Maybe that was a good reason to like Tricia even more.

Yet as he returned to the sink to try another dose of cold water in the face, he couldn't stop wondering if he wouldn't mind sacrificing his father and the company and Tricia and his entire calm, predictable existence for the chance to be driven crazy by Cassie Webber.

CHAPTER SEVEN

THIS WAS NOT going to work.

Seducing Phillip would be easy enough—especially since Diane had persuaded her to run her credit card through the scanners at two boutiques and a Victoria's Secret outlet at the mall last night. Phillip was a heterosexual man, which meant he was biologically incapable of resisting a short skirt. A seduction would be easy, except for one question: who would be seducing whom?

He had no right to seduce her. The SOB was engaged! How dare he kiss her the way he just had, so powerfully her brain melted to syrup, drenching all her thoughts in sticky-sweet goo? She hadn't expected him to respond so enthusiastically to her overture. He should have held back, guilt-stricken that he could even contemplate kissing a woman who was not his beloved bride-to-be. At the very least, he ought to have *tried* to resist her.

She and Diane were going to have to rethink this plan. Stink bombs and mayhem at the wedding were sounding a whole lot more palatable to Cassie. As squeamish as she was about Diane's schemes, she was a whole lot more squeamish about being crushed to an emotional pulp by Phillip.

And she couldn't imagine a seduction that didn't end with her being crushed.

A YEAR AGO, seducing Phillip would have never occurred to her.

They'd been close during the few months they'd
known each other. They'd spent many evenings together, eating pizza, philosophizing about life, arguing
over Buñuel after sitting through a film festival at the
Coolidge Corner Cinema. Cassie had talked to him
about life at the public-TV station, her ideas for mar-
keting dolls and toys related to *Dream Wheels,* her
hope of developing spin-off shows. He'd talked to her
about his courses, his case studies, his intention to return to Ohio after graduation to take the helm of the
family firm. The only time he'd spent the night at her
apartment was after they'd had dinner at a hole-in-the-
wall Thai place and been stricken with food poisoning.
They'd survived that wretched night together, holding
each other's heads over the toilet bowl and pouring
each other glasses of warm ginger ale.

It hadn't been the most romantic night of Cassie's
life, but in some ways, it had been the most loving.
She couldn't think of any other man she would have
wanted to nurse and be nursed by through a bout of
food poisoning.

That night notwithstanding, the attraction between
them had been strong and mutual right from the start.
But Boston was her home, and Phillip had every intention of leaving Boston. They both knew that. The
few times they touched, the few times they hugged
each other good-night and their lips moved toward a
kiss, Phillip always backed off, murmuring, "I want
this, Cassie, but I like you too much. If we got involved, we'd only wind up hurt. There's no future in
it."

She was frustrated—but frustration wasn't fatal.

And his consideration, his sensitivity, his willingness not to take what she would have gladly given him, only made her love him more.

Yet as the date of his departure drew closer, a dull disappointment settled over her. Why had the most exciting man she'd ever met decided he had to go back to Ohio? Why couldn't he stick around and give their relationship the chance it deserved? She knew he had the right to pose the same question in reverse: why couldn't she leave *Dream Wheels* in Diane's capable hands and come to Lynwood with him? Just because developing and producing her very own show had been her dream for years, and she'd achieved it at a remarkably young age, and she was on the cusp of bigger success and expanded opportunity, why wouldn't she simply toss all that away and join him in Lynwood?

Phillip knew her well enough not to ask. And just as she was entitled to her dreams, he was entitled to his.

She hadn't expected to see him his last night in Boston. He'd spent the previous weekend with his parents, who had flown east for his graduation from business school. They'd left, and his final days in town had been devoured by the business of transferring the lease on his grungy apartment in Cambridge to a group of incoming students, selling as much of his ragtag furniture as he could to those students and switching the names on the utilities accounts. He'd phoned Cassie at her production office that morning to tell her he was going to pack up his car with what he couldn't ship, then top off the gas tank and drive back to Lynwood, praying that the decrepit Toyota wouldn't die somewhere along Interstate 84.

"I'd like to see you before I go," he'd told her. "I just don't know how everything is going to play out. Maybe I can stop by your office tomorrow morning to say goodbye. But...I don't know."

She'd understood: he didn't know if seeing her would make it harder for him to leave. She wasn't sure anything could make his departure easier on her. But if not seeing her would make it easier on him...well that was something, she supposed.

"Whatever you think is best," she'd told him, then hung up and wondered why fate had to be so cruel, why long-held aspirations and ambitions had to take precedence over the radiant possibility of a romance. She'd wondered whether bidding Phillip farewell without ever having given their love a chance to blossom was the wisest thing she'd ever done or the most foolish.

The air was muggy that evening, so dense with humidity she felt as if she were swimming home rather than walking. The brick apartment buildings flanking the side street where she lived transformed the block into an oven, magnifying the heat. Allston was a funky part of Boston, the residents a mix of students, working-class folks and yuppies attempting to gentrify the neighborhood, a blend of races and ethnicities that Cassie found bracing. But as she trudged down her block from the T stop on Commonwealth Avenue in the heat, acutely aware that this would be Phillip's final night in Boston, she resented the crowds, the noise, the traffic. Too many shops lined the sidewalks. Too many people clogged her path. All she wanted to do was slog to her building, haul herself upstairs to her apartment, crank up the window-unit air condi-

tioner and collapse in a heap. And grieve over the fact
that he was leaving.

The sight of him, standing in front of her building
with a pizza box balanced in his hands, stunned her.
He was supposed to be across town, closing up his
own apartment and shoving what was left of his Boston life into cartons. He wasn't supposed to be here.

She was too hot, too tired. On her way home from
work, the ventilation system on the T had conked out,
turning the train into a sauna on steel wheels, and her
hair was as limp and dreary as her spirits. Her Museum
of Science shirt was glued to her back with sweat, and
her denim shorts chafed at her waist. The June heat
drained away her appetite. As hard as it was to believe
Phillip had come over, it was even harder to believe
he'd bothered to bring a pizza.

But there he was, holding a flat white box redolent
with spicy steam.

"I couldn't leave without seeing you," he said as
she drew to a halt at the entry to her building. He
looked as sticky as she felt. His polo shirt hung loose
over the waist of his shorts. He wore sandals and sunglasses. His forehead glistened with perspiration.

She wanted to yell at him for bringing her a pizza.
No, she didn't. She wanted to yell at him for aban-
doning her, going back to Ohio, never allowing her to
know what it would be like to kiss him on the mouth.
She wanted to yell at him for being the only man she'd
ever met who could make her want to open up and
share her most private emotions, the only man who
cared more about what she was thinking and feeling
than about the chances he had of scoring with her.

She wanted to grab Phillip by the shoulders and
shake him until he admitted that friendships like theirs

were precious and rare, and that if he drove back to his hometown without ever finding out what would have happened if they'd taken their relationship to another dimension, it would be the biggest mistake of his life.

It was too hot to talk, let alone yell and shake him and scream. "Let's go upstairs and turn on the air conditioner," she said wearily.

He nodded. She unlocked the front door, paused in the vestibule to collect her mail and led Phillip upstairs. The oily smell of the pizza caused beads of perspiration to sprout on her upper lip, and it seemed to add weight to her sneakered feet. The steps were steeper than she remembered. Phillip was going to leave her, and everything felt wrong.

They reached her apartment, three flights up. It was small—one main room plus a kitchenette big enough to accommodate little besides a circular pedestal table Cassie had discovered in a pile of discarded pieces from a set at the studio. While Phillip put the pizza down on the table, she crossed to the air-conditioning unit in the main room and twisted the dial. The motor hummed, but Cassie didn't feel any cooler.

"Help yourself to a beer," she hollered over her shoulder, then kicked off her sneakers and stood in front of the air conditioner with her head rolled back and her arms lifted, waiting for the fan to cool her off. Closing her eyes, she prayed that whatever Phillip said or did, she wouldn't break down and cry.

The air stirred around her. Her hair fluttered against her cheeks. And then she felt Phillip's hands on her shoulders as he approached her from behind. He pulled her gently against him.

"I don't know how to do this," he murmured. His

voice was so soft she almost didn't hear him over the drone of the air conditioner. She scowled. All he had to do was say, "Goodbye." Or, "Here's a slice of pizza. Have a good life." What didn't he know how to do?

As if she'd verbalized her thoughts, he whispered, "I don't know how to say goodbye to you, Cassie. I don't know how to leave you."

Her eyes flew open and she turned to face him. The chill that skimmed down her back had nothing to do with the air conditioner. It had to do with the agony in his eyes, the anguish in his smile.

His eyes and his smile told her as much as his words. Maybe more. They told her that he wanted her, that he wanted more than her friendship and trust. That he'd wanted more for a long time, that his heart ached from wanting so much for so long. They told her that if she took one tiny step toward him, it would be the biggest step she'd ever taken.

She took that step.

His arms closed around her. His mouth came down on hers. The only heat she was aware of didn't come from the sweltering June evening but from Phillip, lean and male and voracious. And from her, just as greedy, just as needy.

His tongue filled her mouth. He groped at her shirt, yanking it free of her shorts so he could slide his hands up underneath. He touched her back, her sides, curled his fingers up over her shoulders and kissed her harder. She clung to him, knowing she would fall if she let go. He was solid and strong, and she needed his solidity and strength. She needed his height, needed the sturdy breadth of his shoulders and the erotic movements of his tongue making love to hers. She needed Phillip, in every way there was to need a man.

He found the clasp of her bra and snapped it open. Her legs went weak and he backed up to the sofa bed, ending the kiss only so he could remove her shirt and bra. She should have felt cooler then, naked from the waist up, but she felt hotter. When he sank onto the sofa, pulling her between his knees so he could kiss her breasts, she felt hotter still.

She dug her fingers into his hair. It was long and soft and beautiful. The sight of his mouth on her breast, his lips tight on her nipple, was even more beautiful. Most beautiful of all was the understanding that he craved her the way she craved him. She hadn't been insane to want him. She hadn't misread the depth of their intimacy. He didn't know how to leave her because of *this,* this passion, this longing.

She didn't remember tearing off his shirt, but somehow it disappeared. She didn't remember sinking into his lap, or feeling him shift and turn her, but suddenly she was under him on the sofa cushions, pulling him down into her arms, spreading her legs so he could settle between them. She didn't remember him removing her shorts or his own, but there they were, stripped bare, nothing between them but yearning and need and love.

She took him in her hands. He stroked between her legs. He was ready for her, and she was ready for him. She felt as if she'd been ready for him all her life. She'd been dreaming about him, wanting him, trying to convince herself every night, after every X-rated fantasy, that she mustn't indulge in the fantasy because it would never come true.

But it was true. It was real. It was Phillip, and with

his first powerful thrust she knew it was love. She
came almost immediately, and he groaned and held
himself still, and then he started again, making her
come a second time before he let go.

For a long moment, they lay on the couch gasping
for breath, their hearts thundering, their hands moving
tentatively on each other and their bodies growing
heavy with lassitude. Carefully, he lifted himself and
peeled off a condom. She hadn't even thought of protection. She hadn't thought of anything except having
him inside her, loving her. "Where did that come
from?" she asked.

He motioned with his head toward the floor. She
rose and peered over the side of the sofa. Atop his
discarded shorts lay an open six-pack of condoms.
"There was a drugstore next door to the pizzeria," he
explained.

"You were planning to do this?" The idea rattled
her. "Before you came here tonight, you were thinking we were going to...?"

"What I was thinking was, 'No, stupid, don't do
it!' I was thinking it would be a terrible mistake. I was
really hoping I'd be able to be sensible. But—" he
smiled sheepishly "—I ordered the pizza, and they
said it would take ten minutes, and...and there was
that drugstore. Maybe those were the ten most crucial
minutes of my life." He twirled a lock of her hair
around his finger, separated the strands and studied
them in the dim light.

"So, was it a terrible mistake? Are you sorry this
happened?" she asked.

"God, no. I'm thrilled."

She smiled. *Thrilled* seemed an understatement, but
she couldn't think of any word strong enough to de-

scribe how wonderful she felt. Wonderful, yet apprehensive.

"We need to talk," she said, pushing herself up to sit. She was beginning to comprehend the ramifications. Phillip was supposed to be leaving Boston tomorrow, and she was madly in love with him. They'd just had sex, and they were lying nude on her couch, their legs still entwined, and he had the most gorgeous, virile body she'd ever seen. They still had five unused condoms. And less than twenty-four hours from now, he was going to be gone.

Unless they could talk things through, figure things out, turn a potential disaster into a triumph.

"This sofa opens up, doesn't it," he said, unwedging his left leg from between her thighs.

Cassie nodded. To her amazement, despite what had just occurred—or maybe because of it—she was hungry. "I'll go get the pizza."

By the time she returned with the wilting pizzeria box, a stack of napkins and a couple of chilled bottles of beer, Phillip had opened the sofa into a double bed and heaped their clothing on the rocking chair across the room. They sprawled out on the sheets, propping the sofa cushions and pillows behind their shoulders so they could recline comfortably.

Phillip lifted two wedges of cooling pizza out of the box and handed one to Cassie. "My life would be a hell of a lot easier if I hadn't come here tonight," he remarked.

"Get over it," Cassie joked, exhilarated but also sympathetic about the mess Phillip's life had become because they'd made love. "The fact that your facing the truth is a good thing."

"And the truth is…?"

"We're perfect for each other."

He took a bite of pizza. "It isn't as simple as that. I've been groomed my whole life to take over Keene Furniture. I worked there summers. I accompanied my dad on business trips. I went to college and business school so I could go back to Lynwood and take the company into the twenty-first century. I'm a son. An only child. My life was all mapped out, and until I met you I was happy with the map."

"It sounds like the most stifling, confining map in the world. Instead of complaining, you ought to be thanking me for saving you from a fate worse than death."

He chuckled, then leaned over and kissed her brow. "You haven't saved me from anything. You've tossed me into the middle of a storm. Don't look so pleased."

But she was pleased. As he gazed at her, his smile waned. His eyes grew darker, his respiration deeper, and she understood in the instant before he shoved the pizza box aside and rolled over, gathering her in his arms, that he wasn't exactly sorry, either.

Sometime later—after they'd made love in the shower, after they'd fallen asleep in her bed, after Cassie had awakened to find Phillip wrapped around her from behind, his hands cupping her breasts and his erection digging into the small of her back, and she'd turned to face him and they made love half-asleep, slowly, lazily, teasing each other with aimless touches and lingering kisses until they couldn't stand the teasing anymore, until they were so aroused they moaned in relief the instant their bodies locked together—it wasn't until then that he said, "I love you, Cassie."

And after that, he'd promised to come back to her.

He'd promised that they would be together forever.
He'd given her his word.

"WHAT DO YOU MEAN, we need another plan?" Diane
looked appalled. She was seated across from Cassie at
a painted wooden picnic table under the awning of
Tilly's Take-out, on the eastern end of Main Street. In
front of Cassie sat a cardboard tray containing a ham-
burger in a boat-shaped cardboard plate, a stack of
French fries in a cardboard pocket and a waxed-
cardboard cup of diet root beer with a straw protruding
from it.

She stared at the food, not quite sure where it came
from. Probably from the window, where Roger lingered, engrossed in what appeared to be a profound
conversation with the high-school girl on the other
side of the glass. Cassie supposed she must have
walked up to that window, recited her order and
handed over a small quantity of money, requesting a
receipt so she'd have adequate records of how she'd
spent *Dream Wheels*' money in Ohio. But she didn't
remember the actual process of ordering her meal and
paying for it.

She didn't remember much of anything she'd done
all day—except for kissing Phillip.

Judging by Diane's satisfaction and Roger's typical
equanimity, the day's filming must have gone well.
Despite being in a trance, Cassie must have said the
right words and done the right things. Everyone was
treating her as if she were functioning normally.

At the next picnic table, a gaggle of wholesome-
looking teenagers were consuming soft-serve sundaes
and laughing. Cassie stared blankly at them. Where
had they come from? Where, exactly, was she?

In Lynwood, Ohio, she reminded herself. In Phillip's town for Phillip's wedding.

Phillip.

She couldn't let him kiss her again. She couldn't risk it. She and Diane were going to have to come up with a different way to wreak vengeance upon him.

"These are the greasiest fries I've ever eaten," Diane said. Cassie wasn't sure if that was a complaint or a compliment, given the way Diane was wolfing the fries down. "Now, explain to me, why do we need a new plan? I thought the plan we came up with was great."

"It won't work," Cassie argued, crossing her legs and then realizing she couldn't do that in her short skirt without displaying more of her thighs than most women exposed on the beach in August.

"Why won't it work?"

"I can't seduce him."

"You don't have to seduce him. You only have to tempt him."

"Semantics," Cassie muttered.

Diane wrapped her hands around her burger and took a bite, her eyes steady on Cassie. "Not semantics. They're two different things. The idea is to have him sniveling and drooling. To reduce him to tics and cravings. To remind him you're the sexiest woman who ever walked the earth and he could have had you once, but he can never have you now." Her lecture came out half-garbled because her mouth was full of food, but Cassie understood enough of it. "The idea," Diane concluded after swallowing, "is to make him regret he turned his back on you."

"I don't want to tempt him," Cassie insisted. What she wanted to do was cross her legs, eat her burger

and kick Phillip in the stomach—or maybe someplace
lower—and then go back to Boston and mope.

"All right." Diane sighed dramatically, then wiped
a smear of ketchup from the corner of her mouth and
sipped her soda. "The thing about effective revenge
is, you've got to hit him where he hurts. You've got
to target his most vulnerable spots."

Great minds think alike, Cassie concluded, although
she suspected that Diane's idea of hitting Phillip's vulnerable spot wasn't quite the same as *her* idea of kicking him someplace below his stomach.

"We know one of his vulnerable spots is the whole
sex thing. If you aren't going to get your revenge by
toying with his uncontrollable lust for you—"

"Which he can control just fine," Cassie snapped,
recalling how calmly he'd washed his hands and face
at the sink in the men's lavatory, how quickly he'd
managed to recover from their clinch—a clinch that,
seven hours later, she still hadn't recovered from.

"So where else is he vulnerable? How else can you
get to him? Tricia?"

"I don't want to hurt her. None of this is her fault."
Cassie nibbled a fry. "At least, I don't think it is."

"Do you want to target his family?"

Cassie considered his parents. They'd been so congenial at the country club last night, so warm and wel-
coming. She'd genuinely liked them. "No," she said,
shaking her head. "Let's leave his family out of it."

"Then what? How are you going to cause him agony?"

"How about his business?"

"Keene Furniture?" Diane arched her eyebrows in
a classic pose of contemplation. "Hmm. Arson's a
possibility."

"No arson," Cassie said. "Nothing illegal." She wasn't sure how she could legally undermine his business, but she, Diane and Roger had access to the building, thanks to Lowell Henley. Maybe they could foment unrest, discontent. Maybe they could smear wood glue in unseemly places.

"You said you didn't want to target his family," Diane pointed out. "Aren't his parents involved in the firm?"

"I think Phil is pretty much running the show now," Cassie told her. "The plan was that he was going to take over the place once he finished business school."

"Then he'd be the one to suffer," Diane said, nodding in approval. "So, what are we talking about? If not arson, what?"

Before Cassie could come up with any viable suggestions, Roger arrived with his tray of food. Cassie glanced at it and grimaced. "Four hot dogs?"

"I like hot dogs," he said amiably.

"Onion rings and a chocolate shake, too," Diane noted with a sniff. "Maybe we ought to stop by the drugstore for some antacids on our way back to Bailey's."

"I'm not going back to Bailey's," Roger reported, maneuvering his long legs under the table. Lowering himself onto the bench, he reached for one of the frankfurters. He devoured half of it in one efficient bite.

"Are you going someplace with her?" Diane tilted her head toward the teenage girl who'd taken their orders. "She's jailbait."

Roger chuckled. "I'm going to the studio to check out the day's tapes," he told her.

"Good boy. We don't want you getting in trouble."

"Roger never gets in trouble," Cassie said, a tinge of envy shading her voice. She was the one in trouble, emotional trouble. And Diane was doing her damnedest to get her into real trouble. As if it wasn't bad enough that Cassie was trying to figure out how she could undermine Keene Furniture in some way, Diane was recommending arson! Without Diane to egg her on, Cassie wouldn't be contemplating criminal acts. She would be kicking Phillip and going home.

And feeling defeated. With arson, she might wind up in jail for a few years, but at least she'd have the satisfaction of evening the score.

But then again, probably not. No doubt Keene Furniture had adequate insurance. The only people who would suffer would be his employees, who'd be out of work until the factory was rebuilt. Meanwhile, Phillip would be happily married to Tricia. They'd go off on their honeymoon, clucking about how poor old Cassie had gone berserk and should never again be left alone with a book of matches, and who would have thought she was a psychopath?

"No arson," Cassie said again, shaking her head.

Roger paused, his hot dog lifted to his mouth. "Huh?"

Lost in her ruminations, Cassie had forgotten Roger was there. "Nothing," she said. "Never mind."

"You think I'm going to torch something?"

"No. I was just…" Cassie eyed Diane, searching for support. Diane grinned and shrugged. "I was just playing with an idea for a script," Cassie answered lamely.

"You want to do a *Dream Wheels* show on arson?"

"Forget it, Roger."

Before he could question her further, a diversion arrived: Tricia Riggs. She cruised into the parking lot of Tilly's Take-out in a fire-engine-red convertible coupe. Steering sharply into a parking space, she sent a spray of gravel flying like a boat's wake. Music pounded from the car's stereo.

Convertibles were so public, Cassie pondered. When you drove one, the world knew your musical tastes. They knew the instant you turned off the engine, the energy with which you yanked on the brake. Of course, Cassie would gladly share that personal information with the world for the chance to own a car like Tricia's.

Wearing sunglasses, her hair pulled back into a ponytail held by a scrunchy, she looked as young as the girl taking orders at the window and the kids eating sundaes at the next table. Cassie wondered if she'd come to Tilly's to gorge on junk food. That seemed like a risky activity so close to her wedding. What if she pigged out on fries and ice cream and wound up with pimples or couldn't fit into her gown on Saturday?

But apparently she hadn't come for food. Broadcasting her general happiness with a huge smile, she jogged over to the table where Cassie and her colleagues sat.

"Hi!" she chirped. "Mind if I join you?"

Under the table, Diane nudged Cassie's foot with her own. Cassie peeked at her. Diane's face registered the question: *What's going on?* Cassie gave an almost imperceptible shrug.

"Pull up a chair," Roger said, putting down his third hot dog and gesturing toward the bench. Tricia's smile grew impossibly bigger as she sat next to him.

"Don't you want to order something to eat?" Cassie asked.

"Here?" Tricia wrinkled her nose. "I wouldn't eat that garbage."

Cassie could have taken offense, but she only laughed and took a hearty bite of her burger.

"It was so cool watching you guys filming today," Tricia said, removing her sunglasses and perching them on the crown of her head. "You didn't mind my watching, did you?" Her question was directed toward all three of them, but her gaze slid sideways, to Roger.

"You were just one onlooker among many," Cassie assured her. "I didn't expect so many people to want to watch."

"Given how crowded it was, we should probably check the sound levels to see if we picked up any background noise," Diane said.

"People were pretty quiet," said Roger. "I don't think we'll have much. Nothing we can't filter out."

Tricia sighed giddily. "I just love listening to you folks talk. It's so show biz!"

Cassie watched the woman who'd received the blessing—or curse—of Phillip's marriage proposal. Tricia was cute. More than cute, she was sweet. And preternaturally ebullient. Cassie could understand why men were attracted to her.

But not Phillip. He was too...smart. She simply couldn't imagine him arguing about the relative merits of Buñuel's *Belle du Jour* with Tricia. The woman was completely lacking in gravity.

Why had he chosen her? Of all the women he could have betrayed Cassie with, why Tricia Riggs?

"I'm surprised you had time to watch us work today," Cassie said cautiously, monitoring Tricia's expression. "Don't you have a million things to do before your wedding?"

Tricia tossed back her head and laughed. The setting sun ignited the copper tone in her hair. "More than a million, but my mother can do them. She'd probably just as soon do them without me anyway. All we ever do is fight about everything." Her laughter waned. "Have you ever been married, Cassie?"

The way Tricia phrased the question gave Cassie pause. Apparently Tricia assumed Cassie wasn't married now, or she would have asked, "Are you married?" Did Cassie project the aura of a divorcée?

Maybe she wasn't all that different from a divorcée. She'd given her love to a man, he'd promised himself to her, and then he'd vanished from her life. "No," she replied, a touch too vehemently. "I've never been married."

"Then you can't begin to know," Tricia said, her lilting tone implying that she had no ulterior motive in inquiring about Cassie's marital history.

Tricia seemed to have no ulterior anything. It took a certain degree of depth to have ulteriorness, and Tricia just didn't seem deep enough.

"My mother thinks everything has to be just so," she explained. "I have to wear this. I have to carry that. These people have to sit here, those people have to sit there. Aunt Loraine can't sit next to Uncle Felix because Aunt Loraine didn't invite Uncle Felix to Joey's graduation party, because when Joey turned twelve Uncle Felix gave him a salt-and-pepper-shaker set for his birthday and there were traces of salt and pepper in the shakers, so he must have used them before he gave them to Joey, and anyway, who'd give a twelve-year-old boy a salt-and-pepper set for his birth-

day? So Loraine and Felix aren't talking to each other,
and they have to be seated as far from each other as
possible. This is all my mother cares about, and it's
just about driving me crazy!''

No depth, but she really was a pleasant young
woman, Cassie admitted. She wished Phillip were
marrying a harridan, not someone so cute and perky.
Perhaps it was punishment enough that he would be
spending the rest of his life with a woman given to
babbling about saltshakers, and that he was marrying
into a family that included Uncle Felix, who gave
tacky used gifts. What fine present would Uncle Felix
bestow on the newlyweds? Used handkerchiefs? Pots
and pans with burned food caked on them?

Cassie and Diane had bought a set of sterling-silver
napkin rings and matching silver candlesticks as a gift
for the bride and groom; the gifts were compact and
unbreakable, ideal for cramming into a suitcase and
taking on a plane. Cassie wondered about maybe burning a pair of bright-red tapers in the candle holders
before she presented them to Phillip. Let them looked
used. Let her be as crass as Uncle Felix. It would serve
Phillip right.

But not Tricia. Tricia seemed so guileless. She
didn't deserve used candlesticks.

Sipping her soda and studying Tricia above the rim
of her cup, Cassie wondered whether Tricia deserved
a lying hypocrite like Phillip. Maybe Cassie ought to
warn her. Maybe she ought to sit Tricia down and tell
her exactly what he'd done in Boston, what he'd said,
what he'd promised. That could be Cassie's revenge.

She vetoed the idea. In all likelihood, Phillip
wouldn't break his promises to Tricia. It was only Cassie who'd been betrayed by him, Cassie who'd been

used like a candle in a silver candlestick, burned until nothing was left of her but a blob of cold wax.

She ought to sabotage his company and leave Tricia out of it. Just because Phillip was a bastard didn't mean Cassie couldn't maintain her principles. A bit of arson, a bit of wood glue, whatever it took—but she would protect Tricia if she could.

CHAPTER EIGHT

TRICIA COULDN'T BELIEVE she was actually sitting at one of the picnic tables at Tilly's with a group of TV people, and they were talking to her as if she was their equal. She wanted to throw back her head and belt out, "Hooray for Hollywood," even though she knew they were from Boston, not Los Angeles, and public TV was a little bit different from the silver screen.

Maybe she ought to belt out, "There's No Business like Show Business," instead. Even children's shows on public TV qualified as show business.

Of course, she wouldn't really sing. If she did, Roger and the women would tell her to get lost. She had an awful voice. Birds flew away when they heard her singing. Puppy dogs whimpered and scampered for cover. People begged her to shut up.

So she just kind of *imagined* herself singing, because watching the filming at Keene Furniture that day had been too exciting not to sing about. She'd seen lights, camera, action. She'd seen Roger filming, and Cassie directing Richard and the other Keene Furniture employees performing before the camera, and Diane racing around with her clipboard, looking terribly important.

The cameras, the folks discussing their areas of expertise and the energy buzzing through the factory all day had been exciting—but even more exciting was watching a genuine artist at work. Roger had looked so confident peering through the camera lens, so smooth moving the camera around, so relaxed between takes. As though the camera were a part of him, an extension of his arm. As though he had cinematographer corpuscles mixed in with the white and red ones in his blood.

For all Tricia knew, the spectacle of filming a children's TV show wouldn't cause even a ripple in Boston. For all she knew, someone was filming something on every street corner in the city, and people acted blasé about the whole thing. If Bostonians saw Roger on a city sidewalk with his camera in his hand, they wouldn't even look twice. His long blond hair? No big deal. His bony scarecrow build? His faded flannel shirt, untucked and unbuttoned, with the sleeves rolled up to his elbows to reveal a glimpse of his flower tattoo, and under it a clean white T-shirt with *plus ça change...* stenciled across his chest in navy-blue script? The black boots that looked like hand-me-downs from a retired marine? In Boston, nobody would pay him any attention at all.

Tricia paid attention. He was so completely different from the people she knew in Lynwood. His eyes were blue—a pale shade, but the French writing on his shirt picked up the color and magnified it. On his left wrist he wore a watch with a humongous face. She wondered if huge watches were a special accessory film people needed, so they could figure out the precise timing of each shot. Cassie had a pretty big watch on, too. Diane's watch looked ordinary, but it was still bigger than Tricia's dainty gold bracelet watch.

Tricia hadn't observed only Roger during the day's

filming. She'd observed Cassie and Diane, also. They were interesting—not exactly riveting the way Roger was, but then, they were women, so there was a limit to how much time Tricia wanted to spend checking them out. She'd enjoyed watching them work, though. Cassie was what Tricia's father would call a "smart cookie"—compact, but forceful. She seemed to tear through the world like a bullet, moving so swiftly she almost caused the air to whistle around her. Diane was calmer, mooring Cassie and waving around her clip-board whenever people ignored her.

Tricia doubted she could ever be friends with women like Cassie and Diane. They were just too dif-ferent from her. Tricia could command attention as effectively as Cassie did, but Tricia's style was noth-ing like Cassie's. Cassie relied more on her person-ality, dominating the folks in the carpentry shop with a smile, never a raised voice or a threat. She radiated authority, and people did what she asked. She didn't flirt with them the way Tricia would.

Tricia glided along on charm. Cassie soared on smarts and savvy.

Savvy. That was what Tricia was missing. She had a great deal going for her—her looks, her father's wealth, her mother's social prominence, her pretty red hair and an abundance of warmth. Tricia had been the captain of the Lynwood High School cheerleading squad, which really said it all.

But she didn't have a speck of savvy. Not a single iota of it.

She wondered if savvy was what it took to impress a city guy like Roger. He didn't seem like the kind of man who was impressed by much. His smile was nei-ther warm and charming nor formidably intelligent. It was...detached but mellow. A little weary, a little weathered, as if nothing much could get to him.

All day at the factory, she'd shadowed him, staying as close to him as she could without getting in his way, so she could examine his technique. She didn't suppose it took all that much technique to film Richard Bausch running off at the mouth on the difference between varnish and lacquer, but still. Tricia would never have been able to do something like that.

"I just think it's so fascinating, what you people do," she said, even though all they were doing at the moment was eating Tilly's Take-out takeout, which had to be the worst excuse for food in Lynwood.

Cassie smiled. Rolling her eyes, Diane said, "It's not much more than what proud papas do with their minicams at their kids' birthday parties. Or weddings. Are you going to videotape your wedding?"

Tricia shook her head emphatically. "We decided that would be tacky. A wedding is a very solemn occasion."

"In a church, maybe. How solemn can you be at a country club?"

Tricia shifted her gaze so she didn't have to look directly at Diane. She decided she didn't like her. No one was supposed to question the bride's choices. It was Tricia's wedding, and she and her mother got to specify what they wanted for the wedding, allowing for a small degree of input from the groom. It was their call whether the ceremony was at a church or a country club, whether the bride was going to wear white or chartreuse, whether someone was going to preserve the event on tape or not. The bride and her mom decided, and everyone was supposed to say, "What a wonderful idea!" They weren't supposed to imply that any decision was less than one hundred percent fabulous.

"I don't blame you for not wanting a videographer there," Cassie said, and Tricia decided that yes, she definitely liked her better than Diane. "When you put a camera into a situation, everyone plays to the camera. Like Richard Bausch at the factory today. He wasn't explaining the properties of the wood to me. He was explaining it to the camera. That's fine when you're filming a TV show, but a wedding isn't a show. You want the bride and groom talking to each other, not to a camera."

"That's so true," Tricia agreed, then turned to Roger so he wouldn't feel left out of the conversation. "Don't you think that's true, Roger?"

"I've never thought about it one way or the other," he admitted.

His smile made his eyes crinkle. If he shaved and trimmed his hair, he would be something. Of course, the beard and the ponytail made him something, too. Something else.

"I really liked watching you film at the factory," she said, hoping she didn't sound like a complete airhead.

He shrugged. His arms were loose, as if controlled by invisible strings, like a marionette. "If you do it often enough, it gets old. We've done it often enough, huh?" He grinned across the table at Cassie and Diane.

"Well, it's not old to me," Tricia insisted. "It seemed so complicated. When you build a chair, for instance—" she considered the process they'd been filming all day "—it's like, one piece goes here, one piece goes there, apply screws and wood glue, sand down the seams and stain it. With a TV show…''

"It's pretty much the same thing," Roger said, glancing at Cassie as if seeking confirmation.

She nodded. "It really is. You stick one scene here, one scene there, glue it together and make it seamless."

"But you don't have pieces," Tricia argued. "You've got film."

"It's videotape, not film," Cassie explained. "We tape in scenes and excerpts, and then we edit, cutting and splicing, putting the tape together in the order we want it."

"So you don't tape everything in order? Like, first pick the wood, then saw it, then shape it, or whatever?"

"It's not like taping a wedding," Diane said.

"We view the tape," Cassie added, "and figure out if we need more of one scene or another, or if something didn't tape well. For instance, if the sound quality is muddled or the light isn't good—if Richard's face is in shadow, that kind of thing. After we've checked it all to make sure we have what we need, we'll bring it back to the studio in Boston, where we'll edit it."

"Do you do the editing?" Tricia asked Roger. He was the cameraman, after all. He was an artist. She'd like to think he edited the film, too.

"Cassie does most of the editing," he told her.

"But we all participate," Diane said.

"We have editors back in Boston who work on it, too," said Cassie. "Roger will be viewing the tape tonight to see if we need to retape any of the scenes we taped today."

"Really? Tonight? Where?"

"Over at the public-access station on Maple Street," Roger told her. "They've been letting us use their equipment."

"Cool!" That Roger could be viewing the day's videotape, right in her poky little town, astonished Tricia. "What's it called? Wait, wait, don't tell me..." She waved her hand palm forward, like a police officer signaling a car to stop. "'The daily rushes,' isn't that right? I've seen movies where they call it 'the daily rushes.'" She loved show-biz terminology.

Roger arched an eyebrow at Cassie, then turned to Tricia and smiled. "If you're interested, maybe you could join us while we review today's tape. That would be okay, wouldn't it?" He lifted an eyebrow at Cassie again.

"Sure, it would be okay."

"I could do that?" Tricia almost gasped. She almost burst into a song—but hearing her honking voice would be enough to make Roger retract the invitation. "You'd let me watch the daily rushes?"

"Aren't you busy with last-minute wedding activities?" Diane asked.

"I'm not busy tonight," Tricia replied, firmly convinced she didn't like Diane. "Everything's been planned up and down and inside out. Everything's been checked and double-checked. And anyway, my grandmother is having her women's club over for coffee and dessert tonight and my mom thinks I should go, but frankly, I deserve a night off." Her mother had hinted that Tricia could win a lot of points by showing up and being pleasant with all the Lynwood ladies. But Tricia knew everyone in the club. They'd seen her grow up. She'd gone to plenty of the club's meetings and helped her grandmother by pouring coffee and serving pastries, and all those blue-haired ladies had made embarrassing comments about how they remembered when Tricia was three years old. They loved to remind her that she'd pronounced her *S*s like *T*s back then, and that whenever she saw a school bus she would bellow, "Look at the big butt!"

If Tricia went to her grandmother's house tonight, she'd have to smile politely while the old ladies told the butt joke for the zillionth time. Whereas, how often did a filmmaker spend time in town? When would she ever again have the opportunity to watch the daily rushes of a genuine TV show?

"I'd really like to come and see the tapes," she said. "If you're sure you don't mind..."

"Actually, this works out great," Diane said before draining her soda with a slurp of her straw. "Cassie and I have some other business to take care of this evening. So maybe, Tricia, if it isn't a problem, you could drive Roger over to the studio in your car, and we could use our car. Would that be okay?"

"Better yet," Cassie said, glancing over her shoulder at Tricia's car, "why don't you two take the rental car and we can borrow Tricia's."

Tricia laughed. "You can't borrow my car. If I let anyone else drive it, my dad would have a cow."

Roger swallowed the last of his hot dog. "Why don't we get going, then. I've just gotta grab some stuff out of the boring old rental car." He eyed Tricia's car, then winked at Cassie and Diane. "Some of us know how to live right."

"Don't gloat," Cassie scolded.

Tricia wanted to gloat herself. To have a real, live, professional cinematographer as a passenger in her car

was such an honor. No one she knew had ever had a
cinematographer in their car, let alone spent the evening watching rushes in a studio. This was definitely
the most exciting thing she'd ever done in her life.

Now, that was a strange thought. She was going to
be married on Saturday, in an elegant, extremely expensive wedding, so classy there wouldn't be a videographer present, and yet here she was, thinking that
spending an evening watching unedited tapes of a children's TV show was the most exciting thing she'd ever
done.

Maybe it wasn't such a strange thought. Everyone
in the world—or at least in Lynwood, which was
pretty much the definition of Tricia's world—got married sooner or later. Everyone thought Tricia and Phillip were the perfect couple. And they were. They'd
get married and live a perfect Lynwood life. She had
nothing to complain about.

Except…it was all pretty ordinary. Expected. A totally Lynwood thing.

As Roger stood and gathered up his trash to carry
to the can near the window, Tricia gazed at her left
hand. The diamond rock on her finger twinkled at her,
reminding her that whatever she did with Roger Beckelman tonight would not be even remotely as significant in her life as getting married. Exciting, maybe,
but not significant. After tonight, after watching the
rushes and maybe learning a few things about show
business from Roger, she'd go on and live the rest of
her calm, unexciting life married to Phillip.

This could be her last chance to enjoy a walk on
the wild side. Or a drive on the wild side, with the top
down and Roger Beckelman in the seat next to her,
his long blond hair blowing in the breeze.

"THIS IS GREAT!" Diane exclaimed. "Unbelievable! Do you see the possibilities here?"

Unfortunately Cassie did see the possibilities—and they made her uneasy. "I know what you're thinking," she warned, "and I just want to make it clear— Roger isn't going to be a part of any plan you and I come up with."

"He already is a part of one of our plans," Diane reminded her. "The plan for coming to Lynwood a few days early, remember? The plan for using this trip to get some footage for *Dream Wheels* so we could case the joint and not have to waste any vacation days."

"Okay. But we're not going to throw Roger and Tricia Riggs together."

"We don't have to." Diane said each word slowly as if speaking to a befuddled young child. "They've thrown themselves together."

"Tricia is a twit." Cassie wanted to shake Diane by the shoulders. "Look at her. She's about to get married, and she's worried about how her father will react if she lets someone borrow her car. She's like a little girl! She doesn't realize what she's doing with Roger."

"Of course she realizes," Diane argued. "What she's doing is contemplating one final fling before her wedding. Now all we have to do is make sure this fling goes as far as it can—and that Phillip finds out about it." Diane rubbed her hands together with gusto. Her smile was strangely malevolent.

"I don't want to use Roger."

"Don't worry about Roger. He's nobody's fool. He knows how to make the best of a situation."

Recalling Roger's first impression of Tricia—that

she was ripe and eager—caused Cassie to subside with
a sigh. Roger would have a grand time with Tricia,
even if all they did was watch the day's tapes. What
man wouldn't enjoy having a ripe and eager woman
gazing at him as if he'd just descended from Olympus
to mingle with the mortals?

Even so, it was one thing for Cassie to target Phillip
for punishment and quite another to involve Roger and
Tricia in her scheme. The phrase "civilian casualties"
flashed like a neon billboard in her skull.

"Stop worrying about them," Diane urged her.
"They can take care of themselves. They're both
adults."

"I'm not so sure Tricia is," Cassie muttered. "Let's
go back to Plan B. Or was it Plan C?"

"Which one was that?"

"Sabotaging Keene Furniture."

"Right." Diane climbed off the bench and scooped
the cardboard debris from her meal onto her tray. "Arson."

"I never agreed to setting a fire."

"I still say you're a wimp." Diane added Cassie's
leftovers to the tray and carried the trash to the pail.
"Why don't we go back to the factory and see what
we can find out?"

Cassie handed Diane the keys to the car and took
the passenger seat. She felt too edgy to drive. She
wasn't sure what unsettled her more: the prospect of
undermining Phillip's business in some way—prefer-
ably one that didn't involve kerosene and a box of
matches—or the notion that Roger and Tricia might
be getting cozy. For some reason, letting the two of
them romp off on their own seemed even more incen-
diary than torching the Keene Furniture factory.

The sun was low in the sky, glowing orange through the windshield as Diane drove west along Main Street toward the factory. Cassie glanced at her watch. Nearly seven. The place would probably be deserted, the gates locked. She and Diane weren't going to be able to gain access to the property—unless they figured out where the river behind the plant flowed. A river couldn't be locked inside a fence. If they could reach the river and hike along its bank, they might be able to enter the grounds that way.

To her surprise, the gates were standing open when Diane steered down the narrow lane to the factory. A few cars were still parked in the lot. Cassie spotted Phillip's Mercedes and cursed. "Phil's here," she whispered.

"Big deal. It's a huge building. We can avoid him if we have to. Or—" Diane rolled to a stop in one of the marked spaces and turned off the engine "—you could try the temptation strategy again."

"That was Plan A. We've abandoned Plan A," Cassie reminded her, struggling not to remember what had happened when both she and Phillip had almost succumbed to temptation.

"Plan A was castrating him. Plan B was inflicting injury to the erogenous zone inside his skull. Plan C is destroying his company. Are we on the same page?"

"We're pursuing Plan C," Cassie confirmed.

"All I'm saying is, don't forget Plan B. Or Plan D, either—that's the Tricia and Roger thing. They could still come in handy." Diane slid the key from the ignition and got out of the car. "Let's split up once we get inside, and have a look around. Maybe we'll be inspired."

"That'll be the day," Cassie grumbled. "Okay. You take the first floor—I'll take the second." She didn't want to wander too near that first-floor men's room, the scene of her near debacle that morning.

They were stymied at the front door, which was locked. A uniformed security guard was posted on the opposite side of the glass, looking proudly official in a starched gray uniform, a walkie-talkie riding his belt where a real policeman would keep his service revolver. He scrutinized the two women through the glass, then inched the door open.

Before he could question them, Diane smiled and said, "Hi. We're from the public-broadcasting crew that was filming here earlier today. We left some equipment behind. We were wondering if we could come in and get it."

Cassie had never realized what a skilled dissembler her friend could be. She wasn't sure whether she was pleased or unnerved by Diane's glib dishonesty.

The guard pushed the door wider. "You'll have to sign in," he informed them.

Cassie forced a smile. Unlike Diane, she had no talent for lying. She was certain she looked as guilty as a cat with canary feathers clinging to its mouth. But if the guard noticed any figurative feathers near her lips, he didn't comment.

She and Diane signed their names in his logbook. Then Diane said, "You get the stuff from upstairs. I'll go collect the gear from the carpentry shop." Given her exaggerated enunciation, Cassie knew Diane was saying this for the guard's benefit.

Unwilling to trust her own voice, Cassie nodded and headed for the stairway. Halfway to the second floor, she glanced over the rail and saw the guard settle his bulky body into a folding chair by the door and open a copy of *Sports Illustrated*. The sight didn't reassure her as much as it should have. Just because she and Diane had gotten past the guard didn't mean they could get past anyone else in the building—especially Phillip.

She shrugged off her nerves and continued to the top of the stairs, treading carefully to make as little noise as possible. She pushed open the fire door and entered a corridor lined with doors. Most were closed, but a few weren't. Through one open door came a wedge of light, landing on the carpeted floor in a misshapen rectangle.

Cassie tiptoed toward the door. As she drew close she heard voices coming from the room. Male voices.

One was Phillip's.

Her breath caught and she darted toward the adjacent rest-room door, this one labeled Women, and gave it a shove, hoping it wasn't locked. But the door swung inward and she ducked inside, refusing to exhale until the door shut behind her.

This bathroom smelled less like antiseptic than the men's room downstairs, she observed once her respiration had returned to normal. She didn't dare to turn on the light; if she did, people might see the light in the crack between the door and the floor. At least there were no urinals to bump into as she sagged against the wall and gathered her wits.

Closing her eyes, she rested her head against the wall. To her surprise she could hear the voices quite clearly. Phillip and his visitor had to be standing right on the other side of the wall.

Eavesdropping was wrong, but she was here to re-

connoiter, wasn't she? So why waste this opportunity?
She pressed her ear to the wall and listened.

"...due the first day of the year 2000," said the
voice that didn't belong to Phillip. It was gruff and
gravelly, not particularly congenial.

"This really isn't the time," Phillip said.

"When *is* the time? The new century is here,
and—"

"And it's going to be here tomorrow and the next
day, too. So stop pressuring me."

"I'm not pressuring you."

"That's exactly what you're doing. Pressure is your
favorite weapon."

"You talk as if this was a war. We're family. Forget
weapons and let's resolve this problem."

"I've said everything I can say. You want to go
after my father, go after him. I can't stop you, Harry.
You're going to do what you're going to do."

"Your father's like a brother to me," the gravelly
voice said. "You're like a son."

"Then get off my back, damn it!"

Silence ensued, long and tense. Cassie wondered
who Phillip was with, who he'd address with such
disrespect. A man who thought of him as a son? A
man who believed they were family?

Phillip sounded angry, although other emotions
seemed blended into his mood. At least, it seemed that
way, although who knew how much the wall was dis-
torting his tone. He might have been smiling when he
told the other fellow to get off his back. He might have
winked immediately afterward or whispered an apology while leading the man away from the wall and
out of Cassie's hearing.

But it was just days before his wedding, and he sounded ready to snap.

Why was he in an office at Keene Furniture at seven o'clock? Why wasn't he with his bride-to-be? She was off making goo-goo eyes at Roger, and Phillip was quarreling about pressure tactics and weapons in his place of business with someone named Harry. It didn't strike Cassie as a promising prelude to a wedding.

The silence was broken by the muted thud of footsteps in the hallway, passing the women's room. She waited a minute longer, then cracked open the door and peeked out.

The hall was empty.

She counted to thirty, just to be sure, and then exited the bathroom. No sound came from the slightly open door to her right. The wedge of light from inside still spilled onto the carpet.

Phillip could be in there.

She scooted past the door and continued down the hallway, her back tingling as if someone's gaze was on it, tickling her. She repeatedly glanced around, but no one was following her. The tingling was just her imagination—or maybe her conscience, urging her to get the hell out of the building before Phillip caught her.

Stifling that nagging voice of caution, she peered into one open doorway: a supply closet. Maybe she and Diane could steal a few sheets of Keene Furniture stationery and write letters that would make the company sound stupid or corrupt.

Cassie hated the idea. She hated everything about seeking revenge. She wasn't cut out for evil. Her back tingled again; a chill played across her nape and her palms grew clammy.

Ignoring her sense of impending doom, she continued down the hall. An unlocked anteroom led to a locked inner office; the sign on the door read Human Resources. Scrambling the employee records could cause Phillip a headache—but he'd probably pass the problem along to his personnel manager to solve; he'd pass along the headache, as well.

Sighing, she turned around and started back toward the stairs. The door to the office where Phillip had been remained ajar. Diane would have the guts to march in and see what Phillip was up to, what he'd been arguing over and who he'd been arguing with. But Diane was downstairs. Cassie was in charge of second-floor espionage, and she'd better do her job. Squaring her shoulders and praying for fortitude, she tiptoed to the door and peeked in.

Ah, an anteroom. An empty anteroom. The door beyond the secretary's desk was half-open, a lamp glowing inside. No sound emerged. It, too, must be empty.

Mustering her courage, Cassie entered.

The inner office was an enormous expanse of brick walls and multipaned windows. She saw a couch, a desk, bookshelves, file cabinets. It was obviously the inner sanctum of an executive.

Phillip or the man with the gravelly voice?

She ventured farther into the room, her curiosity overriding her panic. The low hiss of the ventilation system harmonized with the hum of the computer, its monitor swarming with a screen-saver of abstract shapes and bright colors. Reaching the desk, she hit a key on the computer. The screen went blank and she flinched.

She noticed a spreadsheet lying across the blotter.

Columns of numbers marched down the page: Week of 5/5. Week of 5/12. Orders. Deposits. Returns. Net.

Cassie didn't understand much about finance, but she knew that when the numbers in the Net column were preceded by minus signs, it wasn't good. Maybe one of the company's suppliers was in trouble. Maybe Keene Furniture was owed a lot of money.

So why had that man, Harry, been pressuring Phillip? Why was Phillip talking about weapons and war?

"What the hell are you doing here?" Phillip asked.

Cassie spun toward the door, her foot striking one of the legs of his chair with a clank. Phillip stood on the threshold, glowering at her. The collar button of his shirt was undone and his tie hung loose. His chin was darkened with a five-o'clock shadow and his hair was mussed. He looked rumpled and furious, and absurdly sexy.

She cursed herself. How could she face a man who stared at her with a homicidal glint in his eyes and think only about how sexy he was? Phillip had a way of scrambling her brain, making her forget what was important—making her foolishly believe that loving him was more important than anything else.

She didn't love him. She couldn't. Right now he looked as if he wanted to wring her neck. There wasn't a single romantic impulse in him, as far as she could tell.

She had no handy explanation for her presence in his office. Unlike Diane, she couldn't ad-lib a lie at will. "You know," she said, choosing to evade his question altogether, "I'm getting a little tired of you saying, 'What the hell are you doing here?' every time you see me."

"And I'm getting a little tired of you turning up in

unexpected places, uninvited and unannounced. Besides, I still haven't gotten an answer I can live with.'' He walked slowly into the office.

Backing up, she bumped into his chair again, wincing when her foot struck the chair leg and made another clank. "Diane and I came back here because we left some stuff behind from our taping today,'' she told him, resorting to the story Diane had cooked up for the security guard.

"In my office?''

"No, I just…well, the door was open, so I thought I'd see where you worked. Is that a crime?''

He closed in on his desk, on her. His eyes were dark, stormy. His mouth, the mouth that had kissed •her with such hunger that morning, was grim.

"What stuff?'' he asked.

"What do you mean, what stuff?'' She attempted to keep defensiveness out of her voice.

"What stuff did you and Diane leave behind?''

"Stuff.'' She scrambled for a better answer. "Some notes, and a cable—''

"That cable sat on the floor of the entry all day. I nearly killed myself tripping over it. I told Beckelman to make sure he took it with him when you cleared out, and he did.''

"Yes, well—Diane and I didn't notice it when we got back to Bailey's Bed-and-Breakfast, so we thought maybe…I don't know. Maybe it's in Roger's room—''

"Cassie.''

He still looked angry, but also exasperated. He'd had a long day, she realized. It was after seven and he was still at the office. He'd just endured a heated dispute with someone, and a spreadsheet with minus signs all over it lay across his desk, and Cassie was trespassing. He was entitled to be upset.

And she was going to have to stop apologizing for him, empathizing with him, feeling in any way kindly toward him. He was the man who'd wounded her, right? The man who'd betrayed her and broken her heart.

She only wished she couldn't sense his anguish so clearly. She wished she knew him a little less well, so she wouldn't have to understand why he was feeling what he was feeling.

"I don't want you here," he said. Blunt words, but she heard a struggle in his voice, as if the statement had to be forced through gritted teeth. "I don't want you in Lynwood. I don't want you at my wedding. I don't want you in my office."

"You wanted me this morning," she reminded him.

He closed his eyes, drew in a long breath and then opened his eyes again. Some of the anger was gone from them, replaced by the anguish she'd sensed. "Of course I did," he murmured. A shimmering light seemed to radiate from somewhere deep inside him. "Of course I do," he whispered, cupping his hand around her cheek. He tilted her face up and studied her, as if trying to decide where to land his first kiss.

She couldn't kiss him. Plan B had been scratched. If he kissed her, he'd demolish her before she could demolish him. "Why are there all those minus signs on this chart?" she asked brightly.

He started, frowned and let his hand fall from her face. "Minus signs?"

"Here." She pointed to the spreadsheet on his blotter.

He glanced down at his desk. Sighing, he mulled

over his response. "There are minus signs," he said quietly, "because that store is operating at a loss."

"What store is it? A place that sells Keene furniture?"

"We own it. It's one of Keene's retail outlets."

He stepped back, giving Cassie a little space. Her heart slowed, now that a kiss was no longer imminent.

"It's really none of your business," he thought to add.

"You always used to talk to me about business," she said. "Remember? Back in Boston, you'd tell me about how you'd like to expand the company, how you thought that with more home construction going on, people would be buying more furniture. It was a time of growth, and it would be a great opportunity for Keene Furniture, and you were going to expand into retail." She was surprised that she remembered so much. "Is that what this is?"

"What this is…" He eyed the paper irritably, then stalked away from the desk. "What it is, is a retail expansion that's gone south."

"Atlanta?" she guessed.

"No. Gone south, as in tanked. Fizzled. Flopped."

"Oh." So those minus signs meant a store Keene Furniture owned was losing money. She turned back to the paper and studied it some more. Some of the numbers attached to the minus signs were big. Really big.

"Is it bad?"

He laughed bitterly. "You don't want to know how bad it is."

"Of course I do," she said instinctively. "We're friends, Phil, I—" She cut herself off. How could they be friends when he was determined to marry another woman and she, Cassie, was determined to destroy him?

Yet before he'd decided to marry that other woman and she'd decided to destroy him, they *had* been friends. Before they'd been lovers, they'd been friends. Good friends. Close friends. Caring, compassionate friends. If his company was in trouble, if that was the pressure he was under, the weapon he was facing, the war he was fighting, she wanted to know.

He abandoned the desk and crossed the room to gaze out the window. When he turned back to her, the late-evening light spread behind him, silhouetting him. She could visualize his expression, though. She knew every detail of his face, every nuance. She knew that his eyes were sad, and that his mouth had softened into a wry, humorless smile.

"Keene Furniture is up to its ass in debt," he told her. "My father expanded too fast and borrowed too much. Tricia's father holds most of the notes. If the company doesn't pay its debts, it goes bankrupt and Tricia's father takes the place over."

The words reached her in a calm, even stream, rather like the sluggish river outside. Yet that same river sometimes had perilous rapids that tore at the banks and eroded the rocks in its path.

Tricia's father held Phillip's entire future in his hands.

"Is that why you're marrying Tricia?"

"No," he said quietly, then turned to stare out the window again.

"Then why are you marrying her?" she asked.

An endless minute stretched between them before he spoke, his voice cold and dull. "I'm marrying her because I love her."

The words stung, but they didn't maim—because she didn't believe them. "Her father has nothing to do with it?"

"Her father is a meddlesome son of a bitch. That's irrelevant, though."

"Is it?"

"Go home, Cassie."

Maybe he wanted her to go home because he truly loved Tricia. Maybe because he didn't want to betray Tricia by having sex with Cassie. Maybe he just wanted her to go because she was asking questions he didn't want to face, let alone answer.

In any case, she wasn't going to get any answers from him. He'd just told her, very succinctly, that he loved Tricia.

So she would go. But she wouldn't go home, not yet. Not when she suspected that Phillip was already in worse trouble than anything she and Diane could cause him.

CHAPTER NINE

WHY HAD HE TOLD HER? Phillip asked himself. How had she gotten him to say it? He could scarcely even talk to his parents about the loan situation with Harry Riggs. His father had signed the damned papers, yet Phillip always got angry and frustrated whenever he tried to discuss the company's indebtedness with his father—and he got even more angry and frustrated whenever his father said, "Oh, come on, Phil. I've known Harry forever. He isn't going to pull any fast moves. He knows how much Keene Furniture means to our family."

So Phillip couldn't talk to his father about it.

But he could talk to Cassie.

God, he wished he *could* talk to her—the way they'd talked last year, when nothing limited their friendship, when no subject was out of bounds. When he knew he could unburden himself about anything that was bothering him, whether it was a case study in his management seminar, or a pompous professor, or his landlord's reluctance to deal with the tenant living upstairs from Phillip, a man with very large speakers and a taste for Bing Crosby. All day and all night, Phillip would hear "White Christmas" oozing through his ceiling; when it was eighty degrees outside and eighty-five inside, listening to Bing croon about sleigh bells in the snow was torture.

Phillip used to gripe to Cassie and she used to shower him with sympathy. Sometimes she would offer advice, sometimes a joke that put his problem in perspective. Most of the time, Phillip found relief just by opening up to her, releasing his annoyances in a tirade and knowing that when he was done she wouldn't hate him for complaining. Her eyes would glow with compassion and affection, and she would make a few observations in her husky, sexy voice, and his mood would improve. Sometimes she didn't even have to say anything. It was enough for him to have her beside him, nodding and giving his hand a squeeze, letting him know she cared.

Her footsteps still echoed in his skull, soft but resolute, long after she'd departed from his office. He wanted to chase after her, to apologize for the circumstances beyond his control—and hers—that had drawn him into his current dilemma. He wanted to hug her and hold her and tell her he needed her in his life. He didn't just want her—he truly needed her.

But he couldn't need her. It was impossible. The kindest thing he could do was what he'd just done: tell her he loved Tricia, freeing her to leave him and Lynwood behind, to get on with her life and forget anything had ever blossomed between them. As kind as he'd been to her, she'd also be doing him a favor by disappearing. Having her around only made him regret the choices he'd had to make.

Three days. In three days he would marry Tricia and Harry would no longer pose a threat to his family. In three days it would be too late for regrets.

What had sounded like Cassie's retreating footsteps now sounded like a Grateful Dead drum improvisation in his brain, syncopated tom-toms, deep and resonant.

Cassie never made his head pound. His heart, yes, but never his head. It was her absence that caused the drums to bang inside his skull.

With a sigh he crossed to his desk, ignoring the lingering scent of her, and gathered his spreadsheets. He stored them inside a file cabinet, turned off his computer and left his office, making sure it was locked behind him. What was that bull about Cassie and Diane leaving something at the building that day? Whatever they might have left, no way would Cassie have found it in Phillip's office. As far as he knew, she, Diane and the guy, Beckelman, hadn't been on the second floor all day.

Had Edie brought something of Cassie's upstairs? Edie, always so stolid and somber, had been one step removed from a giggling groupie that morning in the carpentry shop. In fact, pretty much everyone at Keene Furniture had been fawning over the TV crew. Even Tricia. Especially Tricia.

Phillip supposed that to have an episode of *Dream Wheels* filmed on location in the factory was a thrill, especially when constant tension was emanating from the head honcho's office. Lately Phillip had to endure so much pressure from so many quarters he hadn't been treating his employees with the benevolence and good humor they deserved. It wasn't Edie's fault that the Chicago store was in such dire straits. It wasn't Richard Bausch's fault that Harry Riggs was tightening the screws. It wasn't Joe Renkawicz's fault, or Stacy McRae's from human resources, or Cal Springer's from shipping, or Lowell Henley's from public relations.

It was Harry Riggs's fault—and Phillip's father's

fault. And it was Phillip's fault for trying so hard to protect the Keene legacy.

He trudged down the stairs, nodded a farewell to the guard at the door and stepped outside. The sky was pink and dusk gold, but still bright enough to make him reach for his sunglasses. He hesitated when he saw the small cluster of people chatting beside one of the cars in the lot: Cassie, Diane and Harry.

Wonderful. The three people Phillip least wanted to see.

The car they were clustered near was his own. If he wanted to get behind the wheel and leave the premises, he was going to have to acknowledge them. And he wasn't going to flee back to his office and hide as if he was guilty of something—even if he was guilty of plenty.

Donning his sunglasses, he strode across the lot to his car, doing his best to look confident and nonchalant. Diane was the first to greet him.

"Hey, Phil! What are you still doing here?"

"Working," he said laconically.

"It's too late to be working, this close to your wedding day. Don't you agree, Harry?" she asked, already on a first-name basis with Tricia's father. "Harry and I have been discussing cigars," she went on. Harry, Phillip noted, had an unlit cigar clamped between his teeth. "You know, they've got smoking rooms all over Boston now. Cigars are considered a luxurious indulgence. I've been thinking about taking up the habit."

"I haven't," Cassie murmured, her gaze steady on Phillip. "Cigars cause cancer."

"The thing with cigars," Harry pontificated, "as with all good things in life, is to enjoy them in moderation. Now, I appreciate a cigar every once in a while. I don't always light up, either. It's the flavor on your tongue, the texture of leaves on your lips, that offers pleasure. I like your friends, Phil,'' Harry added, patting Diane's shoulder. "Interesting people you socialized with in Boston. Why didn't you tell me Keene Furniture was going to star in a TV show?''

Phillip was in no mood for banter. "Would it have changed anything?''

"What do you mean, changed anything?'' Harry seemed perplexed. "It's an exciting occurrence. I remember Tricia mentioning something about some TV show this morning at breakfast. To tell the truth, I was surprised to see her at the breakfast table so early, but she was all pumped up about this TV thing. She just couldn't wait to come over and watch.'' Harry gazed warmly at Diane, then Cassie. "One thing about my daughter, if you don't mind the father of the bride boasting a little, once she gets pumped up about something, there's no stopping her.''

"Enthusiasm is an admirable trait,'' Diane said.

"She sees something she wants and there's no stopping her, whether it's to watch a TV show get taped or to marry this fellow here.'' Harry pointed to Phillip with his cigar. "I can still recall the first time she saw him—well, of course, she'd seen him plenty when they were children, but he was a few years older than her and he wouldn't have given her the time of day back then. Do you remember, Phil? You used to be so rude to her when our families got together.''

"No, I don't remember,'' Phillip said coolly.

"Well, you *were* rude, but I guess that's how it is with boys and girls. They hate each other. But then everything changes. That day, right after you'd come home from Harvard, you and your father were at my office, discussing business. Remember?'' Harry grew misty eyed as he reminisced. "You were fresh from business school, the ink still wet on your diploma. You'd been in town for, what, a couple of days? So there you were, in my office with your father, and Tricia came rushing in—I don't remember why, but I'm sure she was pumped up about something. And she took one look at you and kind of did a double take. And I knew, right then and there, that my princess was going to make you her husband.''

"Did you.'' Phillip didn't care to wax nostalgic with Harry about that fateful moment, especially not when Cassie was standing just two feet away. Especially not when only minutes ago he'd been perilously close to kissing her.

"Hell, it didn't surprise me when Tricia remarked over dinner that night that you were the best catch in Lynwood. You weren't just a hunk—I believe that was her word—'' Harry winked at Cassie and Diane "—but you also just happened to be the heir apparent to the most successful manufacturing firm in Lynwood. You were the one she wanted from that moment on. And you know Tricia,'' he said with a chummy grin. "Once she decides she wants something, she sure as hell goes after it. I'm not offending you ladies with my language, am I?''

"Hell, no,'' Diane said, provoking a guffaw from Harry.

"I like this gal,'' he said, patting her shoulder again. "Maybe you and I ought to get together for a cigar while you're in town. What do you say?''

"Well, I—''

"Not tonight,'' Cassie announced. She looked paler than Diane, even with the sunset washing her face in tangerine light. Her smile was apprehensive and her eyes darted between Harry and Phillip. "We have things to take care of tonight."

"Um…that's true," Diane said, playing along. "But we'll be in town for the next couple of days, Harry. Can I take a rain check?"

"Any time you want to light up, you just let me know."

Cassie closed her hand around Diane's wrist, as if she thought she'd have to fight Harry for possession of her friend. "Come on, Diane. We've got work to do."

"Okay, okay. We'll have that cigar later, Harry."

"You take care, now," Harry called after them as they moved across the lot. Phillip was glad for his sunglasses; he could stare at Cassie through the dark lenses without Harry's noticing. She still had on her short skirt, but it didn't matter that her beautiful legs were on display. Maybe that morning it had mattered, but not now, not after he'd touched her cheek and talked to her, not after he'd realized how very much he wanted to talk to her, how very much he wanted to say.

She could be wearing long, baggy trousers, snow boots, a lumpy down parka and a ski mask, and he would still want to talk to her. He would still want a whole lot more from her than talk, too.

"I CAN'T BELIEVE IT! I'm in with Tricia's father!" Diane babbled, obviously quite proud of herself.

"You can't begin to know what you're in with," Cassie warned, backing out of the parking space without even glancing in the rearview mirror. The risk of crashing into a car didn't bother her as much as the risk of seeing Phillip in the mirror, shoulder to shoulder with his greedy future father-in-law.

"What am I in with? He wants to have a cigar with me." Diane leaned back in the passenger seat and grinned smugly. "Just think—a public-TV drone smoking fancy cigars like a yuppie millionaire."

"One fancy cigar does not a millionaire make." Cassie continued through town, ignoring the leafy trees, the quaint shops, the Live Crickets sign in the pet-store window. "Listen, Diane. This is important. We're moving on to Plan E."

"What's Plan E? Sipping brandy in club chairs with cigar smoke drifting all around us?"

Cassie turned off Main Street and slowed as the Bailey's Bed-and-Breakfast sign loomed up ahead. "Remember why we went to Keene Furniture this evening?"

"To sabotage the place," Diane answered. "I still think the arson idea has potential. All that wood lying around... They don't make plastic furniture at Keene, you know? They don't make upholstered stuff, either. So if the place went up in flames, we wouldn't have to worry about toxic fumes polluting the atmosphere. If we're going to sabotage the place, I think—"

"Torching Keene Furniture might be the biggest favor we could do for Phil," Cassie said, braking to a halt in the parking lot behind the inn.

"What?"

Cassie climbed out of the car. As soon as Diane was also out, Cassie locked the vehicle and stalked across the lawn, Diane jogging until she caught up with her.

"What are you talking about?" Diane asked. "Phil wants us to set fire to the factory?"

"No. But it might solve all his problems if we did."
She took a measured breath, ignoring the sweet perfume of apple blossoms and recently cut grass mingling with the lighter fragrance of the lilac hedges bordering the porch. On the bottom step she halted and turned to face Diane. "The factory is in financial trouble, and your new best friend, Harry Riggs, is poised to take over the place if the earnings don't improve soon."

Diane stared at her for a moment, her mouth agape. Then she tossed back her head and laughed. "You're kidding. Really? What a hoot!"

"It's not funny." It was near tragic, as far as Cassie was concerned. Phillip might lose everything to that loathsome man: his family's company, his own career and, most important, his chance at a happy future with her. Not that he'd expressed an interest in any sort of future with her, happy or otherwise. Perhaps he'd want to spend a few hours in the sack with her—or on his office sofa, or maybe in the men's room on the first floor. But he'd said he was marrying Tricia because he loved her.

Cassie didn't want to believe him. Until she had proof to the contrary, though, she had to accept what he'd told her: he was in love with the daughter of the man who was threatening to take over Keene Furniture.

"Good grief," Diane mumbled, although she was still smirking. "This is juicy!"

"This is a mess," Cassie argued, not at all amused. "It isn't just Phil and Tricia. It's Phil's history, and his future. His entire heritage is under siege. To say nothing of some store in Chicago that's hemorrhaging cash. And Phil's mother would get hurt if the company sank. She's a terrific lady. If it wasn't for her, we wouldn't even be here now.''

"You're right," Diane said, suppressing her mirth. "People's lives are at stake—and if you ask me, the most important life at stake is yours. Phil's mom may have brought us here, but it's your life we came to save.''

"I thought we came to ruin Phil's life," Cassie corrected her.

"It's the same thing. Now what do we have? Tricia's off making nice with Roger, and Phil's company is going down the tubes because of some store in Chicago. Where exactly does Harry fit into all this?"

"Keene Furniture is in debt to him. Tons of debt, I gather. If the company can't pay, Harry takes over the ownership.''

"You're kidding. This is too good. If we came up with a plot like this for a TV show, the network would tell us it was incredible.''

"It certainly wouldn't be suitable for *Dream Wheels*." Cassie climbed the steps and entered the farmhouse, Diane close behind her.

A message slip awaited her on the mail table in the entry; one of her assistants at the station in Boston had called to update her on goings-on back at the studio. Her animators wanted to talk to her, two agents wanted to set up auditions for their clients and the creator of an on-line encyclopedia wanted to add his sponsorship to the show in exchange for some sort of collaboration. Cassie tucked the square of paper into her pocket and continued down the hall to the kitchen, where diet cola and a package of chocolate-chip cookies awaited her. She had the feeling she was going to

need both to fuel her while she hammered out Plan C
with Diane.

Mrs. Gill was puttering around the kitchen, growl-
ing about a neighborhood cat that had developed the
habit of using her flower beds as its own personal
potty. Cassie gave the woman a generic hello, grabbed
two cans of soda and the cookies and beckoned Diane
out of the kitchen before Mrs. Gill's wrath befell them.
They returned to the porch and settled in two of the
deep wooden chairs to eat and plot.

"Okay," Diane said while Cassie shoved an entire
cookie into her mouth. "Let me see if I've got this
straight—Harry Riggs lent money to Keene Furniture.
The company's in trouble. Some store in Chicago is
causing them problems..."

"Keene Furniture owns the store, and it's losing
serious money," Cassie explained. She recalled the
harsh words she'd overheard while hiding in the upstairs washroom, eavesdropping on Phillip and Harry.
"The loans are overdue. I think they were due on the
first of the year, and Keene Furniture hasn't paid them
yet. Harry could foreclose, I guess. He could say,
'Happy New Year and welcome to the millennium.
Now, pay up or I take title to the company.'"

Diane nodded and reached for a cookie. "And
meanwhile, Harry's princess, the one who thinks Phil
is the best catch in Lynwood, is spending the evening
with another man." Diane studied her cookie, as if
counting the chocolate chips.

"She's not *with* another man," Cassie corrected.
"As far as we know, all they're doing is viewing the
daily rushes. Anything more between the two of them
would put us back in the center of Plan D. We're
supposed to be working on Plan C."

"I don't see why Plan D and Plan C have to be mutually exclusive," Diane argued. "Or Plan E for that matter. Why not foment trouble on all fronts?"

"Because…" Because a part of Cassie—an emotional, sympathetic part; a part growing bigger and stronger, threatening to abduct her soul and return it to its original condition, which was soft and considerate and far from vengeful—recognized that a man who had once been her beloved friend was standing on the edge of a crumbling cliff. And no matter how much she wanted to push him over the edge, that soft, considerate, nonvengeful part of her wanted to save him.

Diane knew her too well. "He broke your heart," she reminded Cassie. "Don't go all mushy on me, Cassie. The man's a duplicitous bastard, remember?"

"Maybe he had to marry Tricia to keep things in balance between Harry and his parents."

"Yeah, right." Diane pulled two cookies from the bag and settled back in her chair. "What kind of a man chooses business over the woman he loves?"

"The kind of man who puts family loyalty and honor above all else," Cassie suggested. "There's something noble about that, don't you think?"

"Give me a break. The guy didn't even phone you and explain what was going on. He didn't even drop you a note to tell you, 'By the way, Cassie, I know I promised to come back to Boston, but I won't be able to. Something noble and honorable has come up.'" She took a robust bite of one of her cookies, then added, "Something named Tricia came up. He's *marrying* her, for God's sake. He promised to marry you, and now he's marrying her."

"He didn't exactly promise to marry me."

"Jeez, Louise." Diane shook her head and gazed heavenward. "Now you're defending him!"

"All I'm saying is, he faced a hard choice."

"And he chose wrong. He didn't choose you." Diane devoured her other cookie and washed it down with a slug of soda. "I'm almost afraid to ask, but what exactly is Plan E? Are you going to rescue him from his own disaster?"

"I don't know," Cassie confessed, then noticed Diane's look of alarm and amended her answer. "I mean, I don't know what Plan E is." The appalling truth was, she just might have been contemplating a rescue. *If* Phillip was truly unhappy with the choice his predicament had forced upon him, and *if* he'd been lying when he said he was marrying Tricia out of love, and *if* Cassie could forgive him for having refused to communicate with her about his difficulties, for having never even tried to contact her, for having disappeared and left her dangling for an entire year—and it would have been forever if his mother hadn't whimsically sent Diane an invitation to the wedding...

That was an awful lot for Cassie to forgive. Maybe she ought to put the compassionate part of her back in its cage and set the vindictive part free.

"Here's the thing," she said, thinking aloud. "If we leave Phillip alone and let his marriage proceed as planned, it solves his company's financial problems—but I think he might wind up miserable. If we interfere with his wedding, he loses his company, but maybe he'd wind up happy."

"You're saying he doesn't want to marry Tricia?"

Cassie's mouth tightened in a grimace. Who knew whether or not he wanted to marry Tricia? He'd said, quite clearly, that he loved her. How could she doubt him?

But she *knew* him. How could she *not* doubt him?

"I think it's a real possibility," she allowed.

"So," Diane summed up, "either outcome solves one problem and creates one problem for him. We have to decide which problem we want to solve and which problem we want to create." She mulled over what she'd just said and wrinkled her nose. "I don't want to solve any of his problems, frankly. I wish we could consolidate all our plans and create more problems than he'll ever recover from."

"You're nasty," Cassie said, then smiled. "Don't take that the wrong way. I didn't mean it as an insult."

Diane laughed. "I'll take it as a compliment, then." She sipped her soda, her amusement waning. "The thing is, you still harbor affection for Phil. I don't know why, after what he did to you—"

"There were mitigating factors."

"See? You're apologizing for him. You're defending him." Diane leaned forward for emphasis. "I'm not nasty, Cassie. What I am is clear-eyed. I know what he did. I know how he hurt you. You cried a hell of a lot harder for him than I ever did for Bobby, who we both know was pond scum, but he didn't hurt me the way Phil hurt you. Now, unlike you, I don't want to make excuses for Phil. This doesn't make me nasty. It makes me clear-eyed and pragmatic."

"All right. The bottom line is, we need to figure out Plan E." Cassie drummed her fingers on the arm of her chair and stared out at the front yard. The colors were fading with the last of the light, and as the sky grew darker, the bug zap-light glowed brighter, an eerie bluish-white glare. The sizzle of bugs getting scorched mixed with the more pleasant sound of crickets chirping.

If only she was as heartless as a bug zap-light, Cassie thought glumly. If only she could scorch Phillip without having to consider all those mitigating factors: not just the financial stress he was under, not just the emotional blackmail he was dealing with, but her own feelings. Nasty or not, Diane had spoken the truth when she'd accused Cassie of harboring affection for Phillip.

More than affection. She actually wanted to make his problems disappear. And then maybe he'd acknowledge how much he loved her, and he'd walk away from Lynwood without a backward glance, return to Boston with her and fulfill the promise he'd made a year ago.

She was in bad shape, she realized. One earnest gaze from him, one gentle caress, one secret revealed, and she was ready to forget all the hurt he'd inflicted upon her. But she mustn't let herself forget what he'd told her in his office that evening, after he'd told her about the store in Chicago and the loans Harry had extended to the company: that he was marrying Tricia Riggs because he loved her.

If he was lying, Cassie should hate him for being a liar. And if he was telling the truth, she'd have to forget her little fantasy about his fulfilling his promise to her.

"Plan E," she said, gathering what few scraps of nastiness she could find within her heart, "is to have everything come crashing down around him. The wedding, the marriage, the company. Everything."

"Now you're talking."

"Tomorrow, we'll try to finish up the taping early.

Then you'll go smoke a cigar with Harry Riggs—''
Cassie winced at the mental image of Diane with a fat
brown cigar protruding from between her lips ''—and
you can pump him for information. Meanwhile, I'll
find Phil's mother and see what I can learn from her.''

''What can she possibly tell you? Do you think
she's in the loop about the company's financial problems?''

Cassie shook her head. ''I don't know how much
she knows about that. But she's Phil's mother. She
can tell me what his relationship with Tricia is really
about.'' If Cassie could be sure that he loved Tricia,
deeply and truly, then she would deem it worth her
effort to wreak revenge on the happy couple. If, on
the other hand, her suspicions were correct and he
didn't love Tricia, she would make sure Plan E entailed a smooth, unchallenged wedding—because if
Phillip didn't love Tricia, vowing before God to be
her husband till death did them part would be the
worst punishment imaginable.

Plan E would work, once Cassie knew which way
to take it. No need to set Keene Furniture on fire; no
need to encourage a fling between Tricia and Roger;
no need to stink-bomb the country club on Saturday
afternoon. All Cassie had to do was figure out what
would happen if Phillip married Tricia, and what
would happen if he didn't, and then decide which alternative would cause him greater grief.

It seemed simple enough when she thought about it
that way. Only one detail stood in the way.

''Just reassure me about one thing,'' Diane said,
prodding that detail into the spotlight. ''Reassure me
that you don't love Phil anymore.''

Cassie opened her mouth and shut it. She drank

some soda. She eyed the bag of cookies wistfully, then drank some more soda.

"Reassure me, Cassie," Diane demanded.

Cassie sent her a grim smile. "I don't know what I feel for him," was all she would concede. "In any case, what I feel for him is irrelevant. We're going with Plan E. We're going to make Phillip Keene regret that he ever left me."

Diane upped the ante. "We're going to make him regret that he ever *met* you."

"That, too."

Diane clicked her half-empty can against Cassie's. "Here's a toast to the new millennium. And here's to Plan E."

"To Plan E," Cassie agreed, then drank.

CHAPTER TEN

LATER THAT NIGHT, alone in her garret beneath the eaves, Cassie was still asking herself that one troubling question: did she still love Phillip?

How could she, after what he'd done to her?

How could she not, when the choice he'd made had demonstrated such valor, such loyalty to his family, such selflessness?

But how valiant could he be if he hadn't even bothered to call her, to tell her what he had decided and why?

Yet if she didn't love him, why did she still respond so powerfully to the lightest touch from him? Why did a single, intense gaze from him turn her on? Why was she still amazed that she'd found the willpower to walk away from him not once but twice today, when she was certain that if she hadn't walked away he would have made love to her?

Her windows were open, allowing tiny whiffs of night air into the stultifying warmth of the attic. It was nearly ten o'clock, and she and Diane had given up waiting for Roger to return to the inn with his report on the quality of the day's tapes. "We've got a big day tomorrow," Diane had pointed out. "A big Plan E day. I'm going to need my beauty rest so I'll be able to puff on a cigar without losing my lunch."

They'd retired to their respective rooms twenty

minutes ago. By now Diane was probably fast asleep; she'd always been unaffected by caffeine-laced soda. Cassie, on the other hand, would probably be awake and jittery half the night.

And caffeine had nothing to do with it, she conceded silently.

Too restless to get into bed, she pulled the local telephone directory from the drawer in her nightstand and flipped to the *K*s. Keene, Phillip was a separate listing from Keene, Jas. & Dorothy. Evidently Phillip no longer lived with his parents. Cassie wondered whether he owned a house or rented an apartment— assuming a town like Lynwood even had apartments. She jotted down both Keene residential addresses, then flipped to the *R*s to see if Tricia Riggs was listed under the same address as Phillip.

Tricia wasn't listed at all. But she must be living with her parents, because her father had said she'd talked about the *Dream Wheels* taping over breakfast. Cassie shouldn't have cared, but she was pleased that Tricia hadn't moved in with Phillip yet.

She closed the directory and slid it back into the drawer. Then she crossed the room to her laptop, moving carefully so she wouldn't bang her head against the gabled ceiling. If she reviewed her notes for tomorrow's taping and made sure everything was in order, she, Diane and Roger could complete their work efficiently, and then she and Diane could move on to Plan E.

On the other hand, if the filming dragged on late enough, she wouldn't have time to visit Phillip's mother—and maybe it was just as well. Cassie wasn't sure she was ready to visit Dorothy Keene and learn

that Phillip really, truly, passionately loved Tricia.
Would she be able to handle such dreadful news?

For heaven's sake, she'd have to consider it fabulous news if Phillip really, truly, passionately loved
Tricia. If he legitimately loved his Fergie-clone fiancée, that truth would liberate Cassie to wreak havoc.
She would be able to avenge herself without a moment's qualm. If Phillip didn't love Cassie, she certainly wouldn't care what happened to him, his furniture factory or his future.

"He doesn't love me," she whispered, almost as
desperate to convince herself as she was desperate to
cling to the hope that he actually *did* love her. "If he
loved me, he wouldn't be marrying Tricia on Saturday."

Through the open window she heard the constant
shrilling of crickets—and another sound, human
voices engaged in conversation. She darted to the window, remembering to duck at the last minute so she
wouldn't hit her head on the ceiling, but the window
afforded her a view of only the south side of the house.
The street was west, the parking area north.

She padded barefoot out of her room and down the
hall to the room that contained the bathtub. Beyond
the tub was another small window, this one facing the
parking lot. Cassie dropped to her knees to protect her
skull from the low ceiling and eased the window open,
wincing when the hinges squeaked.

Two stories below, Roger and Tricia obviously
didn't hear the squeak. Illuminated by the silver moonlight and the bluish radiance of the bug zapper, they
stood at the edge of the parking area next to Tricia's
sporty red roadster, facing each other, Roger towering
above Tricia. His camera tote was slung over his

shoulder; her hands were buried in the pockets of her overalls. The night breeze toyed with her hair—and Roger's—and lifted the sound of Tricia's laughter up to the bathroom window.

Cassie couldn't make out what they were saying, but they remained together beside the car, chatting for much longer than it would take to utter a simple thank-you and good-night. They weren't touching, but they stood close enough that touching would not entail any great exertion by either of them.

What if Plan D kept rolling along? What if Tricia and Roger lingered outside for hours, gazing into each other's eyes? What if one of them made that minor effort and touched the other?

For one thing, Cassie would lose respect for Roger. Tricia was supposed to be engaged, after all. Roger should know better than to flirt with a woman who was already promised to someone else.

Roger wasn't flirting, Cassie admitted. He didn't know how to flirt. He talked to women, listened to women, enjoyed the company of women and slept with women, as far as Cassie knew—but he didn't make plays for women, didn't try lines out on women, didn't employ any of the standard games and courting rituals in his dealings with the opposite sex. He was too straightforward, too guileless.

As for Tricia…well, if Tricia made a play for Roger, Cassie would have to view it as a win-win situation. If Phillip loved Tricia, then Cassie would want his heart broken—and if Tricia made a play for Roger, it would break Phillip's heart. If, on the other hand, Phillip didn't love Tricia, then his marriage to her would be some kind of punishment, and the pun-

ishment would be greater if he wound up marrying a
woman who came on to other men.

So why was she so perturbed by the sight of Roger
and Tricia standing so close together in the moonlight?

A minute passed. Another minute. Their voices,
mostly Tricia's, drifted up to the window, vague and
distorted. What could they be talking about that they
couldn't talk about at the cable-TV studio or on the
drive home? Was Tricia simply prolonging their final
moments together by rambling on about trivia?

Another minute, and then Tricia pulled her hand out
of her pocket and planted it on Roger's shoulder. She
rose on tiptoe and kissed his cheek. Cassie realized
she was holding her breath, praying, yearning...for
something. For Roger to haul Tricia into his arms? For
Tricia to haul Roger into hers?

Whatever Cassie had wished for, she felt disappointed when Tricia took a step backward, then turned
toward her car. Roger said something, waved and
loped around the building to the front porch, out of
Cassie's sight.

A peck on the cheek. Genuine affection or show-
business affectation? Had it been their first kiss of the
night, or their last?

If Diane had been awake, she would have analyzed
every split second of that farewell scene. She would
have calculated all the angles, all the odds, and produced a list for Cassie. By the time Roger had vanished from view, Diane would have spun all sorts of
possibilities: he and Tricia had made wild, sweaty love
in the tech room at the cable studio. Or they'd made
wild, sweaty love in her hot little car. Or Tricia had
tried to jump Roger's bones, and he'd told her she was

too young for him, or too effervescent, or too betrothed.

As far as Cassie was concerned, though, they'd likely spent the evening running the tapes and assessing their quality. Roger had taught her a little about the art and business of video production and she'd kissed him on the cheek to thank him for having edified her.

Maybe it was just as well Diane was asleep. Right now, Cassie didn't want to contemplate any story more convoluted than that simple, innocent explanation for the kiss she'd just witnessed. She was a dreamer, not a schemer, and she preferred upbeat, uplifting stories to sordid tales of revenge—even if revenge was the current motivating principle of her life. She didn't want to think the worst of Roger—or Tricia, for that matter. She actually liked the red-haired airhead.

If she was going to imagine the worst of a person, she'd just as soon have that person be Phillip Keene.

PHILLIP SAT in the kitchen of the house he'd bought for Tricia. Even though his glass of scotch sat staunchly on the table, in no danger of spilling or sliding out of his reach, he kept his fingers curled tightly around the drink, holding it in place just an elbow's bend from his mouth.

He hated this house.

It was a Victorian, with an overabundance of ornamentation inside and out. The outer shingled walls were painted dandelion yellow, the gingerbread trim teal, the front door barn red framed in white. The place looked as if it had been colored in by a toddler who'd run amok with a box of crayons.

Tricia had adored the brightness of the house's exterior. The interior had been a bit more subdued when they'd purchased the house, but she'd handled that in no time.

They'd bought the house in March, and Phillip had moved in right after they'd taken title. Determined to fulfill the role of a blushing bride, Tricia had decided to remain under her parents' roof until her wedding day. But she was frequently over at the Victorian, fixing things, fussing with things, overseeing the installation of new carpets, the arrangement of furniture, the addition of a new dishwasher, a compactor, a washer and dryer in the laundry room. She'd decorated the rooms, cluttering the living-room mantel with porcelain figurines and candlesticks, the bookcases with vases and ornately framed sepia photographs of her ancestors. She'd purchased his-and-hers Barca-Loungers for the den and fragile glass-topped pedestal tables for everywhere else. Not a single piece in the house had been manufactured by Keene Furniture.

Phillip was a firm believer that a little decor went a long way, but when it came to decor, "little" was not a part of Tricia's vocabulary. Every curtain had a contrasting swag, a fringed edge. Every fabric had a pattern embedded in it—sometimes two patterns.

The touch he most despised was the stenciling on the walls. Practically every damned wall in the house was trimmed with a stenciled border near the ceiling, except for the dining room, where the stenciling hovered waist-high. Phillip especially didn't like the kitchen's stencils: vines dripping with triangular bunches of grapes. He always felt as if he ought to be watching his step in the room, checking underfoot for crushed fruit and purple stains.

But he had ceded the decor of the house to Tricia,

because she felt so passionate about the place. She loved the intricate wood trim edging the gables outside, and the faceted leaded-glass sidelights flanking the front door. She loved the pretentious Palladian window in the den. She loved the master bedroom with its nooks and niches, even though those nooks and niches had made it all but impossible to fit the oppressive ebony bedroom set she'd selected into the room. She loved that the living room was sunken, two steps lower than the entry. Phillip had tripped on those steps more times than he cared to count.

Tricia had first seen the house with a real-estate agent in town last Christmas. She'd told Phillip she'd found them a home, *their* home, the perfect residence for them to settle into once they became husband and wife. She'd told him she wasn't going to describe it to him but, instead, would surprise him. Her first surprise of the new century, she'd told him.

On January 2, she and the real estate agent had brought him to look at the house. He'd been more than surprised—he'd been aghast. But she'd loved the place so much and he hadn't been able to bring himself to deny her. Perhaps, subliminally, he'd been thinking, *I can't give you love, but I can give you a house you'll love.*

He took a drink of scotch, held it in his mouth until the alcohol had thoroughly numbed his tongue, then swallowed. He was not pleased with the thoughts that had been plaguing him tonight, ever since Cassie had walked out of his office earlier that evening.

He'd told her he loved Tricia. For the past three hours, he'd been trying to convince himself he did.

He took another belt of scotch, leaned back in his chair and stared at a particularly sinuous-looking vine on the ceiling. If Cassie ever saw this kitchen, she'd double over with laughter. She'd think the grape vines were hilarious, and the glass-topped table with molded wrought-iron vines twining up the legs was ugly. She'd giggle at the café curtains, the fabric featuring bunches of purple grapes and the hems trimmed with a strip of purple fabric from which dangled grape-sized purple pompoms. She'd chuckle over the matching grape-fabric toaster cover, the Tiffany-style lamp—also featuring a grape motif—hanging above the table, and the cookie jar that resembled a fat pink pig with a sprig of green grapes clamped in its snout. The last image a person wanted to see when he was about to grab a handful of cookies was a pig, especially one munching on grapes.

Cassie would recognize immediately how wrong the kitchen—the whole house—was for Phillip.

Oh, God. He didn't want to marry Tricia. He didn't want to spend the rest of his life with a woman whose concept of the ideal home was so different from his. He didn't want to pledge to love, honor and cherish a woman who would decorate her kitchen in Napa Valley modern.

He drained his glass, refilled it from the bottle at the center of the table and tried to remember if it was his second or third refill. It didn't matter; he'd drink until his brain was as numb as his tongue, or until his supply of scotch ran out, whichever came first.

He wouldn't be considering how much he didn't want to marry Tricia if Cassie hadn't come to Lynwood. It was all her fault, this sudden onslaught of doubt and panic. If only she hadn't shown up as a tangible reminder of what he'd had to sacrifice to save his father's company, he wouldn't have had to think about how much he'd rather marry Cassie.

He didn't think he had enough scotch in the house to stop thinking about her. He didn't think there was enough scotch in the world.

That realization made him shove the glass away. Why keep drinking? What good would come from it? It wouldn't change the truth: at one time he'd loved Cassie. A long, trying year had passed since then, and he wasn't sure he still loved her. But he was obviously obsessed with her. Given a choice of who to spend his wedding night with, he'd pick Cassie over Tricia in a second.

She probably wouldn't pick him, though. Unlike Tricia, Cassie couldn't possibly consider him the best catch in Lynwood—or, if she did, she wouldn't think Lynwood's husband supply was worth ranking from worst to best.

It suddenly occurred to him that if he didn't at least explain more to her than he had in his office, he wouldn't be able to live with himself, let alone his bride. He shoved away from the vine-legged table, dug his keys out of his pocket and strode down the back hall to the attached garage.

The neighborhood was quiet. Even on a weekend, Lynwood fell into a coma by ten or ten-thirty. On a Wednesday, most of the houses were already dark, the VCRs taping prime-time shows that the town's residents couldn't manage to stay awake late enough to watch during their regularly scheduled broadcast. Cassie was a city woman, though—she'd still be awake. And if she wasn't, he'd wake her up and get her out of bed. Or maybe wake her up and *not* get her out of bed.

No. He wasn't going to Bailey's Bed-and-Breakfast to make love to her, although that was high on his list of things he'd like to do. He was going to talk to her, explain to her, apologize to her. He was going to make her see why he'd done what he'd done.

Depending on how she reacted, he was going to make good on his year-old promise to her even if it meant consigning Keene Furniture to ruin, or he was going to walk away from Cassie and exile her from his heart forever.

The roads were nearly empty. A few cars and dusty pickups stood in the parking lot of Jake's Tavern, the main watering hole in town. Phillip's bachelor party was going to be held in the back room of Jake's on Friday night. He'd just as soon skip the bachelor party, but his best man and the ushers, old buddies from their high-school varsity days, had insisted on throwing a bash for him. He figured he'd eat a sandwich, play a few rounds of pool, laugh at the dirty jokes and get home early, before any strippers jumped out of cakes.

Jake's parking lot and its neon signs in the windows represented the only pocket of activity in the downtown area. Phillip cruised past the place, past the darkened stores, the bank, the post office looking more tomblike than it did during the day, with its forlorn, empty flagpole. He turned left onto the street where Bailey's was located and slowed as a rectangle of blinding illumination—the antibug lamp—loomed into view.

A few windows of the rambling farmhouse glowed with light. Phillip wondered which room was Cassie's. Would she be reading in bed? Going over her plans for tomorrow's taping? Sitting in the parlor and watching TV? Or curled up in an easy chair somewhere, with a glass in one hand and a bottle of scotch in the other?

No, that was *his* vice, not Cassie's.

He slowed the car, easing to the grassy edge of the road, and shifted into neutral. Through his open car window came the lilt of voices—a familiar voice, in fact. Tricia's voice.

What the hell?

He turned off his headlights and let his car roll forward a few feet. At the side of the building he saw Tricia and Cassie's hippie camera operator, Beckelman, standing very close to each other. He saw Tricia rise on her toes, clasp Beckelman by the shoulder and kiss him.

What the hell!

Beckelman started around to the front of the house, and Phillip immediately pressed the gas pedal, steering the car smoothly and quietly past the front of the building and away. A glance in his rearview mirror indicated that Beckelman apparently hadn't noticed him. On the next block, Phillip stopped and checked in his rearview mirror again. He saw the headlights of a car along the unpaved lane connecting the parking area with the street. Tricia's car.

His original plan had been to speak to Cassie, but he quickly amended it. First he ought to find out what was going on with Tricia. Why had she been with Beckelman? What had they been doing all evening? Why had she kissed the guy?

Not that he was jealous. Not that he was even particularly angry. It just might be that Tricia was as lukewarm about marrying him as he was about marrying her. A gala wedding, especially one carrying a huge price tag, had a way of steamrollering everything in its path, even the second thoughts of the principals.

If Tricia wanted out, then he'd be off the hook. How could Harry blame him and punish his father by calling in Keene Furniture's debts if Harry's daughter was the one to break off the engagement? How could Harry demand instant repayment of his loans if Tricia was the instigator of the breakup and he, Phillip, was the aggrieved party?

He continued to watch his mirror until he saw Tricia hang a right onto Main Street. Then he U-turned and drove after her. He kept as much distance as possible between their cars once he'd followed her onto Main Street; it wasn't as if he could blend into the flow of traffic, since there wasn't any traffic to blend into.

If Tricia noticed him, she didn't indicate it. She cruised her little hot rod at a reasonable speed past the dark, quiet downtown stores and west, toward her parents' house. Phillip still had her in view as she reached the grand brick Georgian where the Riggs family lived. She steered through the gate, not bothering to close it behind her.

Once again Phillip pulled to the side of the road and turned off his headlights. He had to consider his next move carefully. If he followed her in and confronted her, her father might overhear their discussion. He'd go berserk if he knew his princess was spending her off hours with Beckelman, not only because Beckelman wasn't the kind of man Harry would want his daughter associating with but also because Harry had his own plans and they revolved around his being in charge, pulling all the strings and wielding all the power. Of course he would indulge Tricia—but not if indulging her meant losing his leverage with Phillip.

So Phillip wouldn't follow her into her house.

Instead, he continued down the road a few blocks
and around the corner to his parents' elegant Tudor-
style house, perched on a large, verdant square of
lawn. The flower gardens were barely visible in the
amber light from the porch lamps, but when Phillip
climbed out of his car he could smell them, a mixture
of sweet and spicy and tangy fragrances. His mother
was passionate about gardening. She'd served several
terms as president of the Lynwood Horticulture Society, and he knew that even after his father finally
turned the helm of Keene Furniture over to Phillip—
or Harry Riggs—and retired, his mother would refuse
to retire from her hobby. She would still be out on her
knees in her broad-brimmed straw hat, weeding her
flower beds and pruning her shrubs.

He strolled up the slate walk to the front door and
rang. His mother peered through the rectangular window in the door, smiled hesitantly and opened it to let
him in.

"Phillip!" she half exclaimed, half whispered. "Is
everything all right?"

"Yeah," he lied, entering the foyer and closing the
door behind him. "Why are we whispering?"

"Dad fell asleep in front of the TV. Sooner or later
I'm going to have to wake him up and get him upstairs
to bed, but he's so peaceful right now I don't want to
disturb him." She scuffed down the front hall in her
slippers, her robe tied loosely around her waist.

Phillip stifled a laugh. In Boston at this hour, he and
Cassie would have been dawdling over a final cup of
espresso or a glass of wine at some eatery, or a beer
at her apartment. They'd be feeling the wear and tear
of their respective days, but they'd be too engrossed

in their conversation to call it quits for the night. He would be listening to her explain the intricate logic of time travel to him: "We can't have the *Dream Wheels* kids actually change the outcome of anything in the past, because if we did it would have repercussions in the present. So when we send them back to, say, Plymouth Colony, they can't interfere with the lives of any of the real people, the historical people. We have to script the story so they interact with fictional characters but not real people...."

He would be listening to her, and nodding, and wondering if there was some way he could rearrange his life to remain in Boston after he finished business school. He would be watching her, her gaze animated, her smile contagious, her hands gesticulating for emphasis, and he would be trying to figure out a way to tear her from her life in the Hub of the Universe and bring her back to Lynwood with him when he returned home to help his father run the family firm. He would be drinking in her words, her ideas, her shimmering beauty, and wishing he had fewer scruples, because if he did, he would go ahead and make love to her and not care that he would be leaving her in a matter of weeks.

But he'd cared. He'd cared about leaving and he'd cared about Cassie. So he'd sat up late into the night with her, talking and wishing and wondering.

His mother led him through the kitchen to the solarium at the rear of the house. The glass walls framed assorted potted plants and seedlings; at the center of the octagonal room sat a breakfast table and chairs. Phillip instinctively slumped in a chair while his mother returned to the kitchen for a plate of cookies and two glasses of milk.

Ever since he was a boy, he and his mother would come to the solarium to share milk and cookies and conversation. Phillip loved his father, respected him, cherished his memories of the Little League teams his father had coached and the carpentry skills his father had taught him. But conversation was something he associated with Dorothy Keene. When he was young, they would sit at the table, sipping their milk and going over Phillip's homework. As a teenager, they would nibble on sandwich cookies, separating the wafers and eating the cream filling, while Phillip gropingly asked his mother about girls, what they admired most in guys, what it meant if Laurie DiLuca's friends all said she liked him but whenever he smiled at her she ignored him. Or he would ask her whether she thought he should stay in-state for college or apply to Ivy League schools.

His mother had always given him good advice. "If Laurie DiLuca is ignoring you, she probably likes you," Dorothy had told him. And, "I think you should apply to any college you'd like, and if you get accepted, good for you."

Maybe it was because of those long, heart-to-heart talks he used to have with his mother that he'd never had trouble talking to Cassie. Talking to a woman had always seemed perfectly natural to him.

His mother set a plate of oatmeal cookies and a glass of milk in front of him, then sat across the table with her own glass of milk. She smiled and nodded, an invitation for him to open the discussion.

What should he say? *I don't love Tricia. I don't want to marry her. I want to sacrifice you and Dad and this house and everything you stand for in this*

*town for the chance to find out if what I felt for Cassie
Webber a year ago is real.*

Uh-uh.

"I'm having second thoughts about Tricia," was as
much as he'd admit.

His mother sipped her milk and nodded. "Last-
minute panic attack, do you think?"

He shrugged, then shook his head. He pictured Tricia as he'd last seen her, standing in Beckelman's
shadow at the side of Bailey's, reaching up to kiss
him. "I'm thinking maybe she's having second
thoughts about me, too."

"Have you talked to her about it?"

"No." Tricia was one woman he hadn't figured out
how to talk to. "I just…I don't know. It's just not
coming together for me. Something doesn't feel
right."

His mother studied his face above the rim of her
glass. "Is it that you don't love her?" she guessed.

"I don't know. I mean, I don't know if that's what's
bugging me. I just…" He sighed at his own inartic-
ulateness. "I don't know."

His mother smiled. "Well, it's always been one of
those relationships," she said cryptically. "In theory,
it seemed neat and sweet, but it was never what you'd
call a passionate love match." She thought about what
she'd said, then added, "Tricia's a lovely girl, you
know."

"She's a girl," he agreed. "Maybe she's too…I
don't know, unsophisticated."

"This is Lynwood," his mother reminded him.
"Who around here is sophisticated? Other than you, I
suppose. And your friends from Boston."

He didn't think he'd reacted to her words, but he

must have. He noticed his mother shift slightly in her chair and look at him more intently. "It's Diane's friend, isn't it," she said. "It's Cassie."

Unsure what to say, he kept quiet.

"Did you have an affair with her in Boston?"

His mother was too damned shrewd. "It wasn't an affair, Mom. I thought...I thought it might have been the real thing."

"And now she's here, and you're filled with doubts about Tricia." Dorothy sighed. "It's my fault for inviting Diane to Lynwood for the wedding. I thought that would be such a nice surprise for you. I'd been so fond of her that day we spent together in Boston. We exchanged Christmas cards and all." His mother looked sheepish. "I invited her to bring a guest so she wouldn't have to travel all this way alone. I guess she picked the wrong guest to bring."

"What do you think I should do?" Phillip asked, feeling helpless and foolish. There he was, approaching his thirtieth birthday, trying to stave off financial disaster at his father's company, juggling loans and accounts to keep the firm from going under, and he couldn't even manage his own love life without assistance from his mother. What kind of an idiot was he?

She reached across the table and patted his hand. "What you should do, Phil, is trust your instincts."

"My instincts tell me to sell the Chicago outlet," he said, retreating to an area where he felt competent.

"Then do it."

"I'll have to clear it with Dad..."

"Trust your instincts, Phil. In business and in love. You haven't made too many mistakes in your life. There's no need to start making mistakes now."

Wise advice—yet in a way, totally useless. He

didn't know which would be the worse mistake: breaking up with Tricia two days before the wedding and dooming his father's company, or marrying her and spending the rest of his life wondering whether Cassie might have been his one true love.

A year ago he'd been sure she was. This past week, having her back in his life, he'd felt disconcerted. Excited. Occasionally crazed. But more alive than he'd felt since the day he'd left Boston.

"I'll sell Chicago," he said, resolved. When it came to business, he was competent. The decision felt right as soon as he put it into words. The retail outlet needed to go before it dragged the entire Keene enterprise under.

One problem down, one to go. Unfortunately the problem he still had to deal with—the problem eating like acid in his heart—wasn't so easy to solve. He couldn't trust his instincts until his instincts sent him a clear signal, and right now, they were as clear as indelible ink. And whatever decision he made would be just as permanent.

He turned to stare out at the night-black backyard beyond windowpane. All he saw was his own ghostly reflection in the glass.

CHAPTER ELEVEN

"YOU'RE NOT SELLING Chicago," Harry Riggs declared.

Phillip gave him a long hard stare. Who the hell was Harry to be standing in his office, telling him how to run Keene Furniture? Besides being Keene Furniture's biggest creditor, of course.

"It's not open for discussion," Phillip said, exerting himself to remain calm. If Harry hadn't pushed past Edie's desk and barged into the office uninvited, Phillip would have told Edie to send him away. He had a lot to do today, a lot to think about. And the first thing to do, the easiest thing to think about, was divesting Keene Furniture of the most critical drain on its capital—the retail store in Chicago.

As soon as he'd arrived at his office that morning, Phillip had informed his father of his decision. His father hadn't been pleased. Phillip had broken the news gently, explaining how he'd reached his conclusion, reviewing the spreadsheets with his father and relating his recent futile conversations with the manager up in Chicago, who refused to implement any of the reforms or remedies Phillip had requested. James Keene had seemed terribly sad about the whole situation. Phillip tried to persuade his father not to feel as if the expansion he'd instituted had failed. It hadn't. Just this one aspect of it had, at this time. Perhaps they would be able to reopen in Chicago in a few years, once the company's debt was under control.

His father must have telephoned Harry as soon as Phillip had left his father's office for his own. Phillip couldn't blame his father for wanting to share bad news with an old friend, but he would have preferred if his father hadn't shared bad news with a creditor. But James had spilled the beans to Harry, and now Harry was standing in Phillip's office, looming above him only because Phillip hadn't bothered to rise from his chair.

"This isn't your concern," he said, gazing up into Harry's florid face.

"It sure as hell *is* my concern. First of all, if Keene Furniture is in worse shape than I've been led to believe—"

"You know exactly what shape it's in. Selling the Chicago store is going to improve its shape. It's going to reduce the cash outflow. We can sell off some of the inventory, ship some to the other outlets and minimize our losses. We should have done it months ago."

He studied the man who was two days away from becoming his father-in-law. Why wasn't Harry thrilled that Phillip was taking steps to improve the company's financial condition? He ought to be slapping Phillip on the back and saying, "Good for you. That was a tough decision, but you had the balls to make it. Maybe you'll be able to start reducing that debt of yours."

Instead, Harry's face was flushed with anger and twisted into a scowl. He'd traveled all the way here just to argue with Phillip over an eminently sound business decision. It didn't make sense.

"I don't see what the problem is," Phillip finally said.

"You're getting married on Saturday. Why would you want to make such an enormous decision so close to your wedding day?"

"I should have made the decision in January," Phillip answered. "But having made it, I feel good about it. What does it have to do with the wedding?"

"I don't want you dealing with this on your honeymoon." Harry paced to the window and back to Phillip's desk. "What are you going to do—dump Tricia on the beach and go back to your hotel suite to wheel and deal over the phone?"

"There isn't going to be any wheeling and dealing. I have financial people who can oversee the sale. And it's not as if the shutdown has to occur next week. I'm just going to put things in motion, that's all."

"I think it's a terrible decision," Harry argued. "I think you'd be foolish to divest at this time. I think maybe that Harvard education you got inflated your ego, and—"

"Harry, it's not your business," Phillip said quietly.

Harry stopped pacing and glowered at him. Phillip's words hung in the air, unrefuted, undisputed, and yet... Did Harry want it to be his business? Was that what this was about? Making Keene Furniture his business?

Why else would he be so appalled by a decision that would stabilize the company and bolster its bottom line? He *wanted* Keene Furniture to collapse. He *wanted* to seize the company in lieu of repayment. He wanted to own Keene Furniture. He could become more tightly bound to the company by having his daughter marry Phillip, or he could force Phillip's fa-

ther to hand over the keys to the place, once everyone
had agreed that Keene Furniture would never be able
to pay off all the loans Harry had extended. Harry had
to have known he was lending more than Keene Furniture could ever hope to repay on the schedule he and
Phillip's father had agreed to.

The loans had come due on January 1 of the year
2000. The new century had started six months ago,
and Keene Furniture had barely made a dent in its
debt.

The reality struck Phillip with the force of a blow
to the gut: Harry had known all along that Keene Furniture would never be able to pay him back on time.
He was too clever not to have known. He'd planned
it that way, planned to have Keene Furniture default
on its loans so he could take over the place.

To guarantee that Keene Furniture would fall into
his control, he'd brought his daughter together with
James Keene's son—just to dress up the deal, make it
look pretty and as insurance in case a miracle befell
the company and it could pay back the loans on time.
If Harry couldn't usurp the business through a bankruptcy proceeding, he'd edge into it through the marriage of his daughter. Once she became a Keene, he
would have plenty of opportunities to meddle in the
family firm.

"I don't think we have anything more to discuss,"
Phillip said, his anger at a boil but his voice as cold
as dry ice.

Harry must have sensed his dawning comprehension. His expression softened and he planted his hands
on Phillip's desk and leaned over, addressing Phillip
with paternal sympathy. "Don't do anything rash,
Phil. This is much too big a step for you to take with

all the distractions of the wedding crowding your mind. Get married, go on your honeymoon, and we'll discuss the situation in Chicago when you get back.''

"*We* won't discuss it at all,'' Phillip said, his voice chilling to absolute zero. "It's already been decided. Please excuse me now, Harry. I've got a lot of work to do.''

Harry took a deep breath, let it out and straightened. "I'll be talking to your father.''

"If you want.'' Phillip acted as if it was no concern of his. But his heart was thumping in his chest as he swiveled away from Harry and brought up a file on his computer with a tap of the keys. Staring blankly at the monitor, he listened to Harry's footsteps retreating toward the door, then to the click as it opened and the click as it closed. He let out his breath, slowly, with admirable composure—and then slammed his fist on his desk, quickly and with an utter lack of composure. He lifted his phone, punched in his father's extension and said, "Don't you dare talk to Harry.''

"Why? What's going on, Phil?''

"I'm not sure. But he's going to call you,'' Phillip warned. "He's going to tell you I'm a hothead, going off half-cocked. Or maybe he'll tell you they filled my brain with nonsense at Harvard. I don't know—he'll tell you something that implies he thinks I'm an imbecile and you need to convince me not to sell the store in Chicago.''

"Well, I can't say that I'd disagree with him if he—''

"I don't give a damn if you agree or disagree. Just don't say anything to him. He isn't family—not yet. He doesn't deserve any input into this.'' Phillip gave his father a millisecond to respond, then plowed ahead.

"I'm going to be out of the office today. Do your best to put Harry off, Dad, please. I'm doing what I think is best—what I *know* is best, for you and me and the company. Okay?"

His father said nothing for a long moment. Then, "I love you, Phil, and I don't think you're a hotheaded imbecile. But I wish to hell you'd let me know what you're up to."

"I'm up to saving Keene Furniture," Phillip said, hoping he was indeed up to that daunting task. He still wasn't sure how he was going to save it or why Harry wanted to take over the place. All he knew was that his mother had told him to trust his instincts. Right now, his instincts were all he had.

His instincts, and Cassie Webber.

THE STAINING of the wood was executed in a well-ventilated building separate from the main building. Roger had filmed as the foreman explained the process, the machines used, the light buffing applied to the wood between coats, the polyurethane layered on as a protective finish. Even though she had been given a disposable mask to wear over her nose and mouth, Cassie had developed a headache from the faint stench of acetone that laced the air in defiance of all the elaborate exhaust fans.

Roger and Diane insisted the smell didn't bother them. They wandered through the workroom, their faces half-hidden behind pale-blue masks like surgeons in a prime-time TV drama.

"I'm going outside for a breath of fresh air," Cassie told Diane when her headache threatened to sprout runners and overgrow her skull. Two hours in the

staining room, and the smell had so thoroughly soaked
into her she could practically taste it.

"Sure, go ahead." Diane's voice sounded cottony,
muffled by her mask.

"Do we have much more to film here?" Cassie
asked.

Diane glanced at the clipboard. "Final touch-ups.
They use a special brush dipped in varnish. Go on,
Cassie. Go outside and inhale. You look like I'm go-
ing to feel after I've smoked that cigar with Harry."

Plan E, Cassie recalled, glad Diane couldn't see her
mouth curving downward in a reflexive scowl. She
hadn't yet shaken her memory of Harry's rage, the
threatening growl she'd overheard through the wall of
the second-floor ladies' room as he'd quarreled with
Phillip. Diane seemed to have charmed the old man,
but Cassie sensed that he was as charming as a cobra—polite when it suited his purposes, but always
prepared to spring and sink his venomous fangs into
an adversary.

Still, she supposed, if anyone could soften him up,
Diane could. And Cassie's role in Plan E—visiting
Dorothy Keene and pumping her for information about
Phillip's relationship with Tricia—might turn out to
be just as treacherous as a rendezvous with a snake.
Dorothy Keene didn't strike Cassie as venomous, but
she was nobody's fool. She might choose not to tell
Cassie the whole truth. And if she *did* tell Cassie the
whole truth, it might prove more painful than a cobra
bite.

Outside in the warm humid air, she slid her face
mask down around her neck and inhaled deeply. A
drizzle misted the atmosphere, and the sky was dense
with gray clouds. She ought to pay attention to the

regional weather forecasts. Maybe heavy rains were
predicted for Saturday, and the lovely garden wedding
at the country club would be a washout.

She sucked in another refreshing lungful of air and
surveyed the parking lot from her position on the concrete step outside the door of the building. She noticed
only a couple of empty spaces in the lot; despite the
company's alleged cash-flow problems, Keene Furniture seemed to be operating at full capacity.

She heard the sound of a car engine off to her left.
Turning, she saw a Mercedes round the row of cars
and cruise slowly toward her. Its polished cream-
colored roof and hood were beaded with raindrops,
and its long single wiper swept across the windshield
intermittently. Every time it did, she glimpsed Phillip
through the cleared semicircle of glass.

She no longer knew what to think when she saw
him, what to feel. Anger? Resentment? Bitterness? Or
pity and concern? She was still tuned in to his station,
hearing his broadcast, too conscious of him. She was
still responding to his signal, wanting to nod at his
words, wanting to dance to his music.

He rolled to a stop in front of her and pressed a
button on his armrest. The passenger-side window slid
down.

"Get in," he said, angling his head so he could see
her through the open window.

"I'm not—I mean, I just came out to clear the paint
smell from my head. The drizzle isn't bothering me."

His smile was unreadable. His eyes were opaque. It
didn't matter that she was on his frequency; she
couldn't decipher his signal. "Get in anyway," he
said. His words sounded like a command, but his tone
was friendly.

She wanted to get in—and she knew she shouldn't. "I've got to go back inside," she said, gesturing toward the building behind her. "We're still filming."

"They can film without you." He smiled winsomely, beseeching her without words. "Come on. Get in."

He was asking her for something other than simply to take shelter from the rain. He wanted her in his car for some specific purpose, and she couldn't begin to guess what it was. Somehow she understood that her decision—to join him in his car or remain outside, getting wet—carried enormous implications. But she had no idea what those implications were.

His gaze implored her. His posture, his expression, his mussed hair, the hand that had stroked her cheek last night and now rested on the passenger seat as he leaned over and peered through the open window at her—everything in his position, everything in his expression, told her that he desperately needed her to get into his car. That alone was a reason not to get in.

But this was Phillip. The man who had told her last night that he loved Tricia. The man who had lied to her a year ago—or else lied to her last night.

How dangerous could it be to sit in a car next to him for a minute before returning to the smells of the staining workshop? Less dangerous than smoking a cigar with Harry Riggs. Probably less dangerous than interrogating Phillip's mother, too.

Cassie got in.

"Buckle your seat belt," he said, already steering away from the building.

"Phil!" She watched helplessly as the building rapidly receded behind her. "Where are we going?"

"Buckle up. I don't want to get a ticket for driving with an unbelted passenger."

Panic welled up inside her—and then subsided. This was Phillip. A traitor, yes. A liar, definitely. But not a kidnapper. Not a violent man. She'd been the one goaded by his betrayal to violent thoughts of bombs and arson. He wouldn't hurt her.

On the other hand, he'd been quite clear about wanting her out of town. That first evening in Lynwood, when he'd driven her away from Bailey's, the thought had occurred to her that he might be planning to slay her and dump her body in the woods.

But he'd been obviously angry at her then. He didn't seem angry now, at least not at her. He seemed resolute, his mouth set, his jaw steely, his gaze fixed on the wet asphalt in front of him. He exuded determination.

As he put more and more distance between her and her colleagues, she tried to muster at least a modicum of concern. "Where are we going?" she asked again.

He didn't answer.

"That bluff? High Point? I'm not going to make out with you, Phil, so turn the car around and—"

"Chicago," he said.

Her panic returned, full force. "Chicago?" She thought she was screaming, but her voice came out choked with alarm. "What are you talking about?"

"We're going to Chicago."

"Like hell we are! Are you insane?" Fear gradually left her, replaced by healthy anger. "Come on, Phil. This is a joke, right?"

"No joke." He accelerated as they reached the town limits. The road opened into an empty county highway flanked by orchards and farm acreage. No traffic impeded him as he floored the gas pedal; the car's powerful engine hummed as the speedometer needle moved past sixty.

"Phillip." She stared at his profile, searching for signs of dementia. His resolve seemed to thaw the slightest bit; she detected a glint of light in his eyes, a nearly imperceptible softening at the corners of his mouth. But he wasn't offering any explanations, and it occurred to her that "kidnapping" might come awfully close to describing what he was up to. "You aren't serious, are you?"

He flashed her a quick smile. "Oh, I'm serious, all right."

"We'll be driving all day and—"

"We'll be driving less than an hour, to the airport in Columbus. From there it's about ninety minutes by plane. We'll be in Chicago in time for a late lunch."

"You're crazy." She slouched in her seat, stacking her thoughts and knocking them down, then restacking them like a toddler trying to erect a coherent structure out of blocks. Yesterday she'd seen the spreadsheet on his desk, its numbers delineating the river of red ink that flowed from Keene Furniture's store in Chicago. Apparently he needed to go to the store for some reason. To dam the river? To fire people?

Fine. That was his job. Her job was to oversee the filming of a chair's final stages of construction for a *Dream Wheels* broadcast. She had no reason to go to Chicago. Why was he dragging her along? Had he caught wind of her plan? Was he trying to keep her from visiting his mother?

That made no sense. "You really *are* crazy," she concluded, her voice escaping her on a sigh. "Why do you want me with you?"

"I *need* you with me," he said simply. Within the artlessness of his words lay a deep truth. She eyed him thoughtfully. His face was impassive, revealing nothing.

"Why?" she asked.

"I'm selling the store in Chicago."

"Now?"

"I'm going to start things moving. I've got to tell my manager up there to his face. I can't do it over the phone. He knows I'm coming. When I get there, I'll tell him why."

"Okay." Scrutinizing Phillip wasn't telling her anything, so she turned from him to study her knees. Her panty hose had dark spots on them where raindrops had soaked into the mesh. She was wearing another of her new outfits from the mall, purchased back when Plan B or C—whichever plan entailed her playing the sultry siren and reducing Phillip to a defenseless mass of slobbering hormones—was still operational. This skirt wasn't as short as yesterday's, but it had buttons running along the entire left seam, and it was snug enough that the lowest three buttons had to remain unfastened to give her room to walk. Her silk shell blouse was a little more modest than the scoop-necked top she'd had on yesterday. But she'd left her jacket in the vestibule of the staining workshop. It was pure luck that she'd had her purse slung over her shoulder when she'd stepped outside, or she would have left that behind, too. She had never been to Chicago, but she didn't think it was a good place to be without a purse.

"So—" she struggled to keep her voice level "—we're going to fly to Chicago, have a late lunch, you're going to lower the boom on your employees there and then we're going to fly home?''

"That's right.''

"In time for you to get married?'' His schedule didn't matter to her; she'd mentioned it only to remind him that he was supposed to be gearing up for his wedding to Tricia.

"I'll worry about my marriage later.''

"I'm worrying about your marriage now. Why would you take me to Chicago, instead of Tricia? If this is such a big deal you can't handle it alone, why not take her? Or... What's her name? Your secretary. Edie.''

"Edie's more valuable to me in Lynwood, keeping things running smoothly at Keene Furniture and re-assuring my father. He's not exactly thrilled about this. Expanding into Chicago was his idea, and he's griev-ing over how it's all turned out. Maybe we'll reopen in Chicago sometime down the road, but not now, when we can't manage the debt.''

Why was he telling her his rationales? More accu-rately, why was he telling *her,* instead of Tricia? "I'm still not sure what I'm doing here. Unlike you, I haven't got someone like Edie to keep things running back in Lynwood.''

"Sure you do. Diane can oversee the taping. I told you right at the start that this wasn't a good time for you to film an episode for your show at Keene Fur-niture, but you went ahead anyway.'' He shrugged as if to say, *Don't blame me.* "Between Diane and Big Blond Beckelman—to say nothing of all those eager Keene employees who'd jump through hoops of fire just to be a part of your show—you don't have to worry about your project.''

Big Blond Beckelman? Phillip didn't resort to sarcasm casually. Roger must irk him. Cassie grabbed a few more blocks and added them to her teetering tower: did Phillip know that Roger and Tricia had spent yesterday evening together? Did he know that Tricia might be inappropriately attracted to Roger? Did he know she'd kissed Roger's cheek last night?

Cassie ought to spend less time worrying about Tricia and Roger and more time worrying about herself. Despite everything Phillip was telling her, both with his words and his tone, she was still at a loss as to why he'd lured her into his car and was now speeding with her through the rolling farmland that stretched between Lynwood and the airport in Columbus.

"Why me?" she asked. "Why am I here?"

"I trust you."

Nothing between her and Phillip could be that simple. "I don't trust you," she countered.

"I know."

The wiper continued its intermittent sweep across the windshield, clearing away the mist that accumulated on the glass. She wished her view of her situation with Phillip could be cleared with a wipe, too. "You know I don't trust you? Then why did you spirit me away?"

"Closing the Chicago store is going to be hard," he explained, his words coming slowly, almost haltingly. "I'm going against my father's wishes. I'm reversing the big expansion he put in motion. It's like trying to turn an aircraft carrier on a dime. It's hard." He even slowed his driving, as if to concentrate better on what he was saying. "I think Harry's trying to take over the company," he told her. "I think he wants us to drown in debt so he can take over Keene Furniture.''

"Harry? Harry Riggs?'' Cassie gaped at Phillip. ''Your future father-in-law?''

Phillip nodded. ''My future father-in-law and my father's oldest friend. The company's in debt to him, and if we don't pay back the loans in a timely manner, he can take over the company. Keene Furniture is collateral for the loans. The only reason I can think of that Harry wouldn't want me to do something that would reduce our debt is he wants us destroyed by that debt.'' He considered what he'd said, then nodded, apparently convinced he'd guessed right. ''If that's Harry's true motive—to wrest ownership of Keene Furniture from my family—it's going to break my father's heart. Maybe even more than losing the company would break it.''

Cassie suffered a pang of conscience. She'd liked the idea of destroying Keene Furniture as a way of breaking Phillip's heart. But not his father's. Phillip's was the only heart she wanted to break.

''Why would Harry Riggs want to own your company?'' she asked.

''I don't know. He was the chairman of the only bank in town until it got bought out by one of those regional banking conglomerates. He made a fortune on that deal, and he's parlayed that fortune into several more fortunes as a financier. But he's a very... controlling person.'' Phillip seemed to select each word with care. ''When he ran the bank, he controlled most of the town's commerce. Now he's rolling in dough, but he's no longer an essential part of the town. I'm just theorizing, but...I mean, it makes sense, doesn't it? Keene Furniture is the town's biggest employer, its biggest industry. It's the town's economic anchor. I'm figuring Harry wants it because he has nothing else. Except money.'' He shrugged. ''What do you think?''

Cassie mulled over his hypothesis and nodded. ''I don't know Harry as well as you do,'' she admitted. ''But as a psychological theory, it sounds plausible.''

''The fact is, Harry has one of the best financial minds around. He's very cautious about high-risk ventures. He understands the nature of risk. He knows that if you're lending money to a company that's in trouble, you don't expect an immediate return. You're investing for the long haul. But there he was, urging my father to sign for more loans than Harry could possibly think my father would be able to pay back, and setting up unrealistic repayment schedules. Why would he do something so illogical from a business standpoint?''

''Friendship?'' Cassie suggested.

''If he was a straight-shooter, if he was totally scrupulous...if I had that much faith in him, I'd agree with you. But if he'd given my father the loans out of friendship, he wouldn't be tightening the screws on us now, issuing veiled threats about how the loans are overdue. Friends don't do that to each other. Business rivals do.''

It occurred to Cassie that she and Phillip were talking the way they used to talk a year ago. He was thinking aloud, and she was weighing and measuring his ideas, challenging them so he could justify and fine-tune them. She used to love debating with him about business as much as she'd loved debating with him about movies or *Dream Wheels* or the quality of the pizza they were devouring.

They'd fallen in love through their debates, through the rhythm and lilt of their words, through their ideas.

She didn't want to think about how much she'd once loved Phillip. "How do you think Tricia's going to feel if you tell her you think her father is trying to steal your business out from under you?" she asked, mostly because mentioning Tricia seemed like a good way to protect herself from notions of love.

"Who says I'm going to tell her?"

"She'll be your wife. You aren't going to keep secrets from her, are you?"

He pretended to be too busy navigating the ramps onto the highway to respond to her question. Did his silence imply that he intended to keep secrets from his wife? Being able to discuss anything, whether it was business or family or financial pressures—or the state of one's mind and heart—was essential to a good marriage, she believed.

She waited until he'd merged with the flow of highway traffic before goading him. "Phil? How are you going to deal with Tricia if you think her father is trying to stab your father in the back?"

"I don't want to talk about Tricia," he muttered.

"She's a part of this."

"Not at the moment, she's not." He accelerated again, veering aggressively into the left lane to pass a few cars.

Cassie sighed. He could choose to be obstinate, but the reality was, he was traveling to Chicago to stave off a disaster his future father-in-law might have been wishing for. And he was bringing Cassie with him—as an adviser, as a hostage, as a friend.

"As soon as we get to the airport," she said, "I've got to call Diane and Roger and let them know where

I am. They thought I was just stepping outside for some fresh air.''

Phillip opened a storage compartment in the console between their seats and pulled out a cell phone. ''Call them now.''

She took the phone. ''I would guess they're still at Keene. What's the number?''

''It's programmed in. Auto-dial one. That'll connect you to Edie. She can get a message to them.''

Cassie nodded and pressed the buttons. After two rings, Phillip's secretary answered, and Cassie puzzled over what to say. ''Could you please tell Diane and Roger that I—I won't be able to...'' She eyed Phillip's profile, his chiseled features, his flinty, determined gaze. In her mind his voice echoed: *I trust you.*

She'd said she didn't trust him, but if she really didn't, she would have insisted that he turn the car around and take her back to Lynwood. Or she would have pressed the police emergency number on his cell phone the instant he'd handed it to her. So maybe she trusted him, just a little. Just enough to enable her to accompany him to Chicago and pretend they were still confidantes.

''Just tell Diane and Roger that something's come up,'' she said into the phone, ''and I won't be around this afternoon, but they should finish up the taping without me.''

''I'll tell them.''

Cassie imagined they didn't have much more taping to do. She wondered how they would spend the afternoon. Would Roger be waylaid by Tricia again? If he was, that would be Phillip's problem, not hers.

Her problem was Diane. ''Could you also please tell Diane...'' She glanced toward Phillip and chose a discreetly ambiguous phrasing. "Tell her to proceed with caution this afternoon."

"Proceed with caution," Edie repeated. "Will she understand what that means?"

Probably not. "Tell her," Cassie elaborated, "to be very careful if she goes with Plan E."

"Plan E?" Cassie pictured Edie writing the message down, then trying to figure out what it meant.

"She'll know what I'm talking about," Cassie said with more confidence than she felt. "Thanks." She disconnected the phone before Edie could question her further.

"Plan E?" Phillip questioned her, instead.

"It has to do with *Dream Wheels*," Cassie fibbed. She tucked the portable phone back into the console compartment and closed her eyes, attempting to conjure a vision of Diane enjoying a cigar with Harry Riggs. Imagining Diane enjoying a cigar at all was next to impossible. But with Harry? That bluff gruff man who wanted Phillip's company to go under?

Diane was smart and tough. When it came to being scheming, she could hold her own. But what if Harry outfinessed her? What if he finagled information from her about Cassie's defunct relationship with Phillip? How might Harry use that information?

As smart and tough as Diane was, she tended not to exercise caution on a regular basis. She'd fallen for Bobby, the best-looking loser east of the Mississippi River. And she'd adopted Howser, the meanest, mangiest cat west of the Atlantic Ocean. How was she going to fend off Harry Riggs, who possessed more charm than Bobby and Howser combined?

Again Cassie turned in her seat to study Phillip. She'd loved his rugged profile a year ago. She'd loved analyzing business issues with him. She'd loved the smell of him, soap and spice, and the husky edge of his voice, and the graceful masculinity of his hands, his legs, his shoulders. His mouth. His mind.

She'd loved the way he trusted her.

Twenty minutes ago, she had thought he was crazy, absconding with her to Chicago. But now she was thinking maybe *she* was the crazy one, for sitting so calmly in his car, letting him abscond with her while she contemplated the many things she'd once loved about him, all of two days before he was going to marry someone else.

CHAPTER TWELVE

HE WASN'T SURE what he wanted from Cassie.

Like hell. He knew exactly what he wanted from her. Besides all the obvious things, like her mouth crushed to his and her arms and legs wrapped around him and her body hot and tight…. But for the moment, as the plane touched down in Chicago, what he wanted from her was her support. Her wisdom. Her astute mind, her conscience, her empathy. What he had to do was going to be painful for everyone involved, and he wanted her beside him to reassure him that he'd made the right decision.

She'd been quiet during the flight, thumbing through a magazine, handing him her little foil bag of honey-roasted peanuts and sipping on a club soda. But he knew her well enough to recognize that, despite her placid demeanor, her internal engine was running at maximum speed.

She was thinking. Trying to figure out what was going on. Just like him.

Maybe he shouldn't have brought her along. If he hadn't, he would have used his time to rehearse what he was going to say to the folks at the Chicago store. Instead, he'd spent the length of the flight thinking about Cassie's thick dark hair, her pale graceful neck, the swell of her bosom. He'd thought about his wedding, two days from now, to a pleasant young woman who had never done anything to bother him. He hadn't even been particularly upset to see her kiss Beckelman's cheek. People kissed each other's cheeks all the time—especially show-business people. Diane had kissed Phillip's cheek on more than one occasion, and it hadn't meant anything. Cassie...

Cassie only had to flicker an eyelash at him and it meant everything in the world.

He couldn't marry Tricia. He knew that now.

It had nothing to do with her father's duplicity. Harry's slimy tactics weren't Tricia's fault. But Phillip didn't love her. Nor did he feel any sort of passion for her. Whether or not he loved Cassie, her mere presence reminded him of what love and passion could be like. He'd known those joys with her once, and he wasn't going to consign himself to a future without them.

After he ended things with the Chicago store, he would end things with Tricia. Chicago would be good practice for him.

"Phil?" Cassie asked once they were off the plane, caught up in the swarm of passengers surging through the terminal to the escalator that led to ground transportation. "What exactly am I supposed to do while you're chopping off heads?"

He smiled crookedly. "Do you think it's going to be a bloodbath?"

"I think you think it is," she answered. "These things happen all the time, Phil. Stores close. People lose their jobs. Sometimes you have to amputate a diseased limb to save the patient. It stinks, but it has to be done."

"Amputations. Decapitations. You're really cheering me up."

"And you're avoiding my question. What am I supposed to do while you perform surgery? Mop up the blood?"

"I don't know." He gestured toward the revolving door, letting her exit the building ahead of him. Once they were outside, he caught a whiff of rain, refreshing after the processed air of the terminal. "If you want, I can drop you off at a museum, or a movie theater if there's a film you'd like to see." He ushered her toward the taxi stand, where a row of yellow cabs stood waiting for fares.

"I didn't come all this way to go to a museum or a movie," she said, making him wonder why she *had* come all this way—other than because he'd strong-armed her. He hadn't given her much of a chance to refuse.

She'd gotten into his car, though. As far as he was concerned, that had been a yes. And he hadn't heard much in the way of no after that. If she'd given him any real indication that she wanted out, he would have turned the car around and driven her back to Lynwood.

"You're welcome to come to the store with me if you want. I don't think it's going to be bloody enough to require a mop. But it won't be barrel of laughs, either."

"For them? Or for you?"

"It'll be tragic for them. It'll only be lousy for me." He sighed, feeling the weight of his mission pressing on his soul. "I already feel guilty because my father's so bummed out about the whole thing. Added to that, I'm going to have a bunch of unemployed folks on my hands." He helped her into a cab and she scooted across the seat to make room for him. He recited the address for the driver, then gave her what he knew was a miserable excuse for a smile. He wasn't happy about any of this. The only thing that kept it from being even ghastlier was that Cassie was with him; her mere presence gave him courage and fortitude.

"Maybe you could arrange for the employees to work with a relocation counselor," she suggested. "That might make the job loss easier for them."

"I thought about that." Behind her the window was gray, streaked with raindrops. Her face seemed clearer to him in contrast, her features precise, not pretty so much as riveting. He recalled the first time he'd seen her. She was just as beautiful now. Just as enticing.

He remembered that they were supposed to be discussing the fate of his soon-to-be-displaced Chicago employees. "The low-end people don't need relocation counseling. They're a sales staff. They need sales jobs. I'll get them hooked up with an employment agency." He stared out the window for a moment, trying to gauge how hard it was raining. He was wearing a business suit, but Cassie didn't have a coat. Fortunately he'd stashed a folding umbrella in his briefcase. The idea of huddling with her under its protective arch held a definite appeal.

"What about the upper-level people?"

"They're the ones who screwed up. I've been in communication with them constantly since last summer, giving them guidance, explaining what they had to do to get the store back on track. They ignored me. They went to my father behind my back—God knows, maybe they went to Harry, too. I wonder..." Cripes, was he becoming paranoid? Or was it actually possible that Harry had orchestrated the collapse of the store?

Cassie read his mind. That was one of the things he liked best about her: he and she always seemed to be

on the same page. He didn't have to explain everything to her the way he did with Tricia, who rarely
understood his explanations anyway.

"Would you be paying back your loans to Harry on
time if it weren't for this one outlet?" she asked.

"Some of them. Not all. Of course, if the Chicago
store hadn't been opened, Keene Furniture wouldn't
have needed to borrow so much in the first place. So
there's a definite relationship between the two."

"You're nervous, aren't you."

He laughed. Then he gazed into her eyes, and his
laughter waned. He realized that as long as he could
look at her, as long as he could talk to her, listen to
her, rely on her, he wouldn't hear drums banging inside his head. As long as she was with him, he
wouldn't feel nervous, either, no matter how difficult
the task he faced.

"I lied," he said.

Her eyes widened slightly, and she lifted her chin.
It was a magnificent chin, he acknowledged. Sleek and
pointy. She could aim it like a dagger.

"Yesterday," he elaborated.

"Oh?"

"When I said I loved Tricia."

"Oh."

Her mouth shaped a perfect circle. He wanted to
touch his lips to that circle, to taste the perfection of
it. But he didn't dare. "I'm fond of her. She's a good
person. But I don't love her." He wanted to grab Cassie's hands, too. They lay soft and pale against the
dark fabric of her skirt. He wanted just to hold them,
to draw strength from them.

But even without touching Cassie he felt her
strength infuse him. He was going to get through his

meeting with the Chicago staff. He was even going to get through his next conversation with Tricia—the one in which he told her he couldn't marry her. He would survive every ordeal, as long as he carried Cassie's strength inside him.

"You're dealing with a lot right now," she said. "Don't make things more complicated than they have to be."

He smiled, this time a genuine smile. "Okay." He turned to face forward, watching the city thicken around them and imagining he was holding Cassie's hand.

CASSIE WANDERED aimlessly through the Keene Furniture retail outlet while Phillip met with the manager in a back office. The store seemed to be in a convenient location—three other furniture stores shared the block. The quality of the pieces on display was unquestionably high. But the showroom felt cramped and cluttered, chairs stacked upon other chairs, tables so close together a browser could bruise herself trying to move around. The prices seemed steep, too—but then, given that Cassie was only beginning to earn enough money to consider buying new furniture for her efficiency apartment, all furniture prices seemed steep to her.

Someday she wouldn't mind furnishing her home with beautifully crafted pieces of the sort Keene Furniture made. The days she'd spent filming at the factory had given her some idea of why a simple side chair was priced as high as two hundred dollars. Wood was expensive, labor even more expensive.

Outside, rain fell from a low dreary sky. She

checked her watch. Phillip had been in the office for nearly three hours.

She should have been bored. She should have been hungry. But she wasn't. Not in the least. She felt as if she'd slipped through a time warp into another universe. Lynwood seemed unreal to her. Had she actually begun her day with one of Mrs. Gill's leaden bran muffins and a bowl of fruit cocktail that had been marinating long enough for everything—the grapes, the melon, the chunks of apple—to taste like grapefruit? Had she finished breakfast and headed out to the factory with Diane next to her in the rental car's front seat, speaking cryptically but knowingly about the fact that they would have lots of time that afternoon to "take care of business," while Roger had sat oblivious and serene in the back seat? Had Cassie bitten her lip to keep from asking him how his evening with Tricia at the cable studio had gone?

That all seemed like another lifetime. Now she was in the Windy City—at the moment it was the windy, rainy city—with Phillip, who trusted her and told her he didn't love Tricia. Just thinking about it made her feel jet-lagged.

She pressed her forehead against the cool glass of a store window. What was she going to do?

Wait for Phillip, that was what. Wait until he emerged from the office. Then they would go outside in the rain, flag down a cab and travel back to the airport, back to Lynwood. He would figure out what he wanted to do about Tricia, and Cassie would go home to Boston. She shouldn't assume that his revelation about his feelings for Tricia had anything to do with her. It had everything to do with Tricia's father and his own, about the family firm and his family's future. She would be wise to remember that and to keep her emotional distance.

"I promised I'd feed you," he murmured.

She straightened and spun around to find him standing right behind her. He appeared fatigued, his tie loosened and his hair tousled as if he'd been raking his fingers through it. She could see the faintest hint of a five o'clock shadow along his jawline, even though it was only four.

"Are you all right?" she asked, not bothering to put any distance between them, emotional or otherwise.

"I've had happier afternoons in my life. Let's get something to eat." He smiled wearily. "Maybe something to drink, too."

She returned his smile. It took enormous self-control not to extend her arms to him, to give this wounded warrior a hug as he limped off the battlefield. "Okay," she said.

They stepped outside the store and he produced an umbrella from his briefcase. They had to stand close under it, and when he put his arm around her she told herself it was to keep her dry and maybe to lean on her. It wasn't an embrace.

Distance, she reminded herself, although there wasn't even the width of the umbrella's metal shaft between them.

They hurried down the street, sidestepping puddles, keeping away from the curb so they wouldn't get splashed by passing cars. At the corner Phillip spotted a cab and waved it over. They got in and he named a restaurant. The driver turned on his meter and cruised down the rain-slick street.

"I don't know too many restaurants in Chicago,"

Phillip told her. "But I've stayed at the hotel where this place is located when I've been in town on business, and the food was great."

Cassie nodded. She didn't care where they ate. What she cared about was not allowing herself to be anything more than his companion, someone who listened as he vented, someone who offered advice when he asked for it. She shouldn't even want to listen and advise, but as long as she remembered that he had asked another woman to marry him—a woman about whom he was belatedly having second thoughts—she'd be all right.

The cab drove under the hotel's awning to let them out. Cassie stood out of the rain, watching it spill in rippling sheets from edges of the overhang. The air was damp and chilly on her legs, and she hugged her arms around herself for warmth while Phillip paid the fare. As soon as he was out of the cab they dashed inside.

It was early for dinner, but the maître d' assured them that they could be seated and served. He led them into an elegant dining room, all linen and crystal and subtle lighting. Back in Boston, the fanciest restaurant she'd ever patronized with Phillip had been that Thai place where the food, she was certain, had been seasoned with a pinch of e-coli.

The maître d' led them to a small table nestled into a semicircular banquette. He helped Cassie onto the tufted leather cushions, then pushed the table in and handed her and Phillip menus and a wine list. She skimmed the right-hand column of prices and her eyebrows rose reflexively.

"What?" Phillip asked.

She hadn't realized he'd been watching her. "It's expensive," she said.

"That's all right."

"Well, here you are, running a company on the brink of collapse—and you've just spent I don't know how much for an airline ticket for me, and now you're going to spend how much more on dinner for me—"

"This is lunch and dinner combined. Two for the price of one," he joked. "As far as my company being on the brink of collapse, whatever I'm spending on you is coming out of my pocket. The company's paying only for me."

"Yes, but...what happens if the company goes under? You'll be out of a job. Maybe you shouldn't be throwing your own money around."

He chuckled. "I've got an M.B.A. from Harvard. I think I'll be able to find another position."

She relaxed, sank into the upholstery and let herself soak in the dining room's luxurious ambience. Skimming the menu, she noticed one of the appetizers. "Look! They've got pizza here!" Granted, it was goat-cheese pizza on an herbed crust, garnished with sun-dried tomatoes and grilled portobello mushrooms—a far cry from the gooey pizzas she and Phillip had shared back in Boston. The price for the appetizer was more than the cost of a large pizza back in her neighborhood, too. But if the prices didn't bother Phillip with his Harvard M.B.A., she wouldn't let them bother her, either. "We have to order that."

He peered around his menu at her. His smile had lost its shadow of exhaustion. "We certainly do," he said.

By the time the waiter had arrived, they had compiled an impressive order—appetizers, salads, entrées and a forty-dollar bottle of merlot. Along with everything else, the restaurant, empty except for them and the white-jacketed staff milling idly around the dining room, contributed to Cassie's sense of unreality, far from the world of alphabetized revenge plans, far from Lynwood and Saturday's wedding. She was going to savor every gourmet morsel of this meal, every heavenly sip of wine. She was going to pretend nothing existed beyond the cozy semicircular nook where she and Phillip sat.

Two waiters approached, one carrying the wine and another carrying crystal goblets. They were obviously bored, having no other customers to fuss over. If they wanted to fill the time by fawning on Cassie and Phillip, she wouldn't object.

Once the wine was uncorked, tasted and poured, the waiters silently backed away from the table. Phillip lifted his glass and touched it to Cassie's. "Here's to old friends."

"Old friends," she echoed. It sounded like a safe enough toast. And anyway, who cared about safety right now? Outside, rain was spilling from the sky. Outside, a furniture store was going out of business and a romantic debacle demanded vengeance. Outside, it was the first year of the twenty-first century. In here, though, at this secluded table, it was only Cassie and Phillip, old friends.

One of the waiters returned with their first appetizer: the gourmet pizza. Cassie clapped her hand over her mouth to keep from laughing. Whatever that delicate circle layered in red and brown and white was, it didn't resemble a pizza.

"Shh," Phillip scolded. "Behave yourself. This is a classy joint."

"Where's the mozzarella?" Cassie asked as Phillip eased a quarter of the circle onto her plate. "If it isn't all goppy with strings of melted mozzarella, it doesn't count."

"You're just going to have to cope," he said, helping himself to another quarter and taking a bite.

She watched him chew and swallow. "Well?"

"It's interesting," he said tactfully, then grinned. "Actually, it's delicious. But it's not pizza."

She tasted hers. It *was* delicious—and it wasn't pizza, not like the pizza Phillip and she used to eat together. But they weren't who they used to be, either. As much as she wanted to forget that, she couldn't let herself.

"Tell me how things went at the furniture store," she urged him.

He did. Over one course and then another, one glass of wine after another, he told her about his meeting. He described how he and the store manager had gone through the books, figuring out the value of the store's inventory, calculating the cost of breaking the lease, assessing separation packages for the employees. He said it hadn't been as painful as he'd feared, but it hadn't been a barrel of laughs, either. According to Phillip, the store manager had been bracing for this eventuality for a long time, and now that it had happened, he was almost relieved.

He'd also told Phillip that he'd gotten a call from Phillip's father, pleading with him to see if he and Phillip could find any way to keep the store going. The manager admitted he didn't think Phillip's father was being realistic about the prospects. "The manager said that we're too upscale for the location," Phillip told Cassie, "and Shaker and colonial furniture don't go over big in this market. He told my father this, but Dad didn't want to hear it. He said he also got the impression someone else was pulling the strings.'' Phillip said he'd asked if Harry Riggs had been in touch with the manager, but he'd said no.

Cassie was all ears. "Tell me about Harry."

So Phillip did. He spoke like someone desperate to unload his burdens. He told her about other investments Harry had made, most of them conservative and most of them outside of Lynwood. He told her about Harry's long history with Phillip's father, about how they'd grown up together in town and had known each other forever. Phillip told her about his grandfather, who'd successfully expanded the business until it was selling furniture all over the country. He'd told her about his mother, who had encouraged him to trust his instincts.

"That's why I brought you here," Phillip explained, turning his glass around and around in his hand, watching the wine swirl in the bowl. "My instincts told me to, and I trusted them."

"I like your mother," Cassie admitted. She'd lost count of how many times her own glass had been refilled, but she wasn't drunk. She felt a warm glow from the wine, but her mind seemed clear, vividly focused on the man beside her in the banquette. "I was going to visit her today."

"Really?"

"I wanted to get to know her better." Cassie wasn't divulging anything about Plan E. To be sure, she no longer remembered exactly what the plan entailed. Diane was supposed to have a cigar with Harry, and Cassie was supposed to cajole information from Dorothy Keene about Phillip's relationship with Tricia.

But what could Dorothy have told her that Phillip hadn't told her himself? Was Dorothy aware that Phillip didn't love Tricia? Did she have any idea that if the wedding occurred on Saturday it would be a sham?

"My mother is worth getting to know," Phillip admitted. "I trust her as much as I trust you."

"I don't know why you trust me," Cassie muttered. If he'd known about Plan E—and Plans A through D, for that matter—he'd realize how untrustworthy she could be.

"You never lied to me," he said. His voice was low, his eyes dark and steady. "You never deceived me. You never betrayed me the way I betrayed you." He lowered his glass and reached across the table to cover her hand with his. "Do you know how many times I started to call you last year? Dozens. Hundreds. But I knew that the instant I heard your voice, my whole life would fall apart. I wouldn't want to stay in Lynwood and save Keene Furniture. I wouldn't want to rebuild the company and salvage the family's legacy. I would have rejected all that and gone back to you."

"Just from the sound of my voice?" She laughed.

"Yes." He smiled slightly. "It would have made me think about you." His thumb moved across her hand, rising and dipping over each knuckle. "I knew the only way I could make everything work would be to close that door and lock it, to pretend you and Boston had never existed and to stay where I was, living in the present. Forgetting the past." His touch felt too good. She knew she should draw her hand away. But she couldn't. Not in this quiet restaurant, her belly full of gourmet food, her mind singing with wine. "For the sake of Keene Furniture," he said, "I had to make the best of a bad situation. And I did. I was doing fine—until you showed up.''

"So now a bad situation is worse," she said, feeling both apologetic and thrilled that Phillip cared enough about her to stop doing fine the moment she showed up.

"You must hate me," he said, even though he kept caressing her hand.

She shook her head. "I did for a while," she acknowledged. "But I hated myself, too. I thought I had to be the worst judge of character, to believe everything you'd said that night in Boston. I thought I was the world's biggest fool."

"Oh, God—no, Cassie. That honor belongs to me."

"Well." She tried, really tried, to pull her hand away. But her muscles refused to obey her. In fact, they rebelled, forcing her hand to rotate until her palm met his and her fingers wove through his. "It's too late now, I guess. Boston was a whole century ago."

"It's not too late," he murmured, then lifted her hand to his mouth and pressed a kiss to her fingertips.

Heat rose through her like mercury in a thermometer, liquid and silvery. She heard a rush in her ears, the sound of blood searing through her body, rousing every cell to full attention. "Phil," she said, not sure if she was telling him to stop or to continue, not sure he could even hear her because her voice came out softer than a whisper.

"I want you," he said, then brushed his lips over her fingertips again. "I've wanted you every day, every minute since I met you. Even when I tried to forget you, I wanted you. And now you're here. I can't fight it anymore. I'll call off the wedding. I'll sell off the company. I'll go to Boston with you. I love you, Cassie.''

He'd made promises before, dramatic impassioned promises, promises of forever, of love. And he'd broken every promise.

All right, then. She was the world's biggest fool, not Phillip. Because despite everything he'd done, everything she'd learned about him, every damned promise he'd broken, she decided to believe him again.

CHAPTER THIRTEEN

THE ROOM WAS SMALL but nicely decorated, it was available and it was theirs. They'd raced from the restaurant to the registration desk in the hotel's lobby, where Phillip had produced his credit card and the clerk had presented him with the key to this room. Before they'd come upstairs, Phillip had detoured into the convenience store off the lobby. When he'd returned, sliding a small square box into his pocket, he'd been smiling.

He had a smile that could melt an iceberg. A smile that could melt a woman. A smile that could erase Cassie's memory and make her conscious only of the desire powering that smile, the passion, the promises that she prayed wouldn't be broken, not this time.

She heard a click as he closed the door. She was standing in the center of the room, gazing through the window's diaphanous curtains at a city bathed in twilight. The carpet muted Phillip's footsteps, but she felt his approach. The air around her seemed charged. Her skin prickled. Her heart pounded.

"Cassie." Reaching around from behind her, he pulled her against him and sighed into her hair. "I will never leave you again. Never."

She believed him.

He turned her in his arms and took her mouth with his. They had just finished an exquisite meal and savored a well-aged wine, but none of that sublime fare tasted as good as his kiss.

She recalled their first kiss a year ago in Boston. It had felt like a discovery then—a discovery of herself, of everything she knew and was, every magical fantasy she'd ever invented suddenly coming to life. It had been like riding a dream and arriving exactly where she was meant to be. It had been like flying home.

It was the same this time. Kissing Phillip was a homecoming. Looping her arms around his neck and plowing her fingers into his hair was like embracing joy itself. Feeling his breath fill her mouth, and his tongue, his heat and hunger and love, made her recognize her own strength, her own heat and hunger, her own love for him.

She pushed at the collar of his jacket. He released her long enough to shake the jacket down his arms and off. When she reached for the knot of his tie, he groaned. It amazed her that she could turn him on simply by loosening the wound silk at his throat—yet as she slid the knot downward, he brought his hands to her hips and pulled her against him. This must be one hell of a tie, she thought as he pressed into her and let her feel his hardness.

Why wasn't she anxious? Why weren't her hands trembling as she finished with his tie and turned her attention to his shirt buttons? Why were her motions so sure, so easy?

Because this was right. Making love with Phillip was utterly, undeniably, right.

He kissed her again, dug into his trouser pocket and pulled out the package of condoms he'd bought downstairs. He tossed it onto the bed, then went to work on her clothes, untucking her blouse, unbuttoning her skirt, touching her until she wanted to swoon with pleasure. He was a businessman in possession of an Ivy League education, but he had a carpenter's hands. The apprenticeship he had undergone, the summers spent in the shop helping to shape and sand and stain fine pieces of furniture, had textured his fingertips and tempered the muscles in his arms. His were the hands of a craftsman, an artisan.

A lover.

He seemed completely uninterested in the fancy underwear Diane had induced her to buy at the mall earlier that week. Rose-hued satin trimmed in lace, the bikini panties and bra were supposed to have lured him to his destruction. But he didn't even comment on the lingerie, let alone linger over the glossy fabric, the daring cut. With a few deft movements, he stripped the garments off her, apparently interested only in Cassie herself, Cassie naked.

He helped her remove the rest of his clothing, as well. High-quality wool and broadcloth cotton fell to the floor in scattered heaps; dark socks, pale silk boxers, and then she had what she wanted: Phillip himself, naked.

And so beautiful he stole her breath. She couldn't stop gliding her fingers over his body, tracing the sleek contours of his chest, his lean hips, the twin ridges of his collarbones, the taut surface of his abdomen. When she skimmed lower he sucked in his breath, then lifted her, cupping his hands around her bottom and pulling her legs up to circle his waist. His kiss was deep and greedy, expressing a year's worth of pent-up need.

He carried her to the bed and they tumbled onto it together, a tangle of limbs and lips and damp yearning.

How had she survived without him? she wondered. How had she endured all those lonely months without this man, this love? She'd had the challenges of her work, the make-believe stories of her show, but in her life she'd had only emptiness—until now.

He stroked his tongue over her skin. His hair caressed her breasts, his stubbled chin scraped her midriff. His fingers floated, kneaded, danced across her flesh. She nearly came from his touch alone.

But she wanted more. She wanted him, all of him; she wanted Phillip Keene locked inside her, lost inside her, as much hers as she was his. She wanted him to become so intimately bound to her that he could never leave her again, so completely a part of her that he could never choose his family honor and his heritage over her.

But when at last he filled her she was the lost one, a woman who could choose nothing but Phillip. Their bodies moved together, finding each other again and again, sharing every sensation, every spark and spasm, every deep, love-drenched moment. His back flexed; his hips tensed. He breathed with her, strove with her, led and followed until they reached the peak together, gasping and clinging to each other as if their survival depended on it.

Perhaps, Cassie admitted, it did.

Minutes might have passed, or hours. She didn't know and she didn't care. Phillip lay half beside her and half on top of her, one leg flung heavily across her thighs, one arm wrapped possessively around her just below her breasts. His mouth was so close to her ear he was able to nip the lobe without moving his head.

"I feel," he murmured in a ragged voice, "as if I just woke up from a year-long coma."

"You look more like someone ready to fall asleep," she teased, gliding her hand along his arm, which pinned her to the mattress.

"No. I'm just catching my breath. Give me a minute and I'll be ready to conquer the world."

She laughed. "I think you just did that."

He laughed, too, then stopped and propped himself up so he could look at her. "You're right, Cassie. You're my world. Except—" he caressed her lower lip with his index finger and gazed into her eyes "—in this case, the world conquered me."

There was no humor in his expression now. He looked earnest, intense, his gaze as concentrated as a laser penetrating her, reaching deep inside her. She would have liked the laughter to remain, but she knew that as glorious as their lovemaking had been, the implications were serious. Maybe even dire.

"What are we going to do?" she asked.

He brushed a strand of her hair back from her cheek. "We're going to make love. We're going to spend the whole night making love."

"I meant, after that? After the whole night ends?"

"We're going to go back to Lynwood and I'm going to tell Tricia I can't marry her. Once I do that, we'll figure out the rest. We can shuttle back and forth between Ohio and Boston if we have to—until I get Keene Furniture back on its feet. After I've stabilized things with the company, I'll move to Boston."

Cassie could feel her eyes growing round. "You're not going to ask me to move to Lynwood?"

"And give up *Dream Wheels?* I would never ask

you to do that, Cassie. It's your baby.'' He kissed her on the lips, sweetly and gently. "I love you.''

Her eyes stung. He loved her so much he would sacrifice the career that meant everything to him—the career he'd been groomed for, the career that linked the generations of his family into a unified chain—rather than ask her to abandon her own dream. She felt a tear leak through her eyelashes and skitter down her cheek. "I love you, too,'' she said.

HE WAS WASHING UP in the bathroom when he heard her voice. Cracking the door open, he peeked out and saw her seated on the bed, the phone tucked against her ear. "Yes. Bailey's Bed-and-Breakfast,'' she enunciated into the mouthpiece. "Lynwood.'' She listened for a moment, then lifted a pencil and notepad from the night table and jotted down the number.

He loved the arch of her back, the contrast of her dark hair and her pale skin, the sweet roundness of her breasts. He recalled the feel of them in his hands, the taste of them, and he started to get hard again.

Something inside him twisted painfully. He loved Cassie Webber. He'd tried to ignore that truth a year ago, but he couldn't ignore it anymore. She was too essential to him—and not just in bed. All day long he'd needed her with him. He'd been able to think more clearly and fight more effectively because she was close by. He'd enjoyed his meal more. It was as if she fine-tuned him, bringing everything into alignment inside him: his thoughts, his courage, his senses. His body. His soul.

Yet that understanding troubled him, because accepting that he loved her meant bringing pain to other people—his parents, whom he also loved, and Tricia,

toward whom he wished no ill will. He hoped Tricia
would be able to accept his decision. God knew her
mother was going to go berserk, given how much
money she'd sunk into the most spectacular social gala
Lynwood would ever have seen. The wedding's flower
budget alone was more than what Phillip had spent on
honeymoon reservations at a Caribbean resort.

All right. It would be just one more debt Phillip
owed the Riggs family. And he'd lose his deposit on
the honeymoon reservations, and the musicians' fee,
and the tuxedo rentals. No one had ever said love was
cheap.

But plenty of very intelligent people had said that
a marriage lacking in love wasn't a sound investment.
Money was nowhere near as important as happiness,
contentment, the joy of choosing a partner who stim-
ulated you mentally, as well as physically, who kept
you on your toes, who challenged you and showed you
how much your efforts to meet those challenges were
appreciated.

Cassie brought him joy. She made him think and
she made him feel. She made him come alive. What
was money compared with that?

"Mrs. Gill?" she said into the phone. "This is Cassie Webber. Is Diane Krensky there?"

He toweled himself dry but remained in the bathroom, not wanting to interfere with her phone call.

"Could you leave her a message, please? Tell her
I called and I'm fine and...I'll be back tomorrow. Tell
her not to worry, okay?" Cassie listened for a minute.
"Tomorrow," she repeated. "Tell her to forget about
the plan. I'll explain everything when I see her. If I
can." She paused. "I don't know if I'll be able to

explain. But I'll try. Thanks." She lowered the phone into its cradle and fell back against the pillows.

Phillip allowed himself one more minute to admire her body from a distance. She wasn't voluptuous, she wasn't tall and leggy, but as far as he was concerned she was perfect.

Tossing the towel on the edge of the tub, he nudged the door open and stepped into the bedroom. She turned to him and smiled.

"I called and left a message for Diane," she told him, apparently unaware he'd overheard. "I didn't want her to worry when I didn't show up tonight." Her gaze wandered over Phillip's nude body, and her thoughts were transparent. She let out a sigh and shifted her hips on the mattress. "We are going back to Lynwood tomorrow, aren't we?" she asked, sounding wistful.

"I wish we didn't have to," he admitted. "But yes, we'll go back. Tomorrow. Not tonight." He was curious about what plan she'd told Diane to forget. Was it the plan she'd mentioned when she'd called Diane from his cell phone on the way to the airport? Plan E? Something about her work, she'd told him. He wondered whether Diane and Beckelman were still working this late into the evening, or whether Diane was busy renewing her friendship with his mother, and Beckelman was continuing whatever the hell he'd been doing yesterday with Tricia.

What Tricia and Beckelman did tonight was none of Phillip's concern. Whether Diane was ingratiating herself with his mother didn't bother him in the least. He was here, with Cassie, and no matter what hit the fan tomorrow, right now he cared only about where he was and the woman he was with.

He propped a few pillows against the headboard and stretched out beside her on the bed. She snuggled into his arms, her head resting against his chest, near his shoulder. "I feel like we've got a year's worth of talk to catch up on," she said.

He felt like they had a year's worth of sex to catch up on. But talking was fine with him, too. "Have you seen any Buñuel movies lately?" he asked.

Cassie chuckled. Her breath warmed his skin and he tightened his hold on her. "The only movies I've seen lately are flicks with lots of action and explosions in them. I didn't want to watch any emotional foreign films. Or romantic comedies."

"Oh?"

"Romance didn't seem comical to me," she admitted, then pressed her mouth shut as if she feared she'd revealed too much.

Romance hadn't seemed particularly comical to him, either. Actually, he'd exerted himself to avoid thinking about romance at all during the past year. Responsibility had been his guiding principle, responsibility and rescue.

In the process, he'd abdicated responsibility for himself. And now he was the one in need of rescue. Thank God Cassie had arrived in time to save him.

He nestled into the pillows and urged her up onto him. She was light, her slim body resting comfortably on top of him, her eyes bright as she met his gaze. He felt the heat between her thighs, the swollen tips of her nipples brushing his chest, and he experienced a surge of raw male lust.

Her smile told him she was aware of what he felt, what he wanted. It also told him she was in a playful mood. "So ask me about life in the public-broadcasting universe," she said, a dimple punctuating the corner of her grin. "You'll never guess who I met at our last telethon. Think rock-music icons of the sixties."

"Chuck Berry," he murmured, moving his hands up her sides and forward to her breasts.

"Chuck Berry is from the fifties," she argued, propping herself up, giving him full access to her breasts. They were small and round, and when he rolled her nipples between his fingers she moaned.

"Aretha Franklin," he guessed, lifting her so he could take one of her breasts with his mouth.

"She's—ohh," Cassie gasped as he drew her nipple into his mouth. "Soul..." she whispered.

He wasn't sure whether she was referring to Aretha Franklin or something going on between her and himself right now.

He continued kissing her breasts, grazing from one to the other as he moved his hands down her body. "Elvis," he said before sucking hard on her other nipple.

"No Elvis sightings," Cassie managed.

But then he slid his hand between her legs and she was too busy moaning to speak. She opened wider for him, her hips writhing, and he thought he might come just from seeing her so turned on. Her entire body seemed to shimmer with arousal. Her hands fisted against the pillow on either side of his head and her breath grew shallow and tremulous.

He stopped touching her only to grab a condom from the night table. Lucky he could still think clearly enough to protect them—and it was the last clear thought he had before she sank onto him, taking him in, riding him. From then on it was all about sensation, about the heavenly feel of Cassie, the musky scent of her, her hushed cries, her rhythm. The way her body tightened around him, stroked him and shattered in a climax that gave him no choice but surrender.

A long while later, when his brain finally reformed itself into a functioning organ, he realized he was going to have to thank his mother for including Diane Krensky on her invitation list. If Diane hadn't been invited, Cassie would never have come to Lynwood, and Phillip would never have been saved from his own noble, well-intentioned stupidity.

"ARE YOU OKAY?" she asked as the plane touched down in Lynwood.

Their clasped hands rested on the arm separating their seats. He wished that what happened from here on in could be as easy as holding Cassie's hand, but he knew it was going to be hard. At least the rain had ended. The runway was dry, the sun bright in the blue morning sky. The landing had been smooth. If only that meant everything else would go smoothly, too.

"Sure, I'm okay," he said with false confidence. He *was* okay, but that wouldn't last for long. Telling his fiancée twenty-four hours before their wedding that he wasn't going to marry her was not the sort of activity that left a man feeling okay. But he would do it, because not doing it would be an even worse mistake. "I got myself into this," he said, as much to himself as to Cassie. "It's my own fault. I'll deal with it."

"It's not your fault," she reminded him. "Your family and the Riggses put a lot of pressure on you. You did what you thought was the right thing."

"And it was the wrong thing. I just feel bad that

Tricia has to be in the middle of it.'' The plane rolled
to a stop and they unclipped their seat belts.

"You're sure you don't want me to come with you
to see her?''

"No. Absolutely not.''

She looked relieved. ''Then I'll wait at Bailey's,''
she said. ''I'll be there if you need me.''

Damn. He needed her now. He needed her with him
when he saw Tricia and told her he was bailing out
on her. He needed Cassie with him when he faced his
parents and explained to them that, even at the risk of
losing Keene Furniture, he couldn't go through with a
marriage that was so wrong—for both him and Tricia.
He needed her with him when he confronted Harry,
already meddling in the company's decisions when it
came to divesting itself of the Chicago store. Harry
had a temper, and he had inordinate clout. What would
he do to Phillip, the man who was going to break his
daughter's heart?

Whatever Harry did, Phillip told himself, it
wouldn't be as bad as losing Cassie. He would take
his punishment, and he would beg his parents to forgive him for whatever punishment Harry directed at
them—or Keene Furniture.

But he wouldn't compromise his own future happiness. Not anymore.

Cassie said little as he drove through the rolling
farmland to Lynwood, back to the B-and-B where she
and her colleagues were staying. She seemed thought-
ful, dreamy. Maybe it was just exhaustion. They
hadn't slept much last night. He was pretty tired himself.

"So,'' he said as he pulled up alongside the grass
by the Bailey's sign. ''I'll find you here?''

"I'll be waiting." She leaned across the console and kissed him—a light, loving kiss. "Call me if you need me. Anything I can do, Phil—just call."

"I'll be all right," he said in another show of bravado. No man with a conscience would really be all right after doing what he was going to do.

He watched as Cassie climbed out of the car and headed up the flower-lined front walk to the porch. He recalled the day he'd seen her at the Harvest Bounty a few days ago. The familiarity of her back had appalled him then, but now he relished it. He'd explored every square inch of her back last night with his hands, with his mouth. He loved her back, and her front. He loved her inside and out, body and soul. Love would sustain him through his ordeal that morning. Love and trust in Cassie.

Once she vanished into the old farmhouse and the screen door clapped shut behind her, he shifted into gear and headed toward the Riggs house on the west side of town. He tried to take heart from the bright sunshine, the vibrant greens of the grass and foliage, the lively storefronts, the litter-free sidewalks and the flag dancing on its pole in front of the post office. He tried to take every cheerful sight as a positive omen.

It didn't help. He felt grim as he steered through the open gate surrounding the Riggs property, cruised up the driveway to the front door and turned off the engine. Pocketing the keys, he gave himself a silent pep talk. Tricia would be better off in the long run, he assured himself. Why should she marry a man who didn't love her? Why would she want to exchange vows with a man who'd been manipulated by her own father, coerced by his wealth and his threats? Perhaps she would be hurt today, but once she thought about it, once the initial sting wore off, she might be grateful that Phillip had spared them both a travesty of a marriage.

Still, he couldn't even fake a smile as he got out of his car and marched up the brick walk to her front door. The maid answered his ring, and then Tricia materialized behind her, clad in pastel-blue linen walking shorts and a patterned silk T-shirt. Her hair was bouncy and shiny, her sneakers and anklets white enough to make him wish he'd been wearing his sunglasses. Compared with her, he felt rumpled and wrinkled, clad in yesterday's apparel, which had seen him through two flights and a long business meeting.

"Hi, honey!" Tricia chirped as the maid stepped aside. "Come on in! What's up?"

He stepped into the high-ceilinged foyer and took a deep breath. By the time he was done with Tricia, she would never think of him as "honey" again.

"You look beat," she babbled, leading him down a hall to one of the sitting rooms in the house. The Riggs house was tastefully decorated—no grapevine borders marred the walls and no fragile-looking glass-topped tables cluttered the rooms. Even so, there was an oppressive opulence about the place. Phillip had always been afraid to sit on any of the chairs in Constance Riggs's home. They seemed more like decorating statements than actual furniture. He always felt that if a speck of dust or dirt landed on any of the white cushions, an alarm would go off.

"Mom's at Leona's getting her nails done," Tricia reported as she flopped onto a floral-print chair that looked uncomfortable. "Top and bottom, fingers and toes. She's wearing close-toed shoes tomorrow, but she says a woman isn't complete unless she'd had a professional pedicure. I happen to disagree, but you know Mom. Sit down, Phil. I'm glad you're here. You want something to drink? I could have Marcie get you some orange juice, or coffee—or a scotch, if you'd like.''

It wasn't even eleven in the morning, and Tricia was offering him scotch. And talking nonstop, too. He hadn't asked where her mother was, but thanks to Tricia's jabbering, he now knew more about Constance Riggs's toes than he'd ever wanted.

He studied Tricia and decided her smile didn't look particularly authentic. She must have guessed he was here with bad news. ''Where's your father?'' he asked.

Tricia shrugged too nonchalantly, laughed too sweetly. ''Who cares. He's off doing whatever he wants, as usual. Look, Phil...'' She grinned. If her smile got any bigger, she'd need spare cheeks to catch the overflow. ''I'm glad you're here.''

''I'm glad I'm here, too.'' He practically gagged on the words.

''I mean, because it's the day before our wedding, you know? And...well, I feel like we haven't talked in days. Except about things like flowers and stuff. You know?''

''We do need to talk,'' he agreed, watching her.

''Well, so, anyway...'' Her smile made *his* mouth ache. ''You haven't shaved in a while, have you. You look pretty scruffy.''

''No,'' he admitted. ''I haven't shaved.''

''In fact, you look like a bum. But that's cool. I don't care. You might look nice with a beard, actually. I think hair on a man... Oh, never mind.''

What the hell was she babbling about? ''Tricia, look. We need to talk, and—''

"I'm sort of thinking maybe—"

"If you could stop for a minute so I could get in a word—"

"Because I know my mom'll have a cow, but you know what? It's her cow."

"I'm sorry for your mom, but this isn't about her. It's about us."

"Exactly," Tricia said.

Phillip frowned. He leaned forward, rested his elbows on his knees and peered into Tricia's face. Her smile was downright desperate. He took a deep breath, then said, "I don't think we should get married."

"Neither do I."

Silence descended on the room for a full minute. Phillip stared at Tricia, giving her a chance to retract what she'd just said. She only kept smiling at him, that ghastly, angst-filled smile.

"You don't think we should get married?" he asked at last.

"No. I just... Oh, Phil. You look so pale. Are you all right?"

"Um...yeah," he said, gratified when his heart seemed to settle down to a steady beat. "Just a little surprised. Why don't you think we should get married?"

"I'm so sorry." She reached over and patted his knee. "You really are the best catch in Lynwood. I mean it, you really are. I just sort of, well, got to thinking maybe there's more to life than Lynwood."

Where had this come from? When had she come to this great insight? What had happened in the past few days to convince her that ordering flowers for the wedding ceremony wasn't the most worthwhile pursuit to which a woman could devote herself?

What had happened was that Cassie had arrived in town. Cassie and Diane and— "Beckelman?" he blurted.

Tricia's complexion turned bright pink. "What do you mean, Beckelman?" she asked defensively.

He remembered the kiss Tricia had given the cameraman two nights ago. "Do you have something going on with him?"

"I do *not* have anything going on with Roger!" she retorted. "He's just a very nice man."

"Hey, I agree!" Phillip endeavored to reassure her. "I think he's a great guy. Very knowledgeable about cameras."

"He's a true artist," Tricia said.

"I don't doubt it."

"And I just—God, my mom really is going to have a cow, but…well, I just think I need true artists in my life. I'm sorry, Phil. I know that's a really cruel thing to say, but—"

"No, it's not cruel," he insisted.

"—I'm young," she went on, not even acknowledging him. "Except for college, I've spent my whole life in Lynwood. I don't want to spend the rest of my life serving coffee and tea to my grandmother's club ladies, you know? I want to meet artists, and…and guys with hair down their backs. You know what I mean?"

Not quite, but he humored her. "I do, Tricia. I understand."

"My mom will just have to deal with it," she said.

Tricia's mother could be beastly, but she didn't worry him as much as Tricia's father did. Harry had been the one to introduce Phillip and Tricia. He'd been the one constantly making intimidating remarks about

the tenuous balance between Phillip's family firm and
Harry's financial backing, and about Phillip's obliga-
tions to Tricia. "What about your father?" he asked
warily.

Tricia shrugged. "Oh, him—he won't care. He's
got what he wants. He'll get over this."

Phillip sat up straighter. Tension nipped at the edges
of his brain. "What do you mean, he's got what he
wants?"

"Well, I don't know. He and your dad were in
meetings all afternoon and evening yesterday. Weren't
you there?"

"No."

"Well, whatever." She shrugged again. "My dad
came home last night, popped open a bottle of cham-
pagne and said, 'It doesn't get any better than this.
The paperwork's done. I've got what I want. And God
bless Dorothy for inviting those Boston folks to Lynwood.' I'm real glad your mom invited them, too, because Roger...I mean, he's so interesting, and
he's...well, never mind. My dad just seems on another
planet at the moment, so who cares what he thinks. I
sure don't."

"He got what he wants? What paperwork?" Phillip's heart pounded. His head pounded. The inside of
his skull resounded with a marching band's entire
rhythm section. What the hell had happened yesterday
while he'd been in Chicago with Cassie? Had the earth
reversed direction? Suddenly Tricia didn't want to get
married and Harry had *gotten what he wanted.* "What
paperwork?" he repeated, gripping Tricia's hands and
forcing her to look at him.

"How should I know? It was business, I guess. He
doesn't talk about business with me."

Phillip felt queasy. Frenzied. Pumped with adrenaline and dread. What had Harry gotten, and why was he grateful to Phillip's mother for inviting the Boston folks to Lynwood? What did they have to do with Harry's getting what he wanted?

"I've got to go, Tricia," he mumbled, leaping to his feet. He forgot that he had his hands clamped around hers, and he yanked her to her feet, as well. Apologetically, he released her hands and bolted toward the door.

He couldn't just leave without a word. He turned back and gave her a swift hug. "You're a sweetheart," he murmured. "We'll work everything out later. I've got to run."

Before she could respond, let alone hug him back, he was charging down the hall and out of her house.

CHAPTER FOURTEEN

"YOU DID WHAT?" Cassie screamed.

Diane perched placidly atop the dresser in her second-floor room, polishing off the last of Cassie's chocolate-chip cookies. Cassie sat on the edge of the bed, too queasy even to look at the bag of cookies without wanting to throw up. "I'm telling you," Diane said, "it all worked out. We got Phil, and we got him good." She licked a few crumbs from her fingertips, as smug as a cat grooming itself in a patch of sun. "I wish you'd been here. We could have celebrated the victory together."

Cassie shook her head. Maybe she wasn't hearing Diane correctly. Maybe the night she'd spent with Phillip had scrambled her brain so thoroughly that her ears were no longer working properly. "Tell me again," she pleaded, rubbing her hands together to warm them. Nerves seemed to have drained all the blood from her extremities.

"First you've got to tell me what happened last night."

Cassie shook her head again, emphatically. "We're not talking about me. We're talking about you and Harry Riggs and what happened yesterday."

"We had cigars." Diane smiled and swung her legs back and forth, tapping her heels against the bottom drawer of the dresser. "Cigars have to be the most vile indulgence in the world. I can't believe people actually *enjoy* smoking those things. They taste even worse than tequila.''

''Lots of people like the taste of tequila,'' Cassie muttered, thinking that if someone handed her a glass of tequila right now, she wouldn't give a damn what it tasted like. She'd just chug-a-lug the drink and pray for the liquor to kick in fast.

''Okay.'' Diane warmed to her story. ''We couldn't smoke the cigars in his office, because he said some of his clients didn't like the smell and he didn't want it lingering in the air. But the man's got practically an entire floor of a building all to himself. So we went down the hall, past his secretary— Oh, you should see her, Cassie. Forty-Ds, I bet.'' Diane mimed a huge bosom with her hands. ''I don't know how she manages to sit upright. But that's her problem, I guess. She wasn't included in our smoker.''

Cassie scowled in impatience. ''Forget the secretary, all right? So you went down the hall...''

''...into this nice little sitting room. That's where we lit up. I started coughing right away, but I did my best to keep from losing my lunch. And in the meantime, Harry and I got to talking.''

''And he got you to talking, too.'' This was the crucial part of Diane's story, the part Cassie was certain she'd misunderstood the first time Diane had described it.

''It started with Harry getting kind of sappy. He got to talking about his youth, growing up with Phillip's dad. James Keene was always the popular one, he said. James was a gifted athlete, and born to wealth. And of course Dorothy fell in love with him. The prettiest, smartest girl in town. Things always just naturally flowed James's way, like the river flowing past his furniture factory. Harry got a little poetic.'' Diane grinned. ''Anyway, the gist was, he always felt it was a special privilege just to be James Keene's friend.''

Phillip had obviously taken after his father, Cassie concluded. He, too, had been the gifted athlete, the naturally blessed scion of a family dynasty.

''So Harry was rambling on in that vein,'' Diane continued, ''and telling me how he'd always had his eye on Phillip. He said he knew James was going to hand the furniture company over to Phillip, and Harry had thought this wasn't such a hot idea, because Phillip had been to Harvard and his brain was crammed with useless theory. It took a hands-on businessman to run a great company like Keene Furniture, and Harry clearly felt that Phillip didn't fit the bill. He said he'd been watching Phillip for years and wondering whether he could be trusted with that much responsibility. And all I said—''

Cassie sat upright, bracing herself.

''—was, no, Phillip couldn't be trusted.''

''Why did you say that?'' Cassie lamented.

''Because it's true!'' Diane asserted. ''I told Harry that Phillip and you had been an item in Boston, and then all of a sudden he'd hooked up with Tricia. All I said was that kind of behavior can make a person think.''

''Well, it sure made Harry think. What else did you tell him?''

''Only that you'd come to Lynwood to break up his wedding.''

Cassie cringed. ''Why did you tell him?''

''It just sort of—'' Diane shrugged ''—popped out.''

"It just sort of popped out that I wanted to break up his wedding?"

"And maybe seduce Phil, so his heart would be broken."

"Diane. Why didn't you keep your mouth shut and let him do all the talking?"

"Well, because...because he was opening up. I mean, we both were. He was telling me all about the insecure kid he'd been, and how much he envied James Keene, and how people can love and hate each other at the same time...and your history with Phillip just seemed pertinent. And you know, cigars are almost like booze. They loosen the tongue."

Cassie wanted to shake Diane by her shoulders. "I told you to be careful with Harry."

"I was careful."

"You gave him an excuse to destroy the man engaged to marry his daughter. He didn't have to worry about leveling Phil, once he knew Phil would make a lousy husband for Tricia. So he leveled him—and Phil's father, too—by stealing their company right out from under them."

"Well...well..." Diane scrambled for a better defense. "Harry didn't *steal* it. He didn't take anything he wasn't entitled to. He told me how he'd encouraged James to expand his business into retail, and counseled James on the business aspects, and funded him to the tune of a gazillion dollars, using the company as collateral. The loans were due January 1, and they hadn't been paid yet. Harry had waited long enough. I guess he was waiting because he thought Phillip was going to be his son-in-law, but once I told him Phillip had run away for the day with you, Harry decided the time was ripe."

"So he called in his loans."

"I wasn't going to stop him," Diane pointed out. "The plan was to destroy Phil, and this seemed like the best way to accomplish that. Harry would do the dirty work. There would be no blood on our hands. It seemed like the perfect revenge. Anyway, it was Harry's idea, not mine," she continued. "All I did was say, 'Why not?'"

"And tell him Phil and I had been lovers."

"Well, you *had* been. And Phil deserved to be punished."

"So Harry punished Phil's father. Everything Phil had fought for, everything he'd tried to protect—Harry ruined it." Cassie had to force the words past the lump of anguish that clogged her throat.

"It's not as if he took anything he wasn't entitled to," Diane explained. "Phil's father agreed to the terms of the loans, and they were supposed to be paid in full by January 1 of the year 2000. Now it's six months later, and Keene Furniture has barely even *started* repaying them. That's what Harry told me. Was he lying?"

Cassie shook her head dolefully. "No, it's true. Phil's spent this whole year trying to undo his father's mistakes and keep Harry from doing exactly what he did."

"Phil's father agreed to Harry's terms," Diane observed. "He knew how high the stakes were when he accepted those loans."

"Phillip's father accepted those loans under the advice of his supposed best friend! Harry exploited him! He hoodwinked Phil's father! The guy's a swine."

"They're all swine. I told you, before we even left

Boston, that I bet Lynwood, Ohio, would be full of pig dung.''

"Cow dung," Cassie corrected her. "You predicted it would all be soybeans and cow dung."

"Pig dung, cow dung—who cares? You wanted Phillip destroyed, and now he's destroyed. Don't blame me for doing what you wanted me to do. As if I did all that much, anyway," Diane added under her breath.

Cassie groaned. "You told Harry that Phil was involved with me. That was all he needed to know."

She pressed her hands to her eyes, blocking out all distractions so she could focus on what had happened so far and what might happen next. Thoughts tumbled through her head and she tried to sort them, to weigh their significance.

Harry Riggs had forced the loan issue. Phillip's father had defaulted and therefore been compelled to turn over the company to Harry. Phillip had intended his marriage to Tricia to save the company for his father. Last night he'd sworn he couldn't go through with the wedding, but now that James Keene was crushed, might Phillip change his mind? To save what was left of the family firm? To save his father? Would Harry still want to go ahead with the takeover if Phillip was determined to become his son-in-law, if Tricia was determined to go through with the wedding?

If only Phillip had returned to Lynwood yesterday, he might have had a chance to stave off this disaster. He could have stood by his father, giving him *real* advice, advice that would protect the company from Harry. But instead, Phillip had spent the night in Chicago with her, distracted by love when he should have been literally taking care of business.

"Phil suspected that Harry's ultimate goal was to take over the company," she said dolefully. "He was right."

"Who cares," Diane repeated, crumpling the empty cookie bag into a fist-sized wad and tossing it across the room into the trash can. "We came for revenge, and Harry Riggs did our job for us. All I had to do was smoke a cigar, and all you had to do was... What exactly did you do? You were with Phil, weren't you?"

Cassie nodded. Her heart was so heavy it seemed to press down on her diaphragm, making breathing difficult.

"All night?" Diane tilted her head slightly as she assessed Cassie. "Risky."

"No kidding." Cassie sighed.

"Where exactly were you?"

"In Chicago, closing down Keene Furniture's retail store there. That store was a major cause of the company's debt. Harry had convinced Phil's father to open the store. He must have known it would bleed Keene Furniture to the point of anemia, and that would make the company easier to take over. Phil wanted to close down the store to stem the bleeding. Harry was furious with Phil for that."

"Well, Harry got what he wanted, even without the store. We got what we wanted, too. Phil is down for the count. So tell me, Cassie, why are you so upset?"

"I love him," Cassie confessed, then covered her eyes again, this time not to concentrate but simply to hide her tears from her friend.

She heard Diane curse. Then she heard the thud of Diane's feet hitting the floor, and then Diane's footsteps approaching the bed. The mattress dipped as she sat beside Cassie.

"How can you love him?" Diane asked, placing an arm around Cassie's shoulders. "He betrayed you."

"To save his father's company," Cassie explained. "Anyway, it doesn't matter."

"Of course it matters! We came here for revenge, pal, and the reason we wanted revenge was that Phil did you dirt. I don't know what happened in Chicago last night—I don't *want* to know what happened. I do know what happened last year, and that's good enough for me. Phillip Keene is scum. He doesn't deserve your love."

"Phillip Keene was trying to save his father from some stupid mistakes—mistakes he made under the influence of Harry Riggs."

"Phil thought marrying Tricia would save his father from Tricia's father?"

"Yes. And right this minute, while you're telling me all this, he's across town telling Tricia he isn't going to marry her. He doesn't love her. He loves me."

"That's what he said last night, did he?" Diane sounded skeptical.

"I believe him."

Diane let out a long, hissing breath. "You're hopeless, Cassie, you know that? You really are. Thank God you bought cookies, because if you hadn't, I'd consider you worthless, too."

Cassie knew Diane didn't really mean that, but the insult prompted fresh tears. Diane hugged her tighter, offering her shoulder for Cassie to sob into.

"All right, all right," she cooed, stuffing a tissue

into Cassie's hand. "We've got a pretty serious mess here. What do you want to do?"

Cassie didn't know—except that she wanted to stop plotting and scheming. "Phil's going to feel guilty for being out of town when his father was getting the rug pulled out from under him," she predicted. "He's going to feel like it's all his fault. I should probably find him and offer my support."

Diane snorted. "Yeah, right. Be the supportive little lady. Stand by your man."

Cassie pulled away from Diane's embrace and glared at her through tear-blurred eyes. "That's not fair, Diane. I'm not the kind of woman who devotes herself to propping up a man."

"But you want to run to him and help him now."

"Because I love him!" Cassie realized that explanation was insufficient. "Because what happened to him and his father stinks worse than a stink bomb."

"Whereas if we'd executed Plan E, that wouldn't have stunk?"

Cassie struggled to remember the particulars of Plan E. Not that they mattered much. The overriding plan had been to make Phillip suffer.

But she loved him, and the thought of him suffering was unendurable. "I'm going to him, and you won't stop me," she said, shoving herself to her feet and stalking to the door.

"You'd better change first," Diane suggested. "You look like you slept in those clothes—which would probably be better than if you hadn't. No, don't tell me," she insisted, holding up her hand. "I don't want to know."

"Fine," Cassie snapped, already through the door. "I won't tell you."

Now probably would have been a good time to soak in the claw-footed tub beneath the eaves. Cassie would have benefited from spending some time relaxing in a basin full of steaming, soothing water, unwinding, thinking, formulating a new plan. But she'd had it with plans, and she was too anxious to be with Phillip to waste time taking a bath. Instead, she hurried through a shower, put on her khakis and a clean white T-shirt and raced down the stairs of the B-and-B, the keys to the rental car jangling in her hand.

She wasn't sure where Phillip might be, but she wasn't going to just sit here and try to figure out where to look for him. She'd told him she would wait for him at Bailey's; that, however, was before either of them had known what Harry had been up to in their absence. Phillip had said his first task was to talk to Tricia, but Cassie didn't want to track him down to the Riggs house. She would feel awkward confronting Tricia—and homicidal confronting Harry.

She decided to start her search at his parents' house. She still had their address jotted down on a slip of paper and tucked into her purse, where she'd put it yesterday when she'd been prepared to perform her part of Plan E once she was done taping at the factory.

The factory. She contemplated the sprawling building by the river, its distressed-brick walls, its multitude of windows. She contemplated the scenes she, Diane and Roger had videotaped, the enthusiasm of Keene Furniture's employees, the pride they took in their products. Phillip hadn't want her to film there because he'd known the place was in desperate financial straits. But the footage her few days at Keene had produced was not only terrific material for *Dream Wheels,* it was a precious record of what Phillip, his father and his father's father had built. It represented everything they'd stood for: commitment, hard work and faith.

Main Street seemed too sunny, too calm and pleasant, to contain an unfolding catastrophe. Cassie instinctively turned off the road, steering down the narrow lane to the factory gates. They were locked, but through the chain-link fence she saw a few cars parked in the lot.

One of them was Phillip's Mercedes.

Cassie slammed on the brake, yanked the key from the ignition and got out of her car. A couple of evenings ago she had tried to figure out a way for her and Diane to sneak onto the factory grounds if the gates were locked. She'd thought about following the river behind the property and hoping to locate a gap in the fence along the bank.

In the early-afternoon stillness, Cassie could almost hear the river, a hushed, distant white noise. To follow the fence all the way down to the river in search of a way onto the property would take too long. She needed to see Phillip now. She needed to hold him and kiss him, and let him know that no matter what Harry had done, no matter how easily Phillip's father had buckled, Phillip had her standing beside him.

Too impatient to find an easier way in, Cassie wedged one sneakered toe into the mesh of the fence and then the other, determined to scale its ten-foot height and let herself down into the lot.

She was halfway up the fence, refusing to scare herself by looking down, when she saw activity near the main door of the building. The door swung open and a lone figure strode out. She recognized the well-tailored suit, the colorful tie, the thick dark hair caught in a breeze. She couldn't see his eyes from that distance, but she could imagine them. They would be sad, yet steely.

Phillip, she knew, would not accept what Harry had done. He would fight it.

She remained where she was, suspended on the fence, as he stormed across the lot toward his car. Somewhere along the way he must have spotted her four feet off the ground, her fingers curled through the wire, her toes balanced precariously in the squares. He froze, his gaze riveted to her.

She didn't move, afraid she was going to fall. So she clung to the fence and willed him to approach, to help her down and open the gate.

Slowly, he started walking toward her. One step at a time across the black asphalt, across the painted white lines marking the rows of parking spaces. As he drew near she could see the strain in his expression, the lines furrowing his brow, the tension in his mouth. What a horrible morning he must have had. What a dreadful fight he still faced. And on top of that, to have to tell his fiancée he wasn't going to marry her tomorrow...

"Get down," he said. He didn't shout, but his voice carried in the quiet air.

He didn't sound happy to see her, but she refused to take his mood personally. Given what he was going through, she couldn't expect him to greet her with joy.

She cautiously removed one of her feet from its toe-hold and groped downward, feeling for another square of wire to support her. Her fingers were numb from holding the fence so tightly, but she willed them to unfurl, to grip the mesh lower so she could inch her way down.

When she was only a foot above the ground she

pushed away and jumped. Phillip stood directly opposite her, the chain-link between them. "Phil, I heard what happened," she told him, thinking to poke her fingers through the fence so she could touch him. Something about his posture forbade it, though. He didn't look like someone who wanted to be touched.

"Did you?" His voice was harsh, dry.

"Diane told me. She said that while we were in Chicago, Harry made your father hand over the company because he was in default on the loans."

"That's right."

Why wasn't Phillip talking to her? Why wasn't he unburdening himself to her, confiding in her, asking her advice the way he'd asked it about the Chicago store?

"I'm so sorry," she said, squelching the panic that threatened to bubble up inside her. Phillip was upset. He was devastated. She couldn't expect him to smile at her the way he'd smiled at her last night when he'd told her he loved her.

"You're so sorry," he echoed. "Isn't that just swell."

"Phil?" She couldn't suppress her panic anymore. His hostility wasn't merely a spillover from whatever had occurred between him and his father, him and Harry. It was directed at her. "Phil, what's going on?" she asked in a tight, worried voice.

"Plan E? Wasn't that what you called it?"

"Plan E?" She frowned. Why was he bringing up her silly revenge plots? How did he even know about them, other than overhearing the message she'd left for Diane yesterday when he'd lent her his cell phone on the way to the airport? She'd told him Plan E related to her TV show and that had been that.

"This was Plan E, wasn't it?" he asked. "Or was it some other plan? That's the way it was laid out for me, Cassie." His voice was as sharp as a steel blade, and as cold. "Harry told me Diane told him we were lovers."

"Phil—"

"And Harry thought that if that was the kind of man I was, I couldn't be trusted to run Keene Furniture. So once he found out I was out of town, he made his move. I could have been back before my father signed everything over to him. I could have come back to Lynwood in time to stop him. But I didn't. I was with you."

Another emotion blended with the panic rising inside her: rage. "Yes, you were with me," she snapped. "You kidnapped me and dragged me with you to Chicago."

"You got into my car. When I told you where we were going, you didn't put up much of a protest. And afterward, after I'd finished at the store—"

"You said, let's get dinner," she recollected. Once again she wished she could reach through the fence, but not to console him with a loving touch. She wanted to hit him. "You were the one to insist on that restaurant in the hotel."

If she was burning with anger, he was chilling to ice with it. His voice was as taut and subdued as hers was fervent. "When I'm with you, Cassie, I can't think of anything but you. You know that about me. You know that when I'm with you nothing else exists."

"Don't blame me for your own weaknesses!" she shouted through the fence. So what if one of her and Diane's earlier plans had been for her to don her elegant new underwear and a skimpy skirt to tempt him? They'd abandoned that plan. It no longer counted.

"As long as I was with you," he continued, each word ten degrees colder than the previous one, "Harry could have taken over the world. My father could have jumped off a bridge. Keene Furniture could have gone up in smoke. I wouldn't have even noticed. You know that."

All right, so she knew that. But having Harry take over, having Phillip's father cave in, having Keene Furniture undergo so overwhelming a change—none of it had been her plan. Making Phillip believe that nothing else existed but her...well, yes, she'd wanted that. She'd reveled in it. She'd felt the same way about him. But it hadn't been her plan.

She'd come to Lynwood wanting revenge, but by last night, all she'd wanted was Phillip. And now he was blaming her for everything. He was blaming her because Harry had told him that his afternoon with Diane had provided him with the motivation to make his move.

"I didn't know Diane was going to tell Harry anything," she said, suddenly feeling more forlorn than enraged.

Phillip stared at her through the fence. It was like a prison visit, one of them on each side of the barrier, able to see each other and talk to each other but physically barred from each other. She couldn't tell which one of them was the prisoner, though, and which one was free.

"Why did you come to Lynwood?" he asked.

Cassie couldn't lie to him. Not after last night. Not if she wanted their love to survive.

But if she told him the truth—that she'd come to

destroy his life, or at least his wedding—she would lose his love, too.

She said nothing.

"My mother told me to trust my instincts," he murmured. "The moment I saw you here in Lynwood, my instincts told me to look out, because you'd brought trouble with you. I should have trusted those instincts, Cassie." He continued to stare at her, his eyes filling with sorrow but his mouth still tense with anger. "Why did you come? To get back at me? To pay me back for last year?"

She lowered her eyes. She didn't have to tell him the truth; he'd figured it out.

"Well, you sure did a good job of it." The words came out raw, a scrape of sound in the peaceful afternoon. "You got me good, Cassie. Too bad you had to bring down my whole family while you were at it. This isn't *Dream Wheels,* you know. This is reality. I hope you're happy."

With that he pivoted, his footsteps rattling the loose gravel as he stalked across the lot to his car and got in. He didn't start the engine. Cassie understood that he wouldn't until she was gone.

Slowly, fighting off the tide of tears that swept through her, she returned to her car, climbed in and twisted the key in the ignition. She couldn't despise him for accusing her of having sabotaged him, because when she'd come to Lynwood, sabotage was exactly what she'd had in mind. His accusation would have been perfectly legitimate—except for last night.

Last night she'd gotten him, all right. She'd gotten him the way she'd dreamed of having him: all of him, his heart, his soul, his love.

And now she had nothing.

CHAPTER FIFTEEN

PHILLIP WAS NOT a regular at Jake's. He didn't drink much, and on those occasions when he really needed to commune with a glass of scotch, he didn't want to have to behave convivially with others in a public place. But Lynwood was the kind of town where everybody knew everybody, and when he propped himself on a stool at the bar, Jake himself came over to greet him.

"It's the man of the hour," Jake hailed him. A stocky fellow in his late sixties, Jake had too little hair and too much belly, but he kept peace and order in his establishment, and he treated his clientele with respect. "You're a little early for your bachelor party," he told Phillip. "They haven't even started setting up in the back room yet."

Phillip glanced at the clock on the wall behind the bar. The clock face nested in the center of a green windmill, with Heineken printed along the base. The big hand was on the five, the little hand a shade below the two. "I'm not getting married," he told Jake. "Could you give me a scotch on ice? Dewar's, if you have it."

Jake eyed Phillip curiously. Phillip caught his own reflection in the mirrored wall behind the bar. Through the forest of liquor bottles lined up on the back counter, he studied his appearance: wilted shirt, crookedly dangling tie, sagging jacket. He hadn't changed his clothes since getting back from Chicago.

Right now, a drink of scotch was more important than a change of apparel. Right now, a drink of scotch would cleanse him more effectively than a shower. When your world was crashing down all around you, who cared whether your shirt was fresh?

The tavern was gloomy. What appeared to be a couple of farmhands sat at a booth, their duck-billed caps advertising a brand of tractor. Through the open door to the back room Phillip could hear the click and rumble of billiard balls gliding across the felt-topped table; someone was playing in there. But 2:25 on a Friday afternoon was not "happy hour" at Jake's.

Just as well. Phillip wasn't happy.

Jake set a glass of scotch on the rocks in front of Phillip, then nudged over a plastic bowl of pretzels. "I'm here if you need to talk," he said. He gave Phillip a minute to demonstrate such a need, but when Phillip said nothing Jake nodded and moseyed away.

Phillip sipped his drink. A groan vibrated in his throat, and he closed his eyes and waited for the liquor to numb him. What a day. Jesus, what a day.

Had it actually started in a hotel room in Chicago with Cassie in his arms? Had it actually started with a kiss, with the powerful certainty that Cassie was the woman he loved, the woman he wanted in his life forever?

One problem was that even now, after everything, he couldn't quite shed that certainty. In fact, that was such a huge problem, he wasn't going to consider it until he'd considered all his other problems, or until he finished his scotch—whichever came first.

Breaking up with Tricia had been simple enough.

He hadn't expected her to be thinking the way he was thinking, but perhaps he should have. She wasn't an idiot, and she wasn't insensitive. He'd seemed like a decent partner for her before she'd considered the alternatives; she'd seemed like a decent partner for him when he'd thought no alternatives existed.

But when she'd made that cryptic remark about how her father suddenly had everything he'd wanted, warning sirens had joined the symphonic percussion playing inside Phillip's head. He'd broken the speed limit driving the few blocks to his parents' house, where he'd found his mother out in her garden, eradicating the beds of weeds with single-minded ferocity. Without a thought to protecting the lightweight wool of his trousers, he'd knelt down in the damp grass next to her. "Where's Dad?" he'd asked.

Dorothy had twisted around to look at him. She'd been wearing her sun hat, but she'd still sprouted a few new freckles across the bridge of her nose. Her eyes had been fierce. "He's at his office," she'd said. "I don't know what he's doing there. Staring at the walls, probably. Where have you been?"

"Giving word in Chicago that we've got to close the store down. I know Dad didn't want me to do it, but we had to stem the debt flow and shore up our assets, and that was the best place to start."

His mother had turned back to her hydrangeas, fussing with the broad green leaves, inspecting what remained of the puffs of blue blossoms.

"What happened?" he'd asked her.

"Your father got stabbed in the back, that's what happened." She'd yanked another weed, her fingers fisting around the scrawny stem. "I wish you'd been here, Phil. Maybe you could have protected him."

"I thought I was protecting him by selling the Chicago store. Trying to keep it going was a serious drain on the company, and—"

"Oh, the hell with the company!" his mother had yelled. "Who gives a damn about the company? We've got enough money to see us through a comfortable retirement. Maybe we'll sell this big house and move someplace warm, where I can garden year-round." She'd sighed, and he'd heard the tremor of a sob in her breath. "Harry Riggs was your father's best friend. Your father loved that man. And that man betrayed him. Do you know how much a betrayal like that can hurt?"

Phillip filled his mouth with scotch and held it on his tongue. He damned well knew how much a betrayal like that could hurt. He'd gone to the factory, and his father had told him how Harry had demanded the loan repayment yesterday, all of six months into the new century, and Harry had announced that if James didn't pay up right then and there, Harry was going to take possession of the company, and then— with a gloating laugh—Harry had said, "That friend of Phillip's, Diane, sure is a sharp cookie! They grow them smart in Boston, don't they? She told me what kind of man Phillip is, and how ill-suited he is to save the company. If I don't want to lose my investment, I've got to act now."

Phillip had listened as his father went on and on, describing how Diane and Harry had evidently spent a wonderful afternoon together, and how pleased Harry was that Phillip hadn't been in town, in the way... And Phillip had understood exactly what it felt like to be betrayed by someone you trusted, someone you loved.

He took another long drink. An ice cube bumped his tooth and he lowered the glass. Yes, he knew what it felt like to be betrayed. Cassie had betrayed him. She and her friend Diane had set things up so he would wind up out of the way while Harry did his evil work.

But Cassie knew what it felt like to be betrayed, too. One year ago, Phillip had been the betrayer.

Had he hurt her so terribly that she would have plotted with her friend to crush him like this? She must have known that the worst thing she could ever do to him was to go after his family. The worst hurt she could inflict on him would be to hurt his parents.

A shadow fell across his shoulder. He craned his neck to meet the towering gaze of a tall, skinny blond fellow with lots of hair. "Beckelman?"

Cassie's cameraman grinned and gestured toward the empty stool next to Phillip. "Mind if I join you?"

"Go ahead," Phillip said. "I'll be lousy company, though."

"I was looking for some lousy company," Beckelman said affably, lowering his lanky body onto the stool. When Jake came over, he asked for a Budweiser. He said nothing while Jake went off to get his beer.

Phillip studied Beckelman in the mirror facing the bar. So, Tricia thought men looked good with a lot of hair. Beckelman had enough hair for three men.

"Thanks," Phillip said.

Beckelman shot him a bemused grin. "For what?"

"For convincing Tricia she doesn't want to marry me."

Beckelman sat back as far as he could without tumbling off the stool. Jake set a chilled glass mug and a sweating brown bottle of beer in front of him.

Beckelman nodded him off, then nudged the mug aside and took a swig from the bottle. "You're not mad?" he asked.

"I'm relieved."

"It's not like I said anything," Beckelman said, apparently feeling the need to defend himself. "Or did anything. She was into the whole taping process, so I showed her a few things with the camera and some editing equipment. That was all."

"It was enough." Phillip drained his glass, then signaled Jake for a refill. "Tricia and I aren't right for each other. We needed to acknowledge that and figure things out. If it wasn't for you, I'd have had to do the figuring all by myself. You helped her to figure it out with me. I'm grateful."

Jake brought Phillip a fresh drink, his gaze shuttling between Lynwood's Golden Boy and the scruffy stranger from Boston.

"She wants to get an internship at a TV studio," Beckelman told him. "We can always use interns at the station in Boston. We haven't got any money to pay them, but Tricia says money isn't a problem for her."

"It isn't." Especially not since her father took ownership of Lynwood's biggest industry.

"I guess I'll see what I can do for her in Boston, then." Beckelman took another slug of beer. "Strange vibes in this town, I'll tell you."

"Strange vibes? Are you kidding? This is the straightest, most normal, most sedate town in the universe." It was also a hotbed of vengeance and bitterness at the moment, but Beckelman seemed untouched by the deceit and resentment swirling around him. "Tell me about Cassie," he implored.

"Cassie?" Beckelman ruminated for a moment, then said, "She's great. Smart, honest, kindhearted. I'd fall in love with her, except she's my boss. And anyway, she's a bit too decent for me, if you know what I mean."

Too decent? Did Beckelman have any idea of what Cassie had wrought? Did he realize what she was capable of? Keeping a man in Chicago, seducing him, making him promise the world to her, while her best friend was a few hundred miles away, decimating that world—was that Beckelman's idea of decency and honesty and kindness?

"Cassie and I don't talk much," Beckelman went on. "I mean, about personal stuff."

Phillip sipped his drink.

"But I gather she's been through some rough times."

"Oh?" Phillip kept his tone noncommittal.

"Some guy broke her heart. That's my guess, anyway."

Phillip steadied his breath. If Roger Beckelman, who didn't discuss personal matters with Cassie, knew she'd had her heart broken, it must have been really badly broken. Obviously broken. Perhaps irreparably broken. "What makes you say that?"

"She hasn't got anything going with anyone, for one thing. A woman like that—" Beckelman gave Phillip a you-know-what-I-mean look "—should have lovers lining up outside her door. Or at least one steady lover. A man who'd move mountains for her. But there's no one. She's got her deflector shield up. You can just tell someone did a number on her."

Guilt jabbed Phillip in his gut. Someone *did* do a number on her, all right. "Is she the sort of person who'd lash back? Who'd try to hurt the person who hurt her?''

Beckelman chuckled. ''Cassie doesn't know how to hurt anyone. She retreats into her *Dream Wheels* world. Now, Diane—'' Beckelman chuckled again and drank some beer ''—she's the schemer. Whenever there's a problem with a script, Diane's the one who plots the whole thing out. She's the best friend you could have and the worst enemy you could have. I'd love to have her fighting on my side, because you know she'd fight to the death. But I'd hate to have to face her from the opposing side.''

''Diane.'' Phillip lifted his glass, then set it back down without drinking. Was it possible that Diane had plotted the whole scheme with Harry? Was it possible Cassie had been an innocent bystander? As she'd pointed out, it had been his idea to take her to Chicago with him. Not her idea, his. And he'd been the one to ask her to go to the hotel room with him. She had to have known he would ask, but she hadn't suggested it. He had.

She made him crazy. She wielded power over his mind and his heart. But she hadn't forced him to stay in Chicago. All she'd done was be herself, and he hadn't been able to resist.

He stared at the glass. Here he was, in a dimly lit bar in the middle of a Friday afternoon. His wedding was no longer on the agenda. His mother was already planning to sell her house and move away from Lynwood. His father was reeling from his best friend's deceit. And he...

He was drinking scotch and blaming Cassie for the collapse of his life. Cassie, who even Beckelman knew had been through rough times because some guy had broken her heart.

That guy was him. Phillip Keene.

"I've got to go," he said abruptly, rising from his stool and reaching for his wallet. He tossed a ten-dollar bill on the bar, stuffed his wallet back into his hip pocket and patted Beckelman on the shoulder. "Tricia's a great lady," he said. "Make sure nobody breaks her heart, okay?"

Beckelman lifted his beer in a silent toast. Phillip nodded, then strode out of the bar into the blinking-bright afternoon.

He donned his sunglasses before taking the wheel. It didn't seem fair that the sky should be so clear, the sun so strong, when his thoughts were cloudy, his mood overcast. He'd broken Cassie's heart last year—and again today, when he'd assumed that she had participated in Harry Riggs's trickery. Last night Phillip had been madly in love with her, this morning he'd been madly in love with her, but then he'd realized that everything he'd given her up for had been ruined. And in his grief, he'd blamed her, instead of believing her.

Would she forgive him? She had given him a second chance yesterday. Could he even dare to hope she would give him a third chance?

He drove back up Main Street toward Bailey's. Parking at the edge of the lawn, he glanced at the white clapboard farmhouse. A woman sat by herself in one of the oversized Adirondack porch chairs. It wasn't Cassie.

He climbed out of the car, and the woman sat straighter. He recognized her shaggy hair, her athletic build, her troubled expression. If he'd had a spare minute, he would have spent it throttling her. But right now he had more important things to do.

He jogged up the front walk, focusing on the most important thing of all. "Where is she?"

Diane Krensky, he realized as he neared her, had been crying. Streaks of moisture stained her cheeks. "I hate you, Phil," she retorted. "Do you think I did any of it for myself? I did it for her, because you made this past year of her life hell. Anyone who makes my best friend's life hell deserves whatever I can dish out."

"Fine. Sure. Just tell me, is she inside?"

"And you ought to count your blessings," Diane continued. "What I really wanted to do was bomb your wedding. Cassie was the one who insisted on no bloodshed."

Was that supposed to prove what Beckelman had said about Cassie's kindheartedness? "I'm glad there was no bloodshed," he said coolly, aware that even without bloodshed, a fair amount of injury had been inflicted. "Where is she?"

"And besides, when you think about it, the real bad guy in all this was Harry Riggs, right? He was going after your father and the factory long before I said a word. It was only a matter of when. If he hadn't called in the debts before your wedding, he would have found a way to take over the place after you were married. So by making it happen before the wedding, maybe I saved you from a bad marriage. You ought to think about it that way."

"What do you want? A medal?" He stood before her on the porch steps. "Tell me where Cassie is or I'll torture you."

"I don't know where she is," Diane said. "She

came here, told me you thought everything was all her fault, and then she drove off.''

Phillip cursed. Diane jumped, and a few new tears leaked out of her eyes. He couldn't waste time berating her for her stupid meddling, though. He had to find Cassie. For all he knew, she could be halfway to the airport by now, fleeing to Boston. "Did she take her clothes with her?" he asked. "Did she pack a bag?"

Diane shook her head. "The only thing I can think is…" She sniffled and wiped her nose with a tissue. "Maybe she's still thinking about Plan E."

"What the hell is Plan E?"

"I was supposed to have a cigar with Harry Riggs and pump him for information. She was supposed to visit your mother and find out if you were really in love with Tricia."

He didn't stick around to ask why. He sprinted down the walk to his car, jumped in and tore down the street, heading home.

"CASSIE! Come in," Dorothy Keene invited her. "Have some cookies and milk."

Cassie didn't know what to say, but cookies and milk didn't sound like a bad idea, and Diane had already devoured all of Cassie's cookies at the B-and-B.

Actually, she was amazed Phillip's mother would even allow her into the house. Did she know that Diane had precipitated the disaster that had befallen the Keene family? Did she know that Diane's motive had been to hurt Phillip for having hurt her?

His parents' house was spacious and tasteful. Freshly cut flowers filled a round vase in the entry, lending a sweet, tangy fragrance to the air. "Is...is your husband all right?" she asked as she followed Dorothy down the hall and through the kitchen to a sun-filled solarium at the rear of the house. "I heard what happened with Keene Furniture. Is he okay?"

Dorothy gestured toward the table. "My husband is disappointed. Who wouldn't be, to learn that his oldest friend finessed him out of his business?"

"I'm sorry it happened," Cassie murmured. "I feel so bad for him."

"Well, he isn't entirely blameless," Dorothy pointed out. "He should never have expanded so fast and let Harry finance the expansion. Phillip had advised him against it, but Harry kept telling him to think big." She filled two glasses with milk and carried them to the table in the solarium, then returned to the kitchen to fetch a plate heaped high with peanut-butter cookies. "So James decided to think big." She sighed. "Well, there are worse sins in the world."

"Like doing to a friend what Harry Riggs did to your husband."

"Yes." Dorothy took a seat across the table from Cassie, but she ignored her glass of milk as she scrutinized Cassie. "My son loves you," she said bluntly.

The words resonated inside Cassie, making her want to weep. But she'd done enough weeping over the past year—enough even today—to last the rest of her life. Besides, she hadn't come to Dorothy Keene to get her tears wiped. She'd come because she needed to learn how this woman could have raised a son who swore he loved Cassie, yet couldn't seem to believe in her or trust her when life threw him a bad curve.

"I don't know if he loves me," Cassie said, helping herself to a cookie. She bit into it. It was soft and rich, obviously homemade. "He said he did—but he said he did last year and he left me then. What's wrong with him, Dorothy? Why does he do this to me?"

"Why do you *let* him do it?"

"I..." Cassie knew she was trapped, but she wasn't going to lie to Dorothy. "I love him."

Dorothy nodded. "Tricia seems fine about canceling the wedding. Tricia's mother, on the other hand..." She shook her head and laughed. "By the time I got off the phone with her, my ear was ringing. Apparently Linden Hills doesn't give refunds this close to the day of the affair. So we're all stuck with some bills for this mess."

"And you've lost your business..."

"To Constance's husband. Let her get stuck with the bulk of the bills." Dorothy grinned. "As for James and me, we'll survive. We've always lived prudently, and there are trust funds and an ample pension. James's grief is more for Phillip. He always wanted to leave him the business, to keep it in the family. But Phillip will find a way to survive, too—at least as far as finding a good job." She picked up a cookie and took a delicate bite. "I'm not sure how well he'll survive emotionally. That's what I worry about."

Cassie wasn't sure what to say, so she took another cookie.

"Tricia was right about one thing," Dorothy said. "Phillip is the best catch in Lynwood. Quite possibly the best catch in North America, if not the world."

"You're his mother," Cassie said. "You have to say that."

"I'm saying it because it's the truth. What's his worst fault? He's too loyal to his family. Maybe his loyalty blinds him." She nibbled some more of her cookie. "I know he hurt you, Cassie, but when you think about his motivation... All right, maybe that doesn't make it hurt less, but—"

"It does," Cassie admitted. For all her anger at Phillip, all her indignation, all her lust for revenge, she could understand why he'd made the choices he'd made, even if she considered them boneheaded.

"Ah. There he is now," Dorothy said, rising from her chair in response to a chime echoing in the front hall. "I'll be right back."

Frowning, Cassie directed her gaze from Dorothy, hurrying through the kitchen to the hall, to the untouched glass of milk on the table. Was that milk for Phillip? Had Dorothy been so positive he was on his way that she'd filled a glass for him in anticipation?

He entered the kitchen with his mother, then saw Cassie at the table and halted. He looked haggard, drained, his cheeks stubbled with a day's growth of beard and his eyes haunted.

"Sit," Dorothy ordered him. "Sit and talk. The milk is already on the table."

Phillip tossed a wry grin at his mother, who turned and left the kitchen, giving them their privacy. Phillip continued into the solarium. He didn't sit at the chair by his glass of milk, though. Instead, he moved to Cassie's side of the table and dropped to his knees before her. "I love you," he said.

She wanted to reach for him. She wanted him to rest his head in her lap so she could stroke her fingers through his hair. She wanted to touch him, to feel him.

She also wanted to scream at him and pummel him with her fists for having assumed the worst of her— even if there'd been a thread of truth in his accusations. No matter why she'd come to Lynwood, she was furious that he could ever have doubted her love for him.

"Diane did what she did because she was fighting for you," he said. "I did what I did because I was fighting for my father. I'm sorry." He was still wearing his suit from yesterday. He looked disheveled, exhausted and painfully sincere.

That was all she'd had to hear: "I'm sorry." Her rage evaporated. "Phillip—"

He obviously wasn't done. "If it's true you came here to hurt me...well, maybe I shouldn't blame you for that. Maybe I deserved it. But my father—he didn't deserve it, Cassie. He didn't deserve to get hurt like this."

"I know," she said. "It shouldn't have happened." And since he was so busy apologizing, she allowed that she owed him an apology, too. "I *did* come here wanting to hurt you. But not your father, not your family. And last night..."

He looked up at her. His eyes were luminous with hope, with passion, with memory. "Last night," he murmured.

"It wasn't about hurting you." She sighed. "It was about loving you."

He nodded, then took a deep breath, apparently aware that love might not be enough. "If you're not ready to accept me back into your life, I'll earn my way back. I'm going to move to Boston. I'll find work there. It seems I don't have to worry about running the family firm in Lynwood anymore." He smiled sadly. "Maybe that's for the best. Now I can come to Boston and woo you. I don't care how long it takes— I'll convince you I'm worthy."

"I'm already convinced," she said.

He paused as if to memorize her words, to savor them, to tuck them into his heart for safekeeping. Then he said, "Marry me."

"Okay."

His smile grew a little wider, a little brighter, a lot more hopeful. "We've already got the country club lined up for a reception. Food, flowers and musicians—a flautist, not a flutist."

"That's Tricia's party. Not mine."

"True. So what kind of party would you like?" he asked.

She grinned mischievously. "I think we had my kind of party last night."

He grinned back, then pressed a kiss to her hand. "Oh, Cassie, you can't begin to know how much I love you. Even today, when I was stupid enough to think the worst of you…"

"Maybe you had valid reasons to think the worst of me. Diane and I *were* plotting against you."

"'The best-laid plans…'" He stood up and pulled her to her feet. "I guess they went awry, just like my noble plans to save my father's company."

"Maybe we shouldn't make any more plans, then."

"Just one plan," he insisted, enclosing her in his arms. "A plan to trust each other, and believe in each other, and to be together forever."

"That sounds like an excellent plan," she said.

He covered her smile with a kiss, and she realized she didn't need a magic bicycle to make her dreams come true. All she needed was Phillip, forever.

IN UNIFORM

There's something special about a man in uniform. Maybe because he's a man who takes charge, a man you can count on, and yes, maybe even love....

Superromance presents *In Uniform*, an occasional series that features men who live up to your every fantasy—and then some!

Look for:

Mad About the Major
by Roz Denny Fox
Superromance #821
Coming in January 1999

An Officer and a Gentleman
by Elizabeth Ashtree
Superromance #828
Coming in March 1999

SEAL It with a Kiss
by Rogenna Brewer
Superromance #833
Coming in April 1999

Available wherever Harlequin books are sold.

HARLEQUIN®
Makes any time special ™

Look us up on-line at: http://www.romance.net

HSRIU

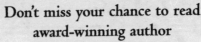

COMING NEXT MONTH

#834 DON'T MESS WITH TEXANS • Peggy Nicholson
By the Year 2000: Satisfaction!

Veterinarian R. D. Taggart is the innocent bystander caught in the cross fire between a blue-eyed Texas hellcat and her vindictive ex-husband. Susannah Mack Colton inadvertently destroys Tag's reputation in what *appears* to be nothing but a vendetta against her ex—and Tag intends to collect on his damages!

#835 THE DOCTOR'S DAUGHTER • Judith Bowen
Men of Glory

Lucas Yellowfly was always in love with Virginia Lake. More than a decade ago, the half-Indian boy from the wrong side of town spent a memorable night with the doctor's daughter. Now they're both back in Glory, Lucas as a successful lawyer and Virginia as a single mother with a five-year-old son. Virginia's looking for a job— and Lucas finds he needs someone with *exactly* her qualifications!

#836 HER SECRET, HIS CHILD • Tara Taylor Quinn
A Little Secret

Jamie Archer has a past she wants to keep hidden. She's created an entirely new life for herself and four-year-old Ashley—a life that's threatened when Kyle Radcliff reappears. Kyle doesn't immediately realize who she is, but Jamie recognizes *him* right away. *Her child's father.*

#837 THE GUARDIAN • Bethany Campbell
Guaranteed Page-Turner

Kate Kanaday is a widow with a young son. Life is hard, but she manages—right up until the day a stalker leaves his first message on her doorstep. Before long she's forced to quit her job and run. And there's only one place to go—to the home of a stranger who has promised to keep them safe whether he wants them there or not. From the bestselling author of *See How They Run* and *Don't Talk to Strangers*.

#838 THE PULL OF THE MOON • Darlene Graham
9 Months Later

Danielle Goodlove has every reason to believe that marriage and family are not for her. As a dedicated obstetrician, she's content to share her patients' happiness. Until one moonlit night, when firefighter Matthew Creed is brought into the emergency room. Now she wishes things could be different....

#839 HER BROTHER'S KEEPER • K.N. Casper
Family Man

Krisanne Blessing receives a call from her ex-lover, Drew Hadley, asking her to come back to Coyote Springs, Texas. Drew is now a widower with a young son— and he's also a close friend of her brother, Patrick. Krisanne is shocked to discover that Patrick wants her and Drew to give romance another try. She's even more shocked when she discovers *why* he's encouraging their relationship.